MW01068525

ON THE EDGE

SCU HOCKEY: BOOK THREE

J.J. MULDER

Print ISBN: 978-1-967245-02-4

E-Book ISBN: 978-1-967245-03-1

Book Cover by Ivanna Nashkolna.

Alpha read by Maya.

Beta read by Lexi, Lucky, and Kim Ruge.

Proofreading by Judy Zweifel.

❀ Created with Vellum

Für Liebhaber von grünen Äpfeln und einsame, ungewollte Herzen

BEFORE YOU READ...

A quick note about the timeline! While this book can be read alone (or out of order), my recommendation would be to start with the first in the SCU series. The main characters of *Shots on Net* and *Save the Game* feature heavily in this book, and the story takes place chronologically from the end of *Save the Game*.

Now, if you really wanted to take the plunge, the full recommended reading order (spanning both the Offsides, and SCU Hockey series) is:

i. *Changing the Game*
ii. *Square to the Puck*
iii. *Between the Pipes*
iv. *Shots on Net*
v. *Save the Game*
vi. *From Coast to Coast*
vii. *On the Edge*

All that being said, thank you for reading! I'm happy you're here, and I hope you enjoy Henri and Atlas' story.

-JJ

1

Henri

4:45 a.m.—wake up, drink a glass of water and get dressed
5-5:15—walk to the hockey complex
5:15-5:30—say hello to Coach Mackenzie (if he is there) when you pass his office on the way to the gym
5:30-6:30—workout (Monday- shoulders and back, Tuesday- legs, Wednesday- cardio, Thursday- back and core, Friday- full body)
6:30-6:45—say goodbye to Coach Mackenzie when you pass his office on the way out
6:45-7—eat post-gym snack on the walk home
7-7:30—shower and get ready for class
7-4 p.m.—classes (see separate schedule)
4-7—hockey practice (except for game nights)
7-8—dinner

8-11—homework

11—bedtime/stress release if you need it

EVEN AFTER NEARLY FOUR years of living here, I still miss the weather in Germany. South Carolina seems reluctant to shift from summer to autumn, no matter that it's late September. The short walk from my dorm to the hockey facility is nice enough, this early in the morning, but will be twice as unpleasant later, when I come back for practice. I long for slightly cooler temperatures, and the rainy days I love in Germany. Gazing around to make sure I won't run into anyone, I pull my phone from the pocket of my athletic shorts to text Carter.

HENRI

Good luck tonight, my friend.

He won't be awake just yet, but at least he'll see it well before his game. I miss Carter rather more than I'd been expecting, and Max's last year on the team is weighing heavily on me. If I'm already feeling lonely before he's gone, that doesn't bode well for next year when I'll be alone in actuality. Sighing, I pull my shoulders back and bury my worries under a bland expression. The lights are already on, which means Coach Mackenzie is here, and I don't want him to think something is wrong.

The hallways are silent as I skirt the rink and walk toward the locker rooms. As I expected there would be, light is spilling from the open doorway of Coach's office. I step carefully into view and tap lightly on the doorframe, not wanting to sneak up and startle him.

"Good morning, Coach Mackenzie," I greet him, smiling. He smiles back, which settles the nerves fluttering in my stomach. I've never been comfortable around authority figures, and no matter that I've played for him going on four years, he still makes me nervous.

"Good morning, Vas. How are you?" He places his cellphone face down on his desk and narrows his eyes at me. I used to think he was mad when he looked at me like this, but now I suspect he's got bad eyesight. It's the same expression my dad uses when he forgets his reading glasses and he has to look at fine print.

"Well, thank you for asking," I answer, the same way I do every morning. I would never complain to him, even if I wasn't doing okay. "How are you?"

Coach's lips twitch like he wants to smile again. He gestures to the chair in front of his desk. "I'm just fine. Have a seat, will you? I need to talk to you, and I knew you'd be here early."

Nerves dance low in my gut again, as I slide into the chair and rest my hands on my lap. I think about the schedule taped above my desk in my dorm, and barely refrain from checking the time on my phone. I'm going to have to cut my workout short if this conversation takes the full fifteen minutes I allow for greeting Coach Mackenzie each morning.

"How may I help you, Coach?" I ask carefully, making sure my voice doesn't waver. God, he makes me nervous.

"You're majoring in broadcasting, right?" He taps a long, thin finger on his desk. There's a folder lying there, but it's closed. He has nice hands—I've always thought so. Like a concert pianist.

"Yes, sir. Broadcast journalism and media. I would like to be a sportscaster for the NHL."

"I thought so." Opening the leather folder, Coach slides out a piece of paper and leans over the desk to hold it out to me. I grab it quickly, before he can strain himself from reaching so far toward me. He points to the sheet as I settle back in my seat. "There is an internship opportunity that will be available next summer with our NHL team. It would be during the off-season, so it would primarily be centering on operations, but also with a focus on media. I thought you might like to apply."

The nervous butterflies in my stomach burn away as my system flushes with pleasure. I'm a distinctly mediocre hockey player, and yet Coach Mackenzie thought of me for this opportunity. I look at the paper and do my best to read it. I hate reading in English when there is someone waiting on me to finish, but I've gotten passably good at it over the years. I'm able to make it through the majority of the words, although there are several that I make note of to look up later. I have no idea what *encompassing* means.

"This would be a very good opportunity," I say, when I've read as much as I can without a dictionary in front of me.

"Indeed. Do you have plans for next summer?"

"I usually go home to Germany, sir." He threads his fingers together and I'm once again distracted by his hands.

"You live in the dorms, correct?" He waits for me to nod before continuing. "You'd have to vacate during the summer, obviously, but if you were hired for that internship, there would be other housing available to you."

I glance back down at the paper. Where did it say anything about housing? My gaze catches on something I missed the first time.

"It is paid, sir?"

"Yes. Not a lot, and certainly not enough to live on, but you'll get something. This is the first year they're doing it. I know the director of the program, and he'd be the one you'd be reporting directly to."

"Oh, I see. Sam Jameson is the husband to Troy Nichols, correct?" I stare at the name, embarrassed to have missed it the first time. Everyone who plays hockey for SCU knows who Sam Jameson is.

"Correct. If you applied and got the position, you'd be welcome to stay with me over the summer. Me and Anthony, that is."

My head snaps up in surprise. "What?"

"You'd need a place to stay and we have plenty of room. Or, I imagine Carter would have a bed for you as well, if you'd be more comfortable." Coach smiles when he sees my baffled expression. "It's an incredible opportunity, Vas. I'll write you a letter of recommendation if you choose to apply, and God knows I've got enough connections there to pull a few strings in your favor."

"I..." Words fail me for a moment, as I flounder for something to say. "There are perhaps others who are better suited."

Coach sighs. "I'd have to disagree. You are exactly the sort of young man they are looking for: hardworking, respectful, intelligent."

"Sometimes I struggle with English, sir. I am still learning."

I don't want to admit that I struggle *a lot* with English; that four years of going to school here and immersing myself have helped, but I still feel barely above proficient. I don't want to admit how hard it is for me to read. I'm a communications student, but communicating is really quite hard.

"You don't give yourself enough credit," he tells me firmly. "And you could think of this job as a learning opportunity in more ways than one. I wouldn't put you in a situation I didn't think you could excel in."

I sit up straighter, clutching the piece of paper. I want to apply, but I know better than to make a decision in haste.

"May I have a day to think about it, sir?"

"Of course. You can come to me with any questions. Also, I admit that I'm unsure of how this would work with your visa."

"Yes, Coach, thank you. I will talk to my brother." I stand, folding the paper carefully and sliding it into my pocket. I glance at my phone as I do, noting the time and feeling a prickle of discomfort. My entire schedule will be off for the rest of the day. "Was there anything else you might need me for?"

"No, Vas. Sorry to take over your morning—have a good workout. Careful with that knee, okay?"

"Yes, sir. I will put on my brace before I start."

He waves me out of his office and I hasten for the locker room. I will have to cut my workout down to the bare bones, but perhaps if there aren't too many homework assignments tonight, I could stay late and finish the gym session after practice. Slightly mollified by this thought, I change quickly, making sure to put the internship information on the shelf where it won't get damaged. I leave my headphones off, knowing my thoughts will be distracting enough to get me through.

By the time I finish and am walking back to my dorm, I've

made the decision to talk to Carter and Zeke first. If they're amenable to having me as a temporary roommate over the summer, I'll apply to the internship.

2

Atlas

ANY COLLEGE PROFESSOR that makes you call them doctor is a fucking asshole. Similarly, any college professor who still uses a chalkboard is an asshole. I scowl and slide a little lower in my seat as I watch Doctor Robertson write his name on the chalkboard in big block letters, as though none of us could read it off the syllabus he emailed out. Give me a fucking break.

When all the seats in the lecture hall are filled, I stare hard at the front of the room as I pretend to be enraptured by what he's saying. Mostly, I'm just trying to deter the girl sitting next to me from talking. She's practically vibrating with excitement, sitting on the edge of her seat and shooting me covert glances each time Doctor Robertson pauses for breath. Pointedly, I ignore her. She's cute, but she reeks of codependency. I would bet every dollar in my bank account that this girl is looking for that Mrs. degree to go with her SCU one. She'll have to look elsewhere. I know better.

I'm so caught up in—admittedly—rude thoughts about my seatmate, that I almost miss what the professor said.

"Wait, what?" I ask, and Perky Girl whips her head toward me so fast, her ponytail almost takes her eye out. "What did the professor say?"

"Doctor," she corrects, and I nearly burst a vessel in my eye from holding back my eyeroll. "He said he's assigned us seats. We're supposed to pack up and he's going to move us around."

"He assigned us seats?" I hiss, as she puts her books back into her bag. She stands, shooting me a look over her shoulder as she moves to the aisle. Annoyed, I toss my shit back into my backpack and follow her. Assigned seating? What is this, kindergarten?

It takes twenty minutes of our lecture time for him to put us where he wants us. Reason number three that a teacher is an asshole: assigned seating. By the time he calls my name, I'm already contemplating dropping the class. This is a two-part course, and if this is how the first day goes, I can't imagine how an entire two semesters will be.

Tossing my bag down next to my shiny new assigned seat, I slump down as far as I can and close my eyes. I'm ready to go home.

"Hello. I believe I am to sit here."

I crack an eye open at the soft, accented voice. There is a freakishly tall guy standing next to me, clutching one of those fancy shoulder bags rich people substitute for backpacks. He's wearing khaki pants and a dark green polo shirt.

"Jesus Christ," I mutter, screwing up my face in distaste. He pulls out the chair next to mine and gently sets his bag on the floor. He looks like every other rich white boy at this school: medium-length brown hair, blue eyes, straight teeth. I make a vow right then and there to ignore the shit out of him all semester.

"I am Henri Vasel," he says in that same quiet voice. In his accent, his name sounds a little bit like Enree. Maybe I'll pretend not to understand that he said Henri, and see if I can fuck with him. "What is your name?"

I ignore him, crossing my arms and facing forward in my seat. Feigning deafness seems like a good way to make him leave me alone.

Dr. Robertson saves the day, pacing in front of the class—he too is wearing a polo and khakis, bringing the count up to two douchebags in the room—and giving us the verbal equivalent to what he already emailed us on the syllabus.

"Now," he says, clapping his hands and rubbing his palms together as though he's about to give us a surprise. "This class will be run a little differently than you're used to in a college course. There will be lecture time, yes, but there will also be an equal amount of seminar time. And by that I mean time to work one-on-one with your seat partner."

Oh dear God, kill me now. I chance a look at *Enree Vasel* and see that he's sitting with hands clasped on the table in front of him, eyes trained on Dr. Robertson as he gives him his full attention. He's wearing leather bracelets on his left arm, three of them looped around his wrist and sliding down a muscular forearm. I look away, because I don't care about his muscles.

"Too often college courses focus on the individual and forget about the collective. And perhaps in mathematics, this approach works. However, this is communications and we must"—Dr. Robertson pauses, gazing around the room and smiling slightly—"communicate. Therefore, half of your grade will depend on group work. Half of your grade will depend on your ability, in short, to communicate."

Several ass-kissers in the room laugh and Dr. Robertson smiles indulgently at them. He turns around to write an assignment out on that damn chalkboard, and murmured conversation breaks out through the room. The frat boy lookalike sitting next to me stays quiet, eyes on the professor as he waits patiently for the lecture to continue.

This is one of my longer classes—pushing two hours—and there is still fifteen minutes left until the end when Dr. Robertson stops his lecture. He awards us with another of his smiles and spreads his hands to encompass what he wrote on the board. He acts more like a politian than a doctor. I think I might hate him.

"For the rest of class today, we'll be doing the simplest of exercises: getting to know one another. You and your partner will be together all semester, whether you want to be or not. There will be no switching. There will be no coming to my office and pleading your case to be paired with your best friend or dormmate. The person next to you will be there all semester, and possibly the next as well." He gestures. "Time to say hello."

Like a dog following his master's orders, Polo Shirt turns to me and smiles.

"Hello," he says obediently.

"Hi," I bite out, crossing my arms tighter and scowling.

"I am Henri Vasel. You may call me Vas, if you wish." He turns in his seat to face me fully as he repeats his earlier greeting. My eyes are drawn to his legs. *Khaki.* Honestly. "What is your name?"

"Atlas."

He waits for me to say more, and when I don't, he nods in

a way that looks like he's bowing to me. I stare at him. Is this guy fucking with me?

"Atlas," he repeats, except on his tongue it sounds sort of like Ahh-tlos.

"Atlas," I correct snappishly, earning myself a quizzical look.

"Atlas," he says, exactly the same way he just said it. I roll my eyes. Whatever.

"I'm not calling you by your last name," I warn him. The moment he told me I could call him "Vas," I clocked him as an athlete. What the fuck is it with jocks and wanting to be addressed by their last name?

"You may call me however you wish," he says equably, doing his head-bowing thing again.

I'm going to do my best not to call him anything at all. Pulling out my cellphone, I make sure the volume is muted and pull up social media. There are still eight minutes left in class. Eight minutes to ignore Polo Shirt.

"May I ask what are you studying?"

"No," I answer, so quickly it catches him off guard, and he lapses into a surprised silence. The rebuke buys me a full minute of peace before he tries again.

"What student year are you in?"

"What the hell is a student year?" I ask, even though I know what he meant. His brow scrunches up in confusion, and he places his hand on the center of his chest.

"I am in year four, and will do another after this year."

I raise my eyebrows. "It's taking you five years to earn your...?" I leave the tail end of the question hanging for him to fill in the blanks, but he only stares at me and waits. Great —I'm stuck with the idiot for a partner. "What degree are you here for?"

"I am earn a dual degree in media and communications, with a minor in foreign language," he answers, punctuating this with another nod, this one joined by a smile. What the hell is he doing, nodding so fucking much?

"Earning," I correct.

"Pardon?"

"You are *earning* a dual degree in media and communications. You should probably learn basic English if you're going to be in the media, yeah?"

He jolts and the smile slips just a bit before he slides it back into place. Instead of rising to the bait, he nods—*again* —and agrees with me.

"Yes. I am still learning basic English. My apologies if I make mistakes."

He says this perfectly seriously and completely without guile, eyes locked on mine in an almost uncomfortable way.

"Whatever." I shrug and look back down at my phone. Less than two minutes left of class. I'm logging into my account and dropping this shit the moment I get home.

3

Henri

MY PARTNER in Creative Communications makes me nervous. I'm good with people—always have been—but from the moment I sat down next to him I felt wrong-footed and unsure. I'm certain I've never met him before, yet it's obvious he doesn't care for me. I don't like that at all.

I know I have an almost pathological need to be liked. My mother tells me I have a dependent personality disorder, and that I have an unhealthy desire to make others happy. She tells me she worries about my self-worth, and that people will take advantage of me if I am not careful. I wonder what she would say if I told her Atlas' clear animosity toward me had me running 5k on the treadmill after practice finished that day, unable to settle myself down.

My palms are a little clammy as I push open the door to the lecture hall. Atlas isn't yet in his seat, which affords me a few moments to get my bearings once I sit down. I'm going to work extra hard to watch my English when I talk to him, and make sure I pronounce his name correctly. Both of these seemed to be black marks against me last time, and I won't make the same mistake twice.

I place an apple on the corner of my desk nearest Atlas' seat, before laying out my notebook and pen. That done, I turn my phone completely off and tuck it back into my bag. Resting my hands in my lap, I sit up straight and watch the door, waiting.

Atlas is one of the last people to enter and he does so with a frown on his face. It's a different frown than the one Carter wears. Carter employs his animosity as a shield to protect himself; it took next to nothing to break it down. Atlas, on the other hand, is all sharp edges. His frown is a knife blade. A warning to stay away.

"Good day, Atlas," I greet him carefully, making sure to soften my accent on his name. I can't tell if I've done well or not—he ignores me and takes his seat, expression never wavering. "How are we today?"

Silence.

I like silence. I am a creature of silence. But this silence is prickly and uncomfortable, and makes me feel vaguely ill. Perhaps he's angry because he's hungry.

"Would you like an apple?" I ask, gesturing to the Granny Smith I brought with me for a snack between lectures. His gaze slides to mine.

"I don't like green apples," he says. I nod. I'll remember that for next time.

"My apologies."

He rolls his eyes and I sigh. When he bends over to dig through his backpack, I watch him. I'm good with people because I'm good at figuring them out. He's an enigma right now, but perhaps not for long.

The first thing I notice is his hair: black. True black hair isn't common, but he has it. There's an almost navy hue when the light hits it just right, and I can tell it's soft by the sheen. I cannot pinpoint just by looking at him, but his creamy skin and almond-shaped eyes speak of a mixed race. His eyelashes are so long and dark, it looks like he's wearing eyeliner. No tattoos, no piercings. His clothes are plain and without any overt logos that might tell me how much they cost. He wears a simple gold band on his pinky finger.

"I like your ring," I tell him, and his eyes narrow nearly to slits.

"Another polo shirt, I see," he responds tartly. I look down at my shirt. It is, in fact, a polo. I have five, all different colors, that I rotate throughout the week. On the weekends I wear my two SCU hockey shirts. I check to make sure the buttons are all fastened, but everything looks in order. Who doesn't like polo shirts?

"Yes," I agree. "I have two blue ones, but this is the darker one."

I grin, trying to bring him in on the joke, but he doesn't even crack a smile. If anything, his eyes narrow further. With his dark irises and dark lashes, it's a distinctly shark-like look. I struggle to maintain my calm, bland expression.

"What?" he snaps. "Why are you looking at me like that?"

I falter, unused to people being so vocal and unpleasant. Most people will smile to my face before talking behind my back. Atlas seems to have no compunctions about being hostile, and makes no effort at all to be friendly. It would almost be admirable, if it wasn't a bit frightening. I remind myself that unhappy people usually take it out on others, and that it likely has little to do with me. It's important that I don't let it get to me.

I fix my smile back into place.

"Do you have many classes today?"

"Yes."

"What is your favorite class?"

"Ceramics."

"Oh?" I sit up straighter, delighted by this. "What are you making?"

"Ceramics."

You did that to yourself, I reprimand myself, giving a mental shake. Atlas is barely maintaining eye contact with me, mouth turned down in a disinterested frown and arms crossed loosely over his chest. His posture screams *you are boring me.* Even so, I can't help but notice and appreciate how pretty his face is.

"Are you an artist?" I try again. He sighs gustily.

"Let's play the silent game, shall we?"

"I am unfamiliar with this, but I shall like to play," I respond gamely, nodding. Maybe if I let him win, he'll be in a better mood.

"No, it's...Jesus Christ, never mind." He slaps his hands down on the table. A sharp report echoes through the room and several people turn around to look for the source of the noise. He doesn't deign to look at them or apologize. The look in his eyes when they meet mine is venomous. "I am majoring in general studies right now, while I figure out what I want to do. Ceramics was something I chose for the hell of it. Turns out I'm actually pretty good, and I like getting my hands dirty."

I can't help but smile as he talks, excited to hear him say so many words in a row. True, he's still looking like he wants to murder me, but at least he's talking. It seems like a step in the right direction, at the very least.

"The polo shirts and khaki pants make you look like a snob," he continues. It takes me an embarrassing amount of time to realize he's talking about *me*. "You look like the kind of guy whose parents own a vacation home, and got you into school by donating money. The kind of guy who drives a fancy car and calls it his *baby*. You look like you're trying to show how much better you are than the rest of us by dressing like that. You look, in short, like a douchebag."

I bite my tongue. Probably best not to tell him I drive a BMW.

"I'll try not to be a snob," is the best I can come up with in reply, but it does little to placate him. Unfortunately, there is nothing I can do about my wardrobe, short of going out and buying all new clothes. Even I know this would be taking things too far. If he doesn't like me in a polo shirt, he probably won't like me in a hockey T-shirt.

"You're fucking weird," he replies, turning and facing forward as Dr. Robertson walks into the lecture hall.

ATLAS SUCCESSFULLY IGNORES me through class, and is packed up and walking away before I've had a chance to say goodbye. I stare morosely at his back, lamenting the fact that we won't have class together again for the rest of the week. I'll have to give it some thought over the weekend, and try to come up with a plan on how to make him like me.

Carefully repacking my shoulder bag, I wait until every student has passed before I step out of the aisle and head for the door. I turn my phone back on as I get outside, see the text message from Zeke, and turn toward the library. I need to speak to him about the internship next summer, but perhaps

I can also obtain his opinion about Atlas. Zeke is smart—he will know what to do.

He's seated in the back of the room at his usual spot, books and flashcards spread across the table. He's looking at his laptop screen as I walk up, clicking the cap of a highlighter idly. I stop several paces away from the table and speak softly, not wanting to startle him.

"Good afternoon, Zeke."

He looks up and smiles, dropping the highlighter and closing his laptop.

"Vas, hi. How are you?"

Pulling out the chair across from him, I sit down carefully and lay my bag on the floor, tucking it between my feet so that it's not a tripping hazard for anyone walking by. Interlocking my fingers, I rest my hands in front of me on the tabletop.

"I am well, thank you for asking. May I interrupt you for a moment?"

"Of course, you're not interrupting. I'm already done with the assigned problems." He laughs sheepishly. "Now I'm just doing the rest of them for fun."

I decide I don't have anything to say about doing math problems for fun, so I merely smile and nod.

"I am considering an internship for over next summer. I have spoken to Coach Mackenzie about it. It would be a very" —I pause, trying to mentally sound out the word—"incredible opportunity as it would provide valuable experience in the NHL."

"Oh, wow! With Carter's team, you mean?"

"Indeed."

"You should do it," Zeke says immediately. "Would you

like me to help you with the application? I can read through and proof it."

"Oh." I pause, having to reorder my thoughts and what I wanted to say. I wasn't expecting him to offer that. "That would be very kind of you, thank you."

"Would you like to stay with Carter and me over the summer? You wouldn't be able to stay in the dorms, probably, but we have an extra bedroom right now. We offered it to my grandma, but she's being stubborn."

I open my mouth to reply and find that English has abandoned me. I came here to ask that, but hadn't expected it to be offered so willingly. The thought of taking advantage of my friend, if I asked him if I could move in, had kept me awake for hours after Coach Mackenzie suggested it. I would not want Carter to feel obligated to say yes. In the spirit of that, I had compiled a list of ways I could make myself useful and pay my way. Apparently, Zeke doesn't even need to see it to offer the space.

"I would not want to make trouble," I tell Zeke, once I am able to formulate a response. Bending over, I pull out the thin folder I tucked my proposal into and slide it over to him. "Here is a list of things I will do and money I will pay. That is, if I move in. I had come here intending to ask you, but you have beaten me to it."

"Household cleaning, including, but not limited to, floors, windows, dusting, and all kitchen appliances," Zeke reads off. He glances up at me and back down to the proposal. "Uhm... this is very thorough and I appreciate the effort, but I already know Carter isn't going to go for this."

Anticipating this, I slide a pen over the table to him. "You may make any edits that you deem appropriate."

"No, I mean...he's just going to say no to *all* of this." Zeke waves a hand over the papers. "He's going to say you can move in and the only thing you have to worry about cleaning is your room and the kitchen if you use it. He's going to be offended if you offer him money, and he's going to be *really* offended if you offer him this amount of money."

Zeke places a finger on the figure I'd calculated for rent and utilities. I nod.

"It is too low."

"No." He laughs. "It's too high, Vas. You're our friend. We'd be happy to have you stay with us over the summer and the only thing you have to worry about paying for is your groceries."

"Oh, no." I shake my head. "That is not fair. I would not want to take advantage of my good friends."

Zeke stares at me for a second, thinking, before tapping the proposal again.

"This would be *us* taking advantage of *you*."

Surprised, I sit back in my chair. I'd thought Zeke would be the easier of them to convince, but apparently that was a miscalculation. Biting the inside of my cheek, I try to think of any possible arguments.

"You will not miss having your own house? You will not mind extra wheel?" I mentally curse myself as soon as I say it. It's *third* wheel.

"Nope."

"I am very quiet. I am also very clean," I tell him, still feeling the need to convince him even though it's obviously unnecessary. "I can make many German foods."

"Sounds great," Zeke replies pleasantly. "Now, trash that before Carter sees it and gets mad at you for thinking he'd make you pay him fifteen hundred dollars to rent a bedroom."

"This is the amount that is the average cost of apartments here," I point out. Zeke merely shakes his head, grinning as he slides the proposal back over to me.

"When he got signed to the AHL, Carter suggested we have my grandma move from her mobile home to our house. They've been arguing about it ever since." Zeke laughs quietly, eyes dancing with happiness. "She wants to pay him, he doesn't want any of her money, and around and around they go. Between you and I, Grandma is going to win, though. Carter is low-key terrified of her."

I smile at that, even though I still feel a little wary about this. Zeke, sensing this, leans toward me over the table and flips the proposal over so that it's no longer visible.

"Vas. Carter won't ever say it out loud, but you're important to him. He isn't the kind of person who has a hundred friends, he's the kind that has two friends he'd do anything for. You're one of those people. Trust me when I say that nothing would make him happier than to be able to help you by offering a home for the summer."

"But you are sure I cannot pay you?" I ask a tad desperately. "It is a paid internship. Coach Mackenzie said so."

"I have never been surer of anything in my life," Zeke answers firmly. "Carter won't take your money, and he'll get pissed if you offer it."

I sigh, sliding the folder off the table and tucking it back into my bag.

"You are good friends."

Zeke beams, sitting back in his chair and pulling his cellphone out of his pocket. He taps out a quick message before laying it face down on the table.

"Summers are the best because Carter is home all the

time. You can teach me to make German dishes and Carter can be our guinea pig."

Frowning, I sort through my knowledge of English phrases. I know a guinea pig is a sort of pet rodent, but I'm unsure of how one relates to Carter eating German food. I hope he's not thinking I will feed them guinea pigs. Deciding it's probably not a distinction that's important to the conversation, I simply smile and nod. It reminds me of Atlas, and his correction of my grammar.

"There was another thing I wished to discuss with you, if you have more time to spare."

"Hit me," he answers, closing his math textbook and sliding it to the side.

"I need assistance with my Creative Communications partner. He dislikes me."

Zeke blinks at me, head tilted a degree to the side. He looks surprised.

"Uhm," he says, "what?"

Sighing, I explain to him all my encounters with Atlas thus far. The more I talk, the more his face scrunches up and his eyes narrow. By the time I fall silent, I've figured out the expression: he's angry on my behalf.

"Well, he sounds rude," Zeke says shortly. "I don't think you should talk to him at all."

"We are partners all semester," I remind him.

"Talk to him the bare minimum to get your work done," he advises, making me grimace. He sighs and takes pity on me. "Kill him with kindness."

This is a saying I'm familiar with.

"Indeed. That is the best plan I have," I confirm.

"Totally unrelated, and has no bearing on the conversation whatsoever, but do you want to know the origin of 'killing with kindness'?" He waits for me to nod, eyes wide with barely contained excitement. "Well, most credit Shakespeare, but a case could also be made that it originates from apes' propensity of hugging their young too tightly and killing them."

"Well then," I say, for want of anything better. And then, because even with my tenuous grasp of the English language, I can recognize an easy joke when I see one: "Perhaps I will simply give Atlas a tight hug."

Zeke laughs, and I love him for it.

"Honestly, it sounds like he needs one," he agrees.

We chat quietly for a few more moments, before Zeke's phone buzzes with a text message. I can tell it's Carter by the way his smile turns fond and his eyes soften. A spike of envy worms through my chest. I wish I had a Carter or a Zeke to text me. I wish I had someone who was my own.

Zeke taps out a reply and looks up at me, catching what must be a telling expression on my face.

"You okay?"

"I have found that college is very alone," I admit. He nods even though that hadn't sounded quite right. "I am glad I have hockey, or I would not have anything. It is hard to make friends."

"Yeah, it is," he agrees sadly. "Meaningful relationships are difficult to cultivate. But they're worth it when you have them."

Zeke unlocks his phone screen, swiping through a few things before laying it flat on the table and sliding it over to me. Angling my head, I look at the text message thread with Carter.

> Vas is applying to an internship with your team for next summer. He won't be able to stay in the dorms though, because campus will be closed.

I'll text him. He should stay with us.

"See," Zeke whispers, after giving me a moment to read the messages. "We want you to stay with us."

"Ask him about the money—"

"No money," Zeke interrupts. "You're a good friend. Let us do this for you."

I stare hard at his phone, trying to think of a way to argue that without sounding ungrateful. It doesn't matter how he words it, the situation still feels wrong to me. It feels like I'll be interrupting what would otherwise be a summer just the two of them.

"Only if you are sure," I stress. "I will not want to be a burden."

"I'll talk to Carter," he reassures me. "But let's just assume that you'll stay with us, okay? You can check that item off your list. Now, when is the application due?"

I give Zeke the information Coach Mackenzie provided me and carefully take notes when he offers advice. We stay in the library, comfortably working together, until the librarian gently reminds us that they close in thirty minutes. Chastised, I hastily put my notebook away and apologize to her. Zeke and I don't speak again until we're standing outside in the evening heat.

"Thank you for your assistance," I tell him.

"Sure, anytime! When is your next CC class?"

"Tuesday," I reply morosely, thinking of Atlas.

"Well, I still don't like that he was so rude to you, but maybe we should give him the benefit of the doubt. I mean" —he grimaces, shooting me a crooked smile—"I'm literally in love with one of the rudest people I've met, so."

"Yes. I am thinking he probably needs a friend."

"Don't take it personally," Zeke warns. "He doesn't even know you. If he doesn't like you, it says more about him than it does about you."

4

Atlas

HENRI VASEL IS ALREADY SEATED when I walk into the lecture hall. He's wearing khaki pants and a grey polo shirt, because, apparently, he only has one wardrobe. Looking at him—with his perfectly styled brown hair, carefully trimmed scruff, and unwrinkled clothing—I just want to throw him down into the mud. I want to filthy him up a little bit and crack the choir boy façade. Maybe also punch him in the face, because for some reason he really rubs me the wrong way.

He smiles when he sees me walking toward him, as though we're the best of friends and I didn't insult him last time we were together.

"Good afternoon, Atlas. Are you doing well today?"

"Fine," I grunt, squeezing around him and tossing my backpack onto the floor between our seats.

"Did you enjoy your weekend?"

"Sure did."

He doesn't seem perturbed by the one-sided conversation.

If anything, he looks happy that I'm engaging at all. I probably should have continued with the silent treatment. Now, he's going to expect me to talk to him every fucking class.

"Do you support hockey?" he asks, angling himself toward me and linking his fingers together in his lap. He looks like he's trying to convince me to vote for him in a student body election.

"Do I look like someone who supports hockey?"

He blinks. "Yes?"

"No."

"I play hockey, but it is not for all people," he says magnanimously. "How is ceramics?"

Of course he plays hockey. He asked me to call him by his last name and both of my thighs put together equal the size of one of his. Not only did I get stuck with the most annoying motherfucker in class, but a jock too. Lucky me.

"Fine."

"What are you making?"

"Pottery."

Instead of being surprised by my less-than-friendly answers, he neatly sidesteps them and fires another question at me. I'm definitely regretting opening my mouth. Next time, I'm choosing silence.

"Would you like an apple?"

"I don't like green apples," I remind him, just as he pulls a red apple from the side pocket of his bag and holds it out to me in his palm. He doesn't even have the decency to look smug for remembering. He waits for me to take it from him, a bland half-smile on his face. "I'm good."

"I shall leave here, yes?" He puts it on the corner of his desk, closest to me. "In case you become hungry."

"Thanks," I answer grudgingly, even though I know I'll

never eat that damn apple. What the hell is he playing at, anyway? Who the fuck brings food for someone that sits next to them in a lecture hall?

He doesn't respond to my thanks, just inclines his head slightly and turns to face the front of the room as Dr. Robertson comes in. Christ, but he is a weird fucker. He remains bent over his notebook the entire class, diligently writing down everything the instructor says or writes on the board. When I peek over at his paper, his handwriting is straight and tidy—rows and rows of perfect penmanship. Unlike earlier, when he was talking to me, he frowns a little bit as he writes, as though he's concentrating particularly hard. He keeps writing even when Dr. Robertson pauses, as though he has to catch up, and every now and then he shakes out his hand like it's cramping.

"Why don't you take notes on a computer?" I ask him as we pack up at the end of class. His head snaps up from where he was bent over his bag, and his eyes widen. I curse myself as soon as I see that stupid, hopeful look on his face. This is the first time I've talked to him without him starting the conversation.

"I am not skilled at typing," he admits. "And writing is to help me remember."

"Got it," I respond shortly, standing up and edging past him. He plasters himself against the desk in an effort to make more room for me.

"I hope you have a pleasant evening, Atlas."

"See you next time, Henri," I call, giving a flippant wave over my shoulder and mimicking his accent when I say his name. He starts to reply, but I'm already too far away to hear and I don't bother to turn around.

Head down and hands shoved into my pockets, I walk

home. The lawn is scattered with various groups of students. Some are lounging in the sun reading, while others throw frisbees or a football. As usual, I feel as detached from it all as if I'm watching a television show that's set in college. I've never had the type of friends who'd willingly spend an afternoon on the grass, aimlessly tossing a frisbee. Half of me wonders if I'm doing college wrong, while the other half wonders why I even care. What would be the point of trying? None of this matters. We're all going to end up in meaningless jobs we hate anyway, and college relationships don't last. It's all a waste of time.

When I get back to the house I share with four other guys, I've got a minor headache and a not-so-minor bad mood. I need a drink and a cigarette—preferably at the same time. I could also use a blowjob, but I'm not sure I have the fortitude to make that one happen tonight. Henri Vasel is so fucking exhausting, he's used up all I have to give for socializing today.

I ignore two of my roommates that are congregated in the living room and head up the stairs to my room. I've got the smallest room in the house—just big enough to fit a full bed and a dresser that I also use as a desk. When I need to spread out, I usually do my homework seated on the floor. Whenever I get annoyed about the situation, I remind myself that it could be worse. I could still be in the dorms, listening to my neighbors fuck through the thin walls, and having to wade through hallway parties to get to the bathroom. Anything is better than that.

I pass Nate Basset's door on my way to my room, cracked open enough to reveal him sitting at his desk—an actual desk, too, because his bedroom is larger than a kitchen pantry. Tossing my backpack in the direction of my closed door, I push Nate's open without knocking. He looks up and makes a face at me, but doesn't bother with a rebuke. We've shared a wall for the last two years—he's well used to my "glooms" as he calls them.

"What's up?" he asks as I close the door behind me and walk over to sit on his bed. He sighs as I flop backward and pull his pillow under my head.

"You play hockey," I start, and he laughs.

"Sure do."

"You know that Henri Vasel guy?"

"Vas!" Nate exclaims happily. "Yeah, he's our top line winger. He's great."

"He's weird as shit," I correct. Nate frowns.

"I mean...okay, yeah, he's a little odd. But he's the most chill dude I've ever met. Nothing gets to that guy, Atlas, *nothing*. I've never once seen him lose his cool, not even when we're down by five in the third and the other team is serving penalties like they're going out of style. Everyone else will be pissed off and then there's Vas—chill as fuck and telling everyone to play our game not theirs."

"Christ, Nate." I roll my eyes. "I don't know what any of that crap you just said means. Be fucking normal for one second."

"He's cool," he says succinctly, shrugging. "We love him."

"He bothers me."

It's Nate's turn to roll his eyes.

"Literally every person bothers you. I hate to break it to you, friend, but Vas is the most inoffensive person I've ever met. If you've got a problem with him, that's on you."

"He's too fucking nice, man. He's like...*fake* nice. Nobody is that friendly all the time."

"Vas is." He shrugs again.

"Well, then he's got a lot of repressed emotions that are going to explode someday. He brought me an apple, dude. I told him he dressed like a prick and then today he brings me an *apple*. What the fuck?"

Nate laughs, shaking his head and swiveling his desk chair back to face his homework.

"God, you're such an ass. You know, maybe if you pretended to be happy every now and again, you might find you're happier by accident."

"Wow." I draw out the O dramatically and raise my hands to slow clap. "That was deep. You should sell that to Hallmark —slap it on a greeting card."

"Fuck you," he retorts, flipping me off over his shoulder. "This is exactly what I mean. You're a dick and you expect everyone else to be as miserable as you are. Vas is nice, so of course something is wrong with him, or he must want something from you—he can't be friendly just because he's a good person. God forbid! Would it kill you to give someone the benefit of the doubt for a change?"

"Probably."

"Maybe just settle for basic manners, then."

"Whatever. I need a fucking cigarette." I sit up and slide over until I'm sitting on the edge of his bed. He glances at me, stretching his arms above his head and groaning.

"If you're going to smoke, shut my window on your way out. I don't want that shit wafting in here."

Scoffing, I step over to his window and slide it down, knocking the latch into place.

"Yeo, I wouldn't want to ruin the sanctity of your precious hockey lungs. You having company tonight?"

"Nah, not tonight. I've got a shit ton of studying to do— like, *a ton*—and I can't put it off. No distractions," Nate says, holding his palms out in front of him and closing his eyes like he's trying to ward off said distractions.

"Me either." I head toward his door. Nate and I aren't friends, exactly. We're more two guys who became friendly by the simple expedient of having bedrooms next to each other in a shared house. We've never once hung out beyond sitting together in the living room or chatting as I pass his room on the way to mine. Pausing in the doorframe, I glance back at him. Maybe we *could* be friends though, if we tried. "You got plans this weekend?"

He spins his desk chair around, looking at me like he's already half checked out of the conversation.

"What? Oh, yeah, I've got hockey like usual. Why?"

"There's a party at Foggers Saturday. You should come."

Nate scrunches up his face in distaste. The stoners all seem to congregate together on campus, so their house was christened Foggers as a subtle nod toward the haze of smoke that seems to hover there like a fog. Not the most creative name, but the few of my friends who live there seem to find it hilarious. Although, since they're usually high, they seem to find most things hilarious.

"Uhm, no, thanks. I don't need to get kicked off the team because Coach decides to randomly drug test us and I piss out bath salts."

Snorting, I shake my head at him. "Pretty sure that's not how drug tests or bath salts work. Or weed, for that matter."

"Thanks for the invite, but I'm going to pass. I've heard what goes on there, and I don't want to be a part of it. I'm not trying to become the next statistic for college overdoses."

"No worries. See you around," I say, trying to backpedal from the conversation. I have no idea what idiocy compelled me to invite a jock to a party at the druggie house. The only time those two worlds collide is when someone wants to buy weed. They don't pretend to be friends.

I leave Nate to his homework, stepping into my bedroom and snatching up my backpack on the way in. Kicking the door shut, I immediately crank open the small picture window beside my bed. My half-empty pack of cigarettes and lighter are sitting on the windowsill, waiting for me. I lean against the wall, making sure to angle my head so the smoke rolls out through the window, close my eyes, and enjoy the burn in my lungs.

I started smoking back in middle school on a dare, and mostly to try and get my dad's attention. I'd nearly made it through an entire pack—weeks of smoking in the backyard of our house and leaving the butts on the patio—before he noticed. The resultant fight hadn't been as satisfying as I'd imagined it would be, and only gave my dad another reason to dislike me. *I have work to do, Atlas, I don't have time to deal with this right now,* he'd said, and then hadn't even bothered to take the pack of cigarettes away. Same shit, different day.

Now, I mostly smoke because I like it. I know I shouldn't —I'm not an idiot—and I don't suck down a pack a week. I'm a casual smoker. The sort of smoker who lights up at the end of a hard day, when their German communication partner drives them nuts for no good reason.

Opening my eyes, I exhale through my nose and wave my hand to waft the smoke toward the window. Fucking Henri Vasel. I know Nate's right, and it shouldn't bother me that he's nice. I also know it shouldn't bother me that he's a little different. But it does. Everything about him—from his hair, to his accent, to his goddamn *polo shirts*—bothers me. Everything about him seems fake to me, like he's putting on a show.

The only time people treat others with that level of respect is when they expect something in return.

Distaste dances in my lungs with the cigarette smoke. Tapping it out in the ashtray, I rest the unsmoked half across the top to save it for later. Leaving the window cranked open, I sit cross-legged on the floor and pull my backpack toward me. I need to at least get a head start on my homework before this weekend, or I'll be stuck doing it with a hangover.

Dr. Robertson presents us with our first team project as though he's handing out blank checks. Beside me, Henri is carefully writing everything down. I can see the tip of his tongue poking out from between his lips, and have to physically drag my eyes away and back to the front of the room. He's so distracting. Even when he's silently working beside me, my gaze seems to track to him like it's magnetized. I have to remind myself that he's not in any way my type, and I'm not going to have my first sexual experience with a guy be with someone like him.

Instead of staring at Henri's profile, my eyes rest on the red apple sitting once more on the corner of his desk. *Not today*, I think waspishly.

"The case studies themselves are unimportant," Dr. Robertson says to the room, pacing in front of us. "The point of the exercise is the discourse they evoke. There are no right or wrong answers. I do not need you to agree with your partner, I merely need you to converse with them. The Dropbox will open tonight and will remain open until Monday."

Papers start to shuffle as everyone realizes class is over and it's almost time to go.

"And one more thing," Dr. Robertson calls, voice cutting through the ambient noise of the room. "Please remember that half of your grade depends on the work you complete with your partner. Take it seriously. That is all—enjoy your weekends."

Henri is still writing as I shut my laptop and slide everything into my backpack. I wait for him, feeling annoyed that he can't write faster than a five-year-old. When he finally sets down his pencil and looks over at me, I scowl.

"You write so fucking slow," I tell him.

"Yes," he replies, nodding. "I apologize if I am in your way."

He scoots his chair into the table, making room for me to walk behind him and leave.

"We have to get together this weekend for an assignment," I remind him. "I'm not planning on wasting my entire weekend on this shit, so let's schedule something and get it over with."

"Certainly. I have two hockey games this weekend. Saturday, the bus leaves at three. Sunday it is here, but I will be going to the rink earlier. Perhaps we could meet in the morning?"

Annoyed that I have to plan my weekend around something as idiotic as a sporting event, I hold my hand out to him.

"Give me your phone."

He does. His background is the standard home screen that comes programmed on all iPhones, and I don't see a single app that I could make fun of him for. Maybe hockey guys don't need dating apps to get laid. He could probably walk across campus and pick up women without even trying. I create a contact and shoot a text message over to myself so that I have his number. When I hand his phone back to him, he smiles.

"Saturday or Sunday? Pick one," I demand.

"Saturday will perhaps work best, if you are agreeable." He does that weird nodding thing and reaches for the red apple he brought. Like he does after every class, he holds it out to me. Like I do every time, I ignore his outstretched hand and stand up.

"Saturday is fine. I'll text you."

With that, I slide past him and walk out the door without looking back. If he wants to pretend to be the nicest man alive, fine. Doesn't mean I have to fall for the act.

5

Henri

MY MORNING with Atlas was a disaster. I hadn't been so foolish to hope that he'd be in a better mood on a Saturday, but he seemed particularly acidic today. Usually, I'd take the responsibility for things moving slowly—I know my English isn't perfect, and I still get tripped up over simple things—but not even I can pretend that I was the problem today. If Atlas and I are to spend an entire semester working together, something will have to change.

The thing is, I am certain that we could get along if he would allow it. He is prickly and rude, yes, but he's also very sharp-witted. Every now and then I get a peek of his dry sense of humor, and I like it. I must also admit that I think he's rather handsome, even despite the bad attitude. I'm certain the real Atlas behind the walls is worth knowing, as long as I can get past the Atlas guarding the gate.

Feeling uncommonly down, I don't bother trying to work on any homework on the team bus. Instead, I stare out the window and listen as my teammates laugh and joke around me. Beside me, Max occasionally jostles my arm when the bus lurches.

"Sorry," he apologizes after a particularly violent jolt that sends him crashing into my shoulder.

"That is no problem," I tell him, smiling. "Will Luke be coming to the game?"

"Not tonight. His car is a piece of crap, so it's better he just watches from home. Wouldn't want him to get stranded." Max smiles and I return it easily.

I play well in the game, able to compartmentalize and focus on the task at hand and not my tumultuous morning. Max—as though spurred on by the knowledge that this is his last year before he joins the NHL—bags five points with two goals and three assists. Nate, too, plays an incredible game and I tell him so when we are waiting to file back onto the bus afterward. He claps a hand on my upper back, smiling wide at the praise.

"Thanks, Vas! You too, buddy," he says, before boarding the bus and finding a seat.

I follow him, taking the spot next to Max as I always do. He looks at me, eyes shining in the dim lighting of the bus. I am suddenly incredibly tired—exhausted from playing sixty minutes of hockey after an equally exhausting sixty minutes spent with Atlas this morning. Max jostles me with his elbow.

"You good?"

"Yes. Merely tired." Max nods in agreement. "Also, I have a communications partner who is difficult. He is not fond of me."

"Really?" He raises his eyebrows. "Huh. Are you sure? I can't imagine anyone not liking you."

"You are very kind, but I am sure. He is not shy about

telling me. I am wondering if perhaps *he* is the communication assignment. If one can speak to Atlas effectively, they shall pass the class."

Max chuckles, turning to face me in his seat. "That bad, huh? Worse than Carter?"

"Carter is easy," I say, waving a hand. "Carter is like...he is like a rose. Thorns, yes, but also a flower. Atlas is only the thorns."

"Oh my god, did you just say Carter is like a flower?"

"It's a metaphor," I explain. Max laughs delightedly.

"Holy shit, I can't wait to tell Luke you said that."

I sigh. "Okay, perhaps that was not quite right. But you understand? Carter needed a friend and was happy when I offered to become that friend. Atlas is not the same. He needs a friend, but does not want one."

"Well, then you don't need him as one anyway."

I nod, because of course he is right. I cannot explain why I want Atlas to like me. I cannot even understand it myself. I just feel like it's important. Atlas is important.

Almost as though my thoughts bring him to fruition, my cellphone buzzes with a text message as we exit the highway and drive toward campus. Beside me, Max is leaned back against the seat, eyes staring sightlessly at the passing darkness through the window. I squint down at my screen, unsure what I'm looking at.

ATLAS

three melbourne place jslkdu big whit house

HENRI

Good evening, Atlas. May I ask for clarification on your previous message?

ATLAS

jesussssss just come hury up

Slightly alarmed, I type out several responses, but end up discarding them all. I wonder if he's texted me by mistake. That makes more sense than him asking me to "just come hurry up." Atlas would never invite me somewhere, unless it was off of a cliff.

HENRI

Did you perhaps mean to text someone else?

There is no response. I stare at my phone, becoming a touch worried the longer I wait. Does he always text like that—with grammatical and spelling errors? I send another message to him, asking for more clarification. Again, I'm left with silence and my stomach erupts with nervous energy. The bus pulls to a stop in front of the rink and Coach Mackenzie rises to standing.

"Great job tonight. Go home and get some rest—I expect a repeat performance tomorrow."

Max nods like Coach is giving him a direct order and several guys cheer. We get off the bus and gather our bags. I wait patiently for my teammates to get theirs before I attempt to grab my own, standing off to the side and nervously staring at my cellphone. Max steps over to me, his own bag slung over his shoulder and mine in his opposite hand.

"Oh, thank you. You did not have to get that," I tell him.

"No worries. Can I give you a ride home?"

"Oh, no, thank you, Max. I am not far. I shall walk."

Halfway back to my dorm, my phone rings. Thinking it might be Max or Coach Mackenzie needing me to come back to the rink, I stop and set my bag on the ground before fishing my phone out. Atlas' name flashes across the screen and I press the answer button with more force than is strictly necessary.

"Hello?"

"Henri-i-i-i," Atlas sings. He's barely audible over the bass of the music playing in the background. "Henri, Henri, Henri-i-i-i."

"Atlas," I interrupt. He's saying my name strangely, dropping the H and giving the I an extended E sound. Disappointed, I realize that I know exactly why his text was so strange. "Atlas, are you drunk?"

He giggles. "Maybe."

"Perhaps you could turn the music down?" I shout into the phone, fighting against the noise. He laughs again. It's an unhinged noise, and I wish he would stop making it.

"Are you coming?" Another laugh. "You're coming, right?"

I bend down to pick up my bag, sliding the strap over my shoulder and continuing to walk toward my dorm. Fatigue settles heavy over me once more. I'm too tired to deal with drunk people right now. I'm too tired to deal with Atlas.

"No, Atlas, I am not coming to the party. I must go to sleep." It's already past the time I'd usually be in bed, and I don't adjust my daily schedule to accommodate late nights. It doesn't matter how late I go to bed, I still get up at the same time.

"You have to come. I need you to come."

His voice trails off as though he's no longer speaking directly into the phone, but letting it hang down by his side. The music stops suddenly, and his voice becomes clear again. He's repeating *please come* over and over again. The back of my neck tingles with unease and I stop walking once more. I don't feel right about this.

"Where are you?"

"Number three Melbourne Place," he says in a singsong, before laughing.

"Atlas, I need you to try and focus, yes?" Turning back around, I peer across the dark campus. Max's car is gone. "I do not want to come to a party. I am just getting home from the game, it is late—"

"I need your help," he whispers, sounding more lucid than he has the entire conversation. Immediately, I pull the phone away from my ear and put it on speaker. When I type the address he gave me into the map app, nothing comes up.

"I need the address, Atlas."

"Number threeeee—"

"No," I interrupt. "That is not correct. Please, just..." I pause, thinking hard. I have no idea what to do, and I wish, more than anything, I'd agreed to letting Max give me a ride. "Share your location, yes? Do you know how to do this?"

He laughs and I barely refrain from cursing in frustration. Changing direction, I walk away from the dorm and toward the lot where I park my car. Tossing my bag into the back, I sit in the driver's seat and desperately try to come up with a solution. At a loss, I try typing different variations of the address he gave me into the map, but none of them work. On the other end of the line, Atlas is singing nonsensically.

"Atlas," I call, trying to get his attention. I keep my voice as even as I can, not wanting to betray my nerves or frustration. "Atlas, please share your location with me, yes?"

"Yes!" he shouts, before devolving into laughter again. Music flares back to life and I hastily lower the volume on my phone.

Tipping my head back against the headrest, I close my eyes and try to come up with another idea. I can't very well drive around campus all night, looking for parties. In fact, I don't even know that Atlas is at a party—he could be anywhere. I'm just coming to the conclusion that maybe I need to call in reinforcements, when my phone buzzes with a text message. I look down and breathe out heavily, dizzy with relief.

"I am on my way, Atlas," I say into the speakerphone, even though I'm pretty sure he is no longer holding it. I can't hear anything other than the indistinct noises one might hear if they were pocket-dialed. Pulling up the location he just shared, I note that it's off campus and an area of town I've never been to before.

The moment I pull into the driveway, I realize there is probably a good reason for that. The house in which Atlas' location has remained stationary looks dilapidated. The front porch is sagging—boards rotting and railing broken. The yard is littered with garbage, overgrown with weeds, and the driveway sports several large cracks that I have to slowly ease my car over. There are lights on inside, but I can't hear any music. Stepping out of the car and adjusting the dress shirt I'm still wearing from the game, I approach the front door and knock briskly.

It takes several minutes of sustained knocking before the door is thrown open by a man who looks far too old to be a college student. Smothering my surprise, I smile politely.

"Good evening. I am here for—to pick up Atlas."

Christ, but I am tired. If the man notices the way I stumbled over the sentence, he doesn't comment on it. His eyes rake over me, top to bottom, and a sneer pulls up one side of his mouth.

"You here to sell fucking Bibles?"

"No, sir, I am here for Atlas," I repeat.

"You look like a Bible thumper," he says, lifting a bottle to his lips and taking a swig. He's wearing a white tank top that looks like it hasn't been washed in this century, and the view I have of the room shows a house in a similar state.

"May you ask Atlas to come to the door?"

"May you ask Atlas to come to the door," he mimics. "Fuck off."

He steps back and goes to swing the door closed. I put my foot between the door and the frame, planting a hand on the wood and shoving it back open. The man stumbles back, liquid sloshing out of the mouth of the bottle he's holding. He rights himself immediately, eyes flashing in anger. I step inside, leaving the door hanging wide open, and make use of every inch of my 6'2" frame—straightening my spine and drawing my shoulders back.

"I do not want to cause any trouble. I would like to pick up my friend," I repeat. I don't want this to get out of hand, but I also don't want to leave without Atlas.

"Get the fuck out of my house," he spits, taking a threatening step toward me. He realizes—the closer he gets—that I'm a good deal taller and wider than him. He might also be cognizant enough to realize that I'm perfectly sober. He narrows his eyes, waves his bottle at the room, and changes track. "Whatever, man."

"Thank you." Stepping past him, and being careful not to touch anything, I quickly peer around the room. It's filthy: carpet and wallpaper yellow with age, drink receptacles discarded around the room, and a white powder scattered across the coffee table. My skin itches, being in this house. I will need another shower before bed, just to scrub away the decay I imagine is already clinging to my body.

"Atlas?" I raise my voice, but none of the people lounging

on the couch so much as raise their heads. It doesn't matter anyway, none of them have hair dark enough to be him.

I tread down the hallway carefully, well aware that this is the sort of place one might step on a used needle. A slight headache is building behind my ears, and my head feels fuzzy with fatigue and nerves. I stick my head into a bedroom and almost gag at the smell of vomit that greets me. Breathing through my mouth, I step far enough in to gaze around at the occupants. A young woman raises her head off the bed where she is tangled up with another woman.

"I am sorry to disturb you, miss," I say softly. "Have you seen Atlas?"

"What?" She sits up a little straighter and the sheet falls down to her waist. She's naked. Politely, I maintain firm eye contact with her even though she makes no move to cover herself back up. Beside her, the other woman hasn't moved an inch.

"Is your companion breathing, ma'am?" I ask, stepping closer and pointing to the unmoving body. People choke and die on their own vomit. I have read about this happening.

"What?" she says again, but obligingly puts a hand on the other woman's shoulder and gives her a vigorous shake. I flinch at the roughness of the gesture, but it does the trick. Her companion sits up, and now I am speaking to *two* unclothed and wasted women.

"Where is Atlas?" I ask firmly, because I know from experience that the best way to deal with drunk people is to project confidence.

"The Chinese guy?" one of them asks.

"He is not Chinese, he...sure, yes, the Chinese guy. Where may I find him?" My headache becomes more insistent. I want to correct her, but I also know that getting into an argument about ethnic profiling with a drunk person will not be fruitful.

"Bedroom down at the end of the hall," she grumbles, pointing a pale arm to the right before flopping back onto the pillow.

"Thank you."

I bypass the rest of the doors until I get to the one at the end of the hall. It's closed, so I knock gently before just letting myself in. The state of this house and its occupants are worrisome. I desperately want to leave. I desperately want to get back to my clean, orderly dorm room and crawl into my non-vomit-soaked sheets.

The moment I walk into the bedroom, I breathe a sigh of relief. Atlas is stretched out on the bed, flat on his stomach, with one arm and leg hanging over the side. His face is turned toward the door, cheek resting against the mattress, and he's breathing softly.

"Atlas," I murmur, placing my palm flat on the middle of his upper back and looking around. There are several small, white pills sitting on the nightstand as well as an empty bottle of cheap vodka. The pills keep my attention far longer than the alcohol. "Atlas, wake up, it is time to be leaving."

"Mm." He mumbles something incoherent and turns to bury his face into the dirty sheets. Alarmed, I grasp his shoulder and pull him back.

"Atlas, do not put your face there. This place is very dirty." The rebuke has him opening his eyes and squinting up at me. A dopey, half-smile crawls across his face.

"En-reeeee," he says, and immediately tries to sit up. I have to help him. He swings his legs over the side of the bed and tips backward until I steady him with my hand on his back. His shirt is damp with sweat and there is a feverish, waxy sheen to his eyes. They look like marbles.

"We are leaving," I say, hooking a hand under his armpit and yanking him to standing. I cannot spend another moment in this place or I will lose my mind.

"Bossy Henri," he says coyly, wrapping a surprisingly firm arm around my waist and plastering himself to my side.

"Do you have your things? Cellphone and wallet?"

He rolls his head until it's lying against my shoulder, so I assume that means he's not going to answer. Gently, I reach down and try to pat his pockets. He giggles.

"That's not a cellphone in my pocket, I'm just happy to see you," he tells me, before devolving into fits of manic laughter.

Sighing, I look around the room. His wallet is in his back pocket, but he's right about the cellphone not being there. Pulling out my own, I call his number and listen for it. After locating his phone—in the closet, of all places—I walk him out the door. He's mostly walking on his own, but still holding tight enough to me that we look like we are competing in a three-legged race. I have to turn him to the side to maneuver down the hallway. Together, we are too wide to fit across.

None of his companions stop us on our way out, and I don't even see the man in the tank top who answered the door. I hope I never, ever have to see him again for as long as I live.

Atlas keeps up a steady stream of gibberish as I help him into the passenger seat of the car, occasionally bursting out into fits of random laughter. When I bend over him to click the seat belt into place, he places his hand on my side and runs his fingertips over my ribs.

"One, two, three, four," he counts under his breath. I

tighten the belt and gently close the door. When I slide into the driver's seat, his dark eyes are shining in the interior light of the car, watching me.

"If you need to be sick, please let me know. We will pull over, yes?" I hand him a water bottle. "You should take small sips of this, please. Do not chug it."

He takes the bottle from me and obediently opens it, sloshing some down his front as he tries to drink. Mentally, I add *clean car* to my to-do list for tomorrow. He holds the bottle out to me as though offering some to share.

"No, thank you. That is for you." I glance over at him after carefully backing us down the driveway. His forehead is leaned against the window, with the water bottle balanced precariously in his lap. "Atlas, do you remember if you took anything?"

He rotates his head enough for me to see one glassy, dark eye. I don't know what to do—take him home or take him to the hospital. I miss Carter and Max with an intensity that burns hot in my chest and makes it hard to breathe. They would know what needs to be done.

"Oh, probably," he responds flippantly.

"What did you take? What are the white pills?"

"Blue ones, white ones, pink ones. I don't remember."

Pulling up to a stop sign, I verify that nobody is behind me and turn to him. He seems less manic now that we're in the quiet, dark car. I put a hand on his shoulder and give him a small, gentle shake.

"You must try to remember, it is very important. You did not take *all* of those, right? Atlas? You did not take multiple pills?"

"Vodka," he says with finality.

"You only drank vodka?"

"Oh, who knows." He sighs. Frustrated, I lean my head down against the steering wheel, and squeeze my eyes shut. A hand pats my back. "Don't cry, Henri. Don't cry."

When I lift my face and look at him, Atlas smiles, hand still patting my upper back mechanically. It makes me sad to see that smile. I hadn't thought it was an expression he knew how to make, and I hate that the first time I've seen it is when he's wasted. Letting my foot off the brake, I continue driving us toward campus.

"Where do you live?"

"Number three Melbourne Place!"

I shake my head, but don't bother arguing with him. We cannot waste the rest of the night driving around aimlessly while I wait for Atlas to provide me with proper instructions. He'll have to come back to my dorm with me.

The campus is deserted by the time I pull my car back into the usual space. Beside me, Atlas is asleep, slumped against the door and breathing softly. He looks so peaceful, I feel badly about reaching across the car and touching his shoulder. I shake him gently, trying not to startle him. After a sustained thirty seconds of jostling, he blinks his eyes open and looks at me.

"We are here," I tell him. He fumbles for the seat belt with shaky hands, and I watch him for a few moments before getting out of the car and walking around to his side. This time, when I lean over him to help, he doesn't touch me.

It takes both of our efforts to unfold him from the car, and once we get there, he leans against the side and closes his eyes as though the movement made him dizzy.

"Where?" he mumbles, squinting around the parking lot.

"I have a single in Simmons Hall," I reply, pointing toward the building. He stares at it, seemingly confused. I grasp a hand around his elbow and pull him gently into motion. "Come. It is late."

He stays quiet as we walk toward my room, bumping against me as he struggles to walk. He stares hard at his feet, apparently confused as to why they aren't working properly. When we get to my room, I lean him against the wall and unlock the door. He steps inside when I gesture.

"Do you have a bathroom?" he asks. Alarmed at the question and the thready sound of his voice, I walk him over to the door and click on the light. It's a small bathroom, but more than most have when they live in a dorm.

"Are you going to be ill?"

"Yeah." He sighs, sinking down to his knees next to the toilet. Trying to give him a little privacy, I leave the bathroom. Taking my shoes off, I line them up by the door, perpendicular with my others.

Pausing to listen at the door of the bathroom, I ascertain that Atlas is still occupied before pulling off my dress clothes and changing into sweats. Biting my lip, I consider laying something out for Atlas as well, but none of my sweatpants will fit him and I'm not sure he's able to function well enough to change his clothes. Deciding I'll wait and see what he wants to do, I rap my knuckles gently on the bathroom door before pushing inside.

He's got his forearms resting on the rim of the toilet, spine arched and head hanging low. I can see sweat beaded on the back of his neck at the base of his hairline, and he's panting like he's just run a race. Silently, I step behind him and wet a clean washcloth in the sink. When I crouch down next to him, he lifts his head and looks at me blearily.

"What are you doing here?" he asks. There's no malice behind the question, just curiosity.

"You called me to pick you up. We are in my dorm." I hold out the washcloth and he takes it from me, wiping it across his face.

"I called you?"

"Yes."

"Sorry," he mumbles, sitting down on the floor and sliding backward until his back comes up against the vanity. He's deathly pale, eyes and hair impossibly dark against his waxy complexion. He looks like a corpse.

"It's all right. Are you going to be sick again?"

"No," he says, before amending it to, "Not yet."

I hold out a hand for him and pull him to standing, keeping hold of him when he sways dangerously. He laughs, apparently finding something funny in the situation. When we get to my room, I'm able to deposit him on the bed without a fight and hand him a fresh bottle of water. Faced with the conundrum of clothes again, I hesitate. Atlas doesn't look at me, just sits hunched on the edge of the bed, hands shaking where they are curled around the water bottle. He will not ask for help, I realize, even though he needs it.

Without speaking, I crouch down and begin untying the laces on his shoes.

6

Atlas

I WATCH as Henri kneels in front of me, swaying like I'm sitting on the deck of a boat. My head feels like it's stuffed full of wool, my brain sluggish and heavy. It feels as though my neck might break from the strain of holding my head aloft.

I feel a strange sort of disconnect from my body as I watch Henri get the laces of one shoe undone before moving to the other one. Maybe it's because I'm wasted, but I feel like I can see a thousand shades of brown in the strands of his hair. I've never seen his head from this angle before. His hair looks shiny, and is a strange mix of wavy and curly. I like it.

Almost as though my arm is being controlled by a puppeteer, I watch my hand lift from my lap and my fingers touch his head.

"Soft," I say, threading my fingers through. He doesn't say anything, just finishes with the laces of my shoes and grasps the heels to pull them off. When he stands up, my hand falls to the bed and I feel oddly sad. He walks over to the door and places my shoes next to his, all lined up in a row. I laugh, even though I'm unsure why it's funny.

"You should get some rest," he tells me, drawing my attention to the bed.

Obediently, I stand up and grasp the hem of my shirt, meaning to take it off. The room jolts and my knees give out, but Henri catches my arm and directs me back to sitting. The bed sways as well, but gently.

"Your room is nuts," I tell him, meaning the way everything is moving. His hand is on my shoulder, putting his forearm in my direct line of sight, and reminding me how muscular they are. "You have nice arms."

Another laugh escapes at that, but Henri doesn't join in. I peer up at him, leaning backward with the motion and feeling my stomach slosh dangerously.

"You should lie down," he says.

Good idea. I let myself fall to the side, legs still off the bed. The room still rocks, but it's better this way. I close my eyes.

"Move up, Atlas." Henri's voice has me cracking my eyes back open to find him bent over me, one hand warm on my arm. He helps me slide up the bed until my head is on the pillow, and my legs aren't hanging off.

His face is so close to mine, with him bent over me like this. It's a nice face, I realize. I reach out and press my fingers to his cheekbone.

"I like your face," I tell him. My mouth is dry and my words are garbled, like I tried to speak around a mouthful of rocks. He sighs.

"No, you do not. You are drunk."

"I do," I say, momentarily distracted by the scratch of his facial hair against my fingers. It feels good. Flattening my hand against his cheek, I repeat the motion with my palm. That feels good, too. "I like looking at you."

"Atlas." He sighs again. He makes that noise a lot. It must be his favorite sound.

He's sitting on the edge of the bed, bent over me slightly. I feel as though I can see all the blues of the ocean in the color of his eyes. I love blue eyes, I decide. They are my favorite eye. I laugh, because having a favorite eye is strange.

"I can't sleep in jeans!" I exclaim suddenly, realizing I'm still fully dressed. My hand isn't touching Henri's face anymore, but I can somehow still feel the scratch of his scruff against my skin. I rub my fingertips together, marveling at that.

"I can help you, if you wish," he offers carefully.

"I wish," I say, mimicking his accent and then laughing. "You talk so funny. You are so funny. You are so *weird*."

"Are you sure you want me to assist you?"

"Yes. I like it when people take my pants off—don't you? Oops. Shhh." I make a motion like I need Henri to talk quieter even though I'm the one who just shouted. "People are sleeping."

He stands up, and slowly reaches for my waist. I lift my hips helpfully off the bed. He barely touches me as he unfastens the button and loosens the zipper. The moment the waist is loose, he moves his hands down to the legs and tugs them down that way. I pout, disappointed that I didn't get to feel the scratch of his knuckles on my abdomen.

I watch as he folds my pants and lays them on his desk chair. He moves the trash can over and sets it next to the bed.

"If you must be sick, use this, yes?"

"You going to sleep with me?" I ask.

"Use this to throw up," he repeats, pointing at the trash can. I nod and pat the bed next to me.

"Time for sleep," I tell him, trying to focus on one of his faces. There are at least three. He's too far away, though, and the room is spinning too much. I flail an arm out, colliding with his stomach, and grasp his shirt.

"No, Atlas," he says, untangling my fingers and resting my arm back on the mattress. I don't understand why he's being so difficult. Doesn't he want to snuggle?

"You don't want to sleep with me?"

"You will be very embarrassed about this, I think, in the morning." He sighs *again*, grabbing my hand before I can tangle my fingers in his shirt once more. "I do not think you will be wanting to sleep with me, if you are sober."

"Just sit." I pat the bed again. "I won't be mad, I pinky swear."

He sits down with his back to the wall, but he's all the way at the end of the bed and I can't reach him with my hand. I poke my toes against his leg, tucking them underneath his thigh and chuckling. He makes a small noise, but doesn't push me away.

"You're like...super fucking nice," I tell him, closing my eyes and pulling his pillow toward me. I remember suddenly that I don't actually like him. Strange, that I forgot in the first place. I hasten to remind him. "I don't like it."

"I know."

"People are going to walk all over you if you be nice like that."

"Okay."

"Do you have a girlfriend?" I don't know why I asked, but now that I did, I want to know. I bet girls love him. Girls love guys that look like him, and have sexy accents. "I bet you do because you have an accent."

"No, Atlas. Perhaps it is time for sleep, yes?"

"Boyfriend?"

"No."

"Me either. But if you weren't so weird, I might try to kiss you. You have a nice face. Nice lips, too. They're just better when they aren't moving and saying odd shit."

He rests a hand down on my calf, patting gently. "Time for sleep."

"All right," I say, turning my face into the pillow. It's a nice pillow, and it doesn't seem to be moving. I like this pillow. "But tomorrow maybe we could try the kissing."

I WAKE up when the contents of my stomach start making their way up my throat. With barely a second's notice, I lean over the side of the bed and vomit into the trash can. It's hardly more than bile, but it burns my throat so badly tears spring to my eyes. I wait until I'm certain there isn't anything more, before rolling onto my back and squeezing my eyes shut against the pain and nausea. My head feels two sizes too small, like my brain is being squeezed to death and is pounding for release against the inside of my skull.

I lie there until my stomach starts to protest once more. Carefully pushing myself to a seated position, I shakily walk to the bathroom, making sure to keep a hand on the wall to steady myself. Bending over the toilet, I dry-heave until my stomach muscles are screaming in pain.

The bathroom is clean, and not one I recognize. There is a tidy row of skincare products sitting on the vanity, and a washcloth lying next to the sink. I try to avoid looking at myself in the mirror, knowing that if I feel this bad, I probably don't look great either. Arm wrapped around my stomach, I shuffle my way back into the dorm and look around.

It's practically empty. Nothing but a desk, a bed, and a wardrobe—standard for a dorm room, but doesn't exactly help me figure out where the fuck I am. Trying to think over the pounding in my head, I walk over to the desk. There's a water bottle sitting on the corner next to a bottle of ibuprofen. I down four before my eye catches on a picture taped above the desk.

"What the fuck," I mutter, squinting at Henri Vasel's smiling face, his arms around two sweaty guys I don't know. Given that I'm not wearing pants, and I can't remember a single thing that happened after I left the stoner house last night, I almost hope I'm in the dorm of one of those strangers and not Henri's. I can't imagine a world where Henri and I ended up at the same party and left together. Hell, I can't imagine him at a party at all.

Picking the water bottle back up and taking a few sips, I start to sit back down on the bed before my eyes catch on a piece of paper also taped to the wall. It's a schedule, broken down by time increments and very detailed. Even "stress release" has a scheduled time, although I'm not altogether certain what that entails. I read through it twice, stomach beginning to flip unpleasantly once more. Why do I get the impression that this is something fucking Henri would do?

Feeling like I might pass out if I don't sit back down, I half collapse onto the bed and rest my forearms on my knees. I need to get out of here before the occupant of this dorm comes back. I need to take a shower, eat something greasy, and sleep for the next twelve hours. Unfortunately, I can't manage to do any of those things right now, because I feel like I was hit by a car. Twice.

The sound of a key turning in the lock almost has me throwing up again. I look down at my bare legs and curse the fact that I didn't think to put my damn pants on. God, I really hope I was too drunk to hook up last night.

Henri walks into the room, paper bag clutched in his hand and a wary look on his face. When he sees me, he smiles carefully and holds his arm up.

"Good morning, Atlas. I have breakfast."

"Hey," I croak. My throat feels like someone took sandpaper to it. He approaches the bed slowly, arm held out as though the food is a peace offering and I'm a wild animal.

He looks unfairly good in sweatpants and an SCU hockey shirt, hair still damp from a shower and face freshly shaved. When he gets close enough to hand me the paper bag, I get a whiff of something fresh and clean, like laundry detergent. The way his shirt fits a little tighter than his usual polos holds my attention. He's pretty muscular from what I can tell; certainly not as soft as me. Swallowing roughly, I look away.

"Thanks," I mutter, opening the bag and groaning as the smell of bacon grease wafts out. Inside are two breakfast sandwiches—perfect hangover food. I pull one out, take a bite, and only just remember to chew before I swallow. Henri sits on his desk chair, facing me. He leans forward and places my folded jeans on the bed next to me. I flush, embarrassed. I can't believe I have my legs out in front of this guy right now.

"Do you feel all right?" he asks.

"I puked in your trash can." I nudge it with my foot and he nods.

"Yes," he agrees, likely because he was able to figure that

out by the smell. Feeling unmoored and defensive, I take a bite of breakfast sandwich and point a finger at his wall.

"What is 'stress release'?"

His eyes track over to the schedule and his head angles to the left slightly, like he's thinking. He fidgets a little bit, sucking his bottom lip between his teeth like he's embarrassed.

"I like to stay organized," he says slowly.

Obviously, I think, glancing around at the nearly sterile room. The dirtiest thing in here is me.

"That is when I will sometimes..." He trails off, closes his eyes, and sighs. Lifting his right hand off his leg, he does a short jerking motion before dropping his hand back into his lap. Swallowing my half-chewed bite, I raise my eyebrows.

"You schedule a time to jerk off?"

He looks embarrassed by me saying it out loud. Normally, I'd probably balk at having this conversation—or any—with him. But I'm hungover as fuck, my puke is between us in the trash can, and I'm not wearing pants. We've gone beyond modesty, and now I'm curious.

"Porn guy?" I ask, smirking around my bite of sandwich as he blushes.

"No. I do not like that so much."

I take another bite of sandwich and a swig of water. This conversation is doing more to perk me up than any greasy food ever could. Who knew talking to prim-and-proper Henri about wanking would be so much fun?

"What's wrong with porn?" I ask.

He stares at me for a second, clearly trying to decide whether or not to answer me. Seemingly deciding that he wants to take advantage of my apparent chattiness, he crosses an ankle over one knee and leans back in the chair.

"Porn is distracting, because I start to wonder if they are fairly compensated and having a good time. It is not so enjoyable for me. Also, it is not...I do not...well, it does not work for me, that is all. I do not like it."

I laugh, but immediately have to stop when my head threatens to explode. "Christ, only you."

"Are you feeling better?" he asks, deftly changing the subject. I shrug, reaching for the second breakfast sandwich.

"Not really. Sorry, by the way, for...you know. Calling you," I mumble around a mouthful.

"It is fine. But I do not like your friends or the place you were at. It was not safe." He pauses, thinking. "Or clean."

I don't remember where I ended up last night, so I stay silent. There'd been a party at Foggers—that much I remember—but parties there didn't always stay there. I hadn't been having a great day yesterday, which means I probably made some questionable decisions about what I ingested and whom I ingested it with. I'm not known for having good judgement when I've been drinking, which would also explain why I called Henri, of all people, to pick me up.

"Where did you pick me up from, anyway?" He taps through his phone before holding it out to me to show me the map app. Squinting down at the screen, I try to decide if I recognize it or not. "I don't know that address."

"Atlas!" Henri protests. "You should not be going to strange houses when you have been drinking. What if something bad happened to you?"

Nobody would have given a fuck. I shrug. "It's fine."

"No, it is not fine. I am thinking your friends are not really friends at all and they should be taking better care of you. There was alcohol *and* drugs at that house. It was filthy!"

Feeling strange about the turn this conversation has taken, I look away from him. Why the hell does he care so much? He's not even faking it. Earnestness rolls off of him in waves, and the air is thick with his concern. Taking another sip of water, I nod toward him and change the subject.

"No polo shirt today, I see."

"It is the weekend," he replies, as though this matters at all. Setting the bottle back down, I wipe the back of my hand across my mouth. I'm feeling better, whether from the water and food, or from the strangeness of this encounter. I'm also feeling oddly glad that I called him. There isn't an ounce of judgement in his eyes, nor does he seem unduly put out by me sleeping in his bed or emptying the contents of my stomach into his trash. Apparently, Nate was being truthful when he said nothing can phase this guy.

"I do anything crazy here last night?" I ask. "I can't really remember."

"No, you were fine," he answers, but averts his eyes in a way that tells me it's a lie.

"Did I hit on you?" His gaze snaps back to mine and I shrug. "I'm a flirty drunk and you're hot."

His eyebrows wing upward at my admission that I find him attractive. I roll my eyes. Just because I don't like him doesn't mean I'm fucking blind. I'm not going to act on it, but I can certainly enjoy the view.

"You did, but nothing happened," he reassures me hastily.

"I still don't like you," I tell him, even though I have to force the words. It's hard to hate someone who fed you, and took care of you when you were sick. Crumpling up the empty paper bag, I drop it into the trash can. Finishing off the water, I toss that in as well. "I'll hit on anyone and anything when I'm drunk. It doesn't mean anything."

"I understand."

Feeling like I've had about as much of this as I can take, I stand up. Immediately, Henri follows suit and raises his arm as though to catch me were I to fall. Biting back the inclination to slap his hand away, I glare at him until he drops it. He looks away as I shakily pull my pants on. Even so, I angle my hips away to try and hide how difficult it is for me to get the button done.

"I shall give you a ride home," he says once I turn back around and meet his eyes.

"I'm fine." I'm not, but I'll be damned if I ask him for more help. Relying on people is a good way to be let down.

He frowns, but doesn't argue. Silently, he slides my cellphone and wallet toward me from where they were resting on his desk. I'm surprised when my phone lights up as I touch it, assuming that it would have died. When I check the battery, it shows 100%. Henri must have charged it. Tucking everything away in my pockets—and trying to ignore the churning in my stomach that has less to do with alcohol and more to do with Henri—I take a step toward the door.

"Thanks again," I mumble, trying to look anywhere in the room but at him. My eyes catch on the trash can. *Fuck.* "Uhm...do you want me to take care of that?"

I point at it, but Henri is already shaking his head without even looking to where I'm indicating.

"No, that is fine. Are you sure I cannot give you a ride?"

"Positive," I say firmly, turning for the door. "See you in class."

7

Henri

IF I WONDERED whether Atlas would be friendlier after his drunken call for help, I do not have to wonder long. Classes the following weeks have followed much the same pattern as they usually did, with me desperately trying to make conversation and Atlas desperately trying to avoid it. He seems embarrassed about what happened, or perhaps just my part in it, shooting wary glances at me out of the corners of his eyes as though waiting for me to bring it up. I only hope, at the very least, that he learned a lesson and won't go back to that house; also, that he reconsiders his choice of friends.

Swinging my legs idly from where I'm seated on the trainer's table, I look up at the clock hanging above the door. Barely three minutes have passed since Coach Mackenzie sent me in here to be checked out, but I'm already impatient to be done. There's no reason to think I won't be cleared to play in our game, but the longer I sit here alone, the more I worry about what they might say. I might not be the most dynamic player on the ice, but I love it and I'm in my last two seasons—I want to make the most of the time I have left.

Aaron, our head athletic trainer, opens the door and steps inside with a smile. Straightening my spine, I smile back.

"Good afternoon, Aaron," I greet him, ignoring the way my stomach flutters with nerves. He's asked me multiple times to not use an honorific, and to call him by his given name. Even so, I hate doing it. I was raised to always use the proper deference when speaking to anyone in a position of respect.

"Hey, Vasel, how are you doing?" He straddles a wheeled chair and scoots it over to where I'm sitting on the raised bed.

"I am well. How are you?"

He smiles, reaching a hand out and tapping my knee.

"I'm good, but we're not here to talk about me. How's that knee been feeling at practice? Nico said you might have tweaked it?"

"Oh, it has been fine. No issues." I pause, realizing that every athlete who has ever been injured probably says those very same words. "I promise. I would not lie to you, Aaron."

Standing, he chuckles. "What's crazy is I actually believe you when you say that. Lie flat for me, let's take a look."

He slides a bolster under my knees as I comply. Resting my hands on my abdomen, I try to relax as he gently manipulates my left knee. After checking the range of motion on the left, he moves to the right and does the same. When he asks if something hurts, I tell him no. It hasn't bothered me all summer, and I was cleared by my surgeon back in Germany to play. But I understand why Coach Mackenzie wants to be sure, and I appreciate the concern. Only my brother has shown more concern than Coach Mackenzie has.

"Range of motion is excellent," Aaron says, raising his

voice above the mutter he was using to talk to himself. "You must have been diligent with your physical therapy over the summer."

"Yes, sir. Aaron," I correct immediately. "My mother is a cardiologist in Germany, and I know how important it is to follow all instructions your doctor may give you."

"Does it hurt when I do this?" he asks, pushing my bent leg slowly back toward my chest and watching my face carefully. I shake my head and he nods, satisfied. Changing his grip so his hand is wrapped around my ankle and the other is pressing on the inside of my thigh, he changes the angle and tries a different rotation. "How about now? I'm going to press here, and I want you to push back—don't let me move you."

We spend ten minutes on the table before he's satisfied with that. He then has me work through a series of basic strength exercises so he can watch me move. By the time he's content, I've had a thorough warm-up and am feeling more than ready to take the ice with my teammates. Aaron bends over a folder on his desk, scribbling notes, before straightening and clapping a hand on my shoulder.

"All right, Vasel, I'll talk to Nico. You're good to go, for now. But any discomfort—any at all—and you say something, okay?"

"Yes," I agree, nodding. "I will. You have my word."

"Have fun tonight," he says, waving me out the door. "I'll find Nico and let him know you've got the green light."

I head straight for the locker room, where I can hear the sounds of my teammates readying for the game. I step inside and a cheer goes up, as though everyone was waiting for me. Shaking my head, I walk over to my stall and start to undress. I'm far behind everyone else, after spending nearly forty minutes with Aaron.

"You good?" Max asks, leaning over so that he doesn't have to raise his voice to be heard. I smile at him before grasping the neckline of my shirt and pulling it over my head.

"Yes, I am good. I will be fine to play. Thank you for asking."

"Thank God." He breathes a sigh of relief. "I need you."

When he holds a hand out, I bump my knuckles against his softly and grin. He really doesn't need me. Max has more skill in his pinky finger than I do in my entire body. But I appreciate the words more than he could possibly know.

"You are a good friend, Max."

He gives me a strange look and opens his mouth to reply, but Coach walks into the room before he can get the words out. We both fall silent, Max sitting down on the bench and me continuing to change with increasing urgency. I hate that I'm the only one not ready to go; the only one holding us up. When Coach Mackenzie is close enough to hear, I mutter an apology.

"I am sorry, sir. I will be ready very quick."

He narrows his eyes and looks down at his watch. Again, I'm struck with the thought that he probably needs glasses. Does he not get his vision checked regularly?

"No need to rush, Vas. We have plenty of time. I know you were with the training staff."

Gratefully, I nod. But I also continue to dress at twice my usual pace. Every other person in the room is ready to step onto the ice.

"You going to Carter and Zeke's house tomorrow?" Max asks, scooting a little closer to me and raising his voice to be heard over the hubbub of the locker room. In the opposite corner, Nate has the goalies bent over their padded legs in fits of laughter. I can only imagine what he said to get Micky to laugh like that.

"I am! You and Luke as well, I presume?"

"Yeah. I'm excited."

"Yes," I agree. "It is always good to see Carter. When you are playing for Detroit, you will still come visit? Or perhaps we shall come to you."

"Both sound good to me," he says, grinning.

"And although I will have to remain impartial on the broadcast when I am a sportscaster, I will secretly be cheering for my friends Max and Carter, always."

He stands up and starts to shake out his legs. The smile on his face is one that I'm still not quite used to seeing. Max has changed a lot since I first met him. He is less shy and withdrawn, more likely to join in when the team has fun on the ice or in the locker room. And although he still turns down all invitations to team events, he always agrees to come out with Carter and me when it's just the small group of us.

"What about when Carter and I play each other?" he asks mischievously.

"Aye." I sigh, finishing with my gear and feeling my chest loosen as a result. *Relax, they aren't waiting for you to finish,* I tell myself. "I will truly be impartial then."

Max is still smiling when we line up in the chute and head out onto the ice for warm-ups. DU—although a formidable team—relies too heavily on their size. Coach Mackenzie had us reviewing hours of tape, each one showing a team of behemoths who were skilled at blocking shooting lanes and stopping pucks, but severely lacking in footwork and speed. We aren't small, necessarily, but our tallest player is Micky and he will be in goal. However, we are fast and we are excellent at moving the puck.

We also have Max.

He scores seventeen seconds into the game by slipping past DU's winger and sending the puck straight through the five-hole of their goalie. Max skates down the bench grinning, tapping the outstretched gloves of our teammates. Even Coach Mackenzie looks like he is fighting a smile.

Resetting, we line up to take another face-off at center ice. Bolstered by being the first on the board and so early in the game, we again gain possession of the puck and force DU to play in their defensive zone for the second time in less than a minute. As though trying to learn from their earlier mistakes, they put pressure on Max immediately.

But Max's ability to score goals was only part of the reason he was drafted into the NHL so young. His biggest abilities lie in footwork and speed. Turning so rapidly it shouldn't even be possible on a blade, he spins away from the defensemen trying to pick his pocket and passes the puck to me. As familiar as I am with Max's strengths, so too do I know my own—instead of taking a shot, I send it over to Nate.

By the time we leave the ice for first intermission, we are up by three goals and two of those were scored by Max. I hope Luke is watching and that he is proud. When we sit next to each other, I lean my shoulder against him companionably and pass him a towel to wipe his face.

"Slick pass," he says, grinning. "You should have kept it and gone for a goal."

"And robbed you of the chance to bag such a beauty? I am not so selfish as that!"

The opposition manages to sneak two by Micky, but we win the game 4–2 and one of those goals was tallied by me. I don't score often, so I always try to savor it when I do. I love feeling like I'm pulling my weight on the ice and there is proof of that work on the scoreboard. I especially love when Coach Mackenzie claps me on the shoulder and tells me I did a good job.

"Thank you, sir." I nod, pulling off my gloves and resting them in my stall.

"How's the knee?" he asks sternly, changing tracks and becoming serious.

"It is fine! No pain."

He puts a hand on the back of my sweaty head, giving me an abnormally fond look as he ruffles my sticky hair. I feel unduly warm, all of a sudden. I know Coach likes me, but at times like these I'm struck by the realization that he might also be proud of me. I hope he is. I don't often make people proud, but I always strive to do so.

"What's up, hockey star!" Luke calls as he hops out of Max's car and waves at me. I wave back, easily matching his cheerfulness. Luke is always so joyful. I love being around him.

"Hello, Luke. You are looking well."

"Thanks for noticing," he says, throwing his free arm over my shoulder and tugging Max along by their linked hands. "I love watching you guys' games. Don't tell Cranky, but I sometimes prefer them to watching the NHL."

Max gasps. "Blasphemy."

"I think both are quite enjoyable," I say equably, and Luke snorts. I don't bother asking who he means by "Cranky." There is only one person in our friend group who might be nicknamed as such.

"Whatever you say, Switzerland."

I knock gently on the door and wait for Zeke to let us in. He does so with a twist to his mouth, telling me he's thinking of all the times he told me I could just let myself in and that I didn't have to knock.

"Carter is not home yet?" I ask Zeke, bending over to slip my shoes off and place them neatly by the door. Luke kicks his off as well, so I wait for him to pass by before I arrange them next to mine, making sure the shoes are all in a row.

"Not yet," Zeke says, closing the door softly behind us and waving me toward the living room. "Carter was just going to order food like he usually does, but I actually ended up cooking."

"You did?" I arch a brow at him, and he shrugs, sheepishly. "You made food for five people all by alone? Yourself," I correct automatically.

"Well, I've discovered that I'm pretty awesome at making lasagna, and that's something that can feed a lot of people. I made four, because..." He waves an arm through the air in a visual representation of the stomach capacity of three hockey and one baseball players.

"I shall help you clean up," I tell him, feeling a little bad that he went through the trouble to make *four* lasagnas. I don't know how to make lasagna, but I can't imagine it's easy.

"No, Vas, you're here to hang out, not do chores. It's already done. Food is in the oven," he says, raising his voice to be heard by Max and Luke as well. Luke lets out a *whoop whoop* from where he is sprawled on the couch next to Max.

"What are you working on here, Little Z?" he asks, nudging the coffee table with his foot. Luke loves giving people special names.

"Well, I'm working as a TA this semester, so I'm assisting

the professor with lesson plans. Right now, we're covering axiomatic geometry, which is *fascinating*."

"Oh dear God," Luke mutters.

Max grins at me from the opposite side of Luke as I take a seat next to him. Zeke crosses his legs and drops onto the floor in front of the coffee table, which is likely where he'd been before we showed up. I listen quietly as they chat, simply enjoying how it feels to be around them. They are my favorite people.

"Did you submit the application for the internship, Vas?" Max asks, leaning around Luke to look at me.

"I did, yes. Zeke was very helpful."

"I didn't do anything," Zeke corrects. "Just read it over. Have they called you yet?"

"Actually, yes. I will be having an interview with Sam Jameson next week." My stomach gives a little flutter of nervousness at the thought, but is chased away by my friends.

"Hell yes, good for you," Luke says. Max leans around him further, eyes alight with excitement.

"I wonder if your interview will coincide with practice. How cool would that be? Maybe they'd let you skate with the team."

"Oh, I do not think they would want me. Perhaps they might let me watch, though." I shake my head, chuckling. I'm not good enough to skate with an NHL team, not even at practice. "I am nervous for this meeting. I do not want to make any mistakes."

"It's normal to be nervous," Zeke tells me, smiling. "But I don't think you have to be. Your application and reference letters will speak volumes for themselves, and nobody who meets you could dislike you."

I nod, even though Atlas is living proof that he is wrong.

All I can do is hope Sam Jameson is friendlier than my communications partner.

"Hey, how did your date go?" Luke asks, nudging me with his foot and leaning his head back against Max's shoulder.

"It was fine, thank you for asking." All of my dates are fine. I like going out and chatting with people, even though I never feel any sort of spark or attraction. Dates, for me, are more of a way to make friends. To not be alone for a few hours. Luke stares at me, waiting for more, and I try to come up with a way to explain it to him that he might understand. "I do not have bad dates, really, but I...I do not feel that anyone is my Max. I do not like anyone."

Everyone stares at me silently for a protracted moment. I think if they all spoke German, I'd be able to clarify it better. It's hard to find the correct words to explain that I've never been interested in sex or relationships beyond those of close friends. I try. I ask people out and go on dates, but I never feel anything. Going out to dinner for a date feels no different to me than going out to dinner with my brother.

It's never bothered me before, and I've never really questioned whether there was something wrong with me. I've never before looked at other couples and wondered if I was missing out. But after spending time with Carter and Zeke, and now getting to see the way Luke is with Max, I do sometimes wonder if there is something absent from my life. I question whether I am fated for a life spent searching, only to wind up alone. Perhaps I will *never* feel something.

"What are you looking for? Like, a type," Luke asks, lifting his head off of Max to look at me properly. "Hair color? Eye color? Height? Sex? Any preference at all?"

I open my mouth to tell him that no, I don't think I have any preferences like that, when a picture of Atlas pops into my head. Black hair. Hair so dark, it is the embodiment of a complete absence of color. The way his black eyelashes resemble makeup around equally dark eyes. The sharp-boned, narrow cast of his features.

"I like to look at black hair," I admit. "But it does not mean anything. I do not have a type, in that way. And no, I am not so much interested in the sex things."

Max's cheeks turn pink and Zeke rolls his bottom lip into his mouth, biting on it. Luke gives a little cough, valiantly trying to fight the smile that is tugging at the corner of his lips.

"Uh, right, that's fine. But I was actually asking if you had a preference in gender?"

"Oh. My apologies. No, I am not thinking that matters so much to me."

Luke smiles and winks at me. He leans his head back against Max's shoulder again, and the other man reaches up to play with his hair. I watch the gesture and feel that sharp pain, low in my stomach, that has recently been happening quite a lot around my friends. I turn to Zeke, because I think he will understand what I am saying better than anyone.

"I think I am mostly wanting someone that I might like to talk with, and maybe lie under a blanket with to watch hockey, and also touch my hair."

Gamely, Luke reaches his arm out and threads his fingers through the hair on the back of my head, kneading my scalp gently. It feels amazing. I knew it would.

"Someone nice," Max puts in, and I nod very carefully, not wanting to dislodge Luke's hand. I wouldn't mind someone nice, but again I think of Atlas. He always accuses me of being "fake nice," which is funny because it's one thing

I appreciate about him. He never fakes being nice. He doesn't ever pretend to be something he's not.

The front door opens, and judging by the abject joy on Zeke's face, it's Carter who walks in. The thought of what his face must look like when he sees Luke's hand on my head makes me smile. I bet he is glaring.

"Cranky's here," Luke announces. A tattooed arm swings into view, and Luke's too tangled up in Max and me to dodge before he's smacked on the side of the head. He drops his hand from my head to rub his own. "Ouch."

"You earned that," Max says, although he does lean over and kiss his temple. I turn around so I can see Carter.

"Hello, my friend. How are you this day?"

"Good. Hey, Max."

That's all the greeting we get, before he's skirting the couch and saying a much more friendly hello to Zeke, whom he is always the happiest to see.

"We were discussing dating with Vas—" Zeke starts, but Carter raises his hand.

"I really don't need to know about Vas' love life," he says, scowling. The timer on Zeke's phone goes off, and he bounds to his feet, heading into the kitchen with Carter trailing after him like a huge, tattooed shadow. Luke nudges me.

"Come here," he says, and scoots a little closer to me. Holding his phone out, he snaps a picture of us together. After a few minutes, his phone dings and he grins. "Got you another date. Might not be a love match, but you'll have good conversation and she'd be game for some hockey talk, too."

Max leans over to peek at his phone and smiles. "Oh, good call."

I give them an inquisitive look, and wait for Luke to find something on his phone and hold it out to me. There is a picture on the screen of himself standing next to a small girl with a purple streak in her blond hair. She must be wearing Luke's baseball jersey because it hangs off her small frame. Dark paint is smeared underneath her eyes and they are both flexing their biceps for the photo.

"That's Margot," Luke explains. "My ride or die."

"Oh," I say, not familiar with this, but thinking it's probably bad if someone is dying.

"His friend," Max clarifies.

"I asked if I could give you her number and she said yes."

"Really?" I'm surprised. I do not think I am hideous, but I am not as handsome or interesting as others. Mostly, people's eyes just slide right past me. Once, I was told I was like the white rice of SCU hockey players. I am not fun, like my teammate Nate, or good at making people smile, like Luke.

"Yeah, really. She said, and I quote, *if that's the way they make them in Germany, why are we all living here?*" Luke tells me, grinning. "No pressure, but you can have her number if you want. She's great. Super nice and smart, too."

"Well, actually, I was not made in Germany. I was born in Germany, yes, but I was made in New Zealand while my parents were on holiday," I correct. Max snorts and I smile at him. "But yes, thank you, I think I will take Margot's number."

"Cool. She said she'd love to hang out sometime," Luke says, holding his phone out so I can copy the number into my own. I put her contact in as "Margot—Luke's friend."

"You guys ready to eat?" Carter yells from the kitchen. Luke jumps up and holds a hand out to Max, pulling him to his feet. I trail after them to the kitchen, stomach growling at the smell of Italian. Zeke is a good cook—the few times I've eaten something he's made, I have been impressed.

"You are a skilled chef," I tell Zeke, inhaling deeply as I take in the massive pans of lasagna laid out on the island. In answer, he smiles and passes a plate to me.

I shuffle to the side, letting Max and Luke go first. This puts me next to Carter, who is leaned against the counter and drinking a glass of water like his life depends on it. I wait for him to drain it.

"Practice was tiring?"

"Yeah, but fun," he says, leaning over and flicking the sink on to refill the glass. He glances back at me. "Nice work on getting an interview. It's with Sam, right?"

"Yes, right." I nod. Carter reaches behind himself to grab another glass, filling it with water and handing it to me.

"He's pretty chill," he says gruffly. "Cool guy."

"I will try and make a good impression. I am wanting to make sure you are certain it is okay for me to stay here over the summer months? I do not want to be a bother, Carter."

He scowls at me, drinking down another glass of water. I take a sip of my own and wait.

"You're not a bother," he mutters.

"I should also like to pay you," I tell him.

"Absolutely fucking not," he retorts. I sigh as he sets his cup down on the counter so forcefully, I'm surprised the glass doesn't shatter. "Vas, I know you already talked to Zeke about this. The answer is *no*. I'm not taking your money, okay? Buy your own gas and groceries, and whatever else you need, but you can sleep here for free. Don't argue with me about it."

He puts a hand on my shoulder and turns me toward the island.

"Get something to eat," he mutters, squeezing once before dropping his hand.

I do as he says, placing a slice of lasagna on a plate and

sitting down next to Max. When I glance up at Carter, he looks embarrassed the way he always does when he has to say more than four words in a row. I smile at him softly, waiting for the very small smile I get in return before I bend over my plate and take a bite.

"This is very delicious, Zeke," I tell him.

"Seriously," Luke agrees around a groan, reaching for a pan and sliding it close enough for him to dish out more onto his and Max's plates. He swallows, points his fork at Carter and says, "I fucking love watching you play this season."

Max, after swallowing a mouthful and coughing a bit from the size of the bite, eagerly jumps in.

"Okay, so I've been paying close attention to the save percentages, shutouts, and GAAs of the starting tendies this season, and if you keep playing the way—"

Zeke's eyes, which had brightened at the mention of statistics, slowly take on a glazed look as Max and Carter jump into a spirited hockey discussion. Luke chimes in every now and then, but mostly just sits and watches Max with a smile on his face. For myself, I simply eat and listen, enjoying the presence of all my friends in one place.

I like seeing the way Carter's face has become softer these last two years, and his mouth is quicker to smile. I like seeing how animated Max has become, as though Luke is a battery he's drawing energy from. I like how happy they all are and I like that I am a part of it. I love them.

8

Atlas

MY FAVORITE TIME TO be on campus is after midnight; bonus points if it's a night like tonight and the moon is full. Tipping my head against the back of the bench, I stretch my legs out in front of me and look up at the stars. It's not perfectly dark, what with the lamps positioned along the walkways, but the stars are still visible. It's beautiful.

Taking another drag of my cigarette, I fiddle with my cellphone in my other hand. I'd called my dad earlier, struck with a sudden madness that left me feeling strangely homesick. He hadn't answered, and only just texted me back (seven hours after my call) to let me know he was busy, and that if I needed money, he would put some in my checking account. I shouldn't be surprised. Our relationship is little more than a transactional one, at best. It's a good reminder of who *not* to call, should I ever find myself in an emergency.

I could just call Henri again, I think, and like I'm some sort of magician, the thought makes him appear out of the mist.

He's strolling along the path, hands tucked into his pockets and chin tipped upward as he looks at the sky the same way I just was. He's wearing a polo shirt, because of-fucking-course he is, and khaki pants. Even from a distance away, I can tell he looks good.

Taking another slow drag from the cigarette, I watch him. He hasn't seen me yet, and there isn't any reason for me to call out and make him aware of my presence. Twisting my phone around in my hand, I think of my dad. I think of my call history from the night Henri picked me up from the party. How I'd called seven other people before him, but none of them had answered. Only him. I think of the gentle way he took my shoes off, and how he let me sleep in his bed.

"Polo Shirt," I yell, just loud enough for him to hear and know I'm talking to him. He looks around, sees me, and smiles. When he raises a hand in greeting, I don't return the gesture, but continue watching as he makes a beeline toward me.

"Good evening, Atlas," he says once he reaches me.

"You lost?" I ask, gesturing around the dark, empty quad. His dorm is on the complete other side of campus.

"No. I was with a friend and walked her back to her house. It is a lovely night." He shrugs. "I thought a walk might be nice, instead of driving."

"A friend, huh? Good for you." Tapping the ashes off to the side, I gesture to the other half of the bench. He hesitates and I see his eyes flick to the smoke curling up from my fingers. I feel like I can see the actual war going on in his head as he tries to decide whether he wants to be friendly or health-conscious.

Friendliness wins out and he sits next to me. I give it a solid minute before I glance over at him, eyebrow raised.

"What, no lecture on smoking?"

He shrugs. "You already know you should not be smoking, I think. I do not need to tell you."

"True." Sitting up and bending over, I stub it out on the sidewalk before pocketing the butt. I'm not so much of an asshole that I would smoke this close to someone I know won't like it. I'm the one who called him over, after all.

"How are you this night?" he asks.

"Fine. I got laid, too." Hooking a thumb over my shoulder, I indicate one of the dorms behind me. He glances behind us, mulling this over for a minute before speaking.

"That sounds like you've enjoyed yourself," he says evenly. I snort. Jesus, this guy.

"Sure, yeah. It was fun. What about you? Must have gotten lucky since you walked her home."

He looks surprised, eyebrows crawling up his forehead in an almost comical way. Again, I notice how fucking nice his face is. What sort of genetics does this guy have, to look like this?

"We had a pleasant evening. It was merely a date, and there was no...getting lucky," he says, shifting on the bench so he's facing me with one leg pulled up. The man has the meatiest thighs I've ever see. It would take both of my hands to circle one.

"Such a gentleman," I tease. "No banging on the first date and you walked her back to her house. Love match?"

"Oh, I do not think so. Probably just friends. And yourself?"

"No. I don't do repeats. No point, when we're all going to end up miserable and alone anyway."

Henri sighs, but doesn't say anything. I let it go. Having an orgasm puts me in a good mood, so I'm less inclined to pick at him tonight. Closing my eyes, I tip my head back and breathe in the cooler night air. Maybe I'll sleep out here.

"Did you wish to get together and work on communications this weekend?" he asks carefully, voice low. Similar to his face, he's got a nice voice. I can't explain it, but it's a warm voice. The kind of voice that makes you feel like you swallowed a mouthful of hot coffee. A pleasant sort of burn.

"Sure," I agree, surprising myself. "Want to meet up somewhere off campus?"

"I could pick you up, if you prefer?" he offers. I shrug. It doesn't matter to me either way. Smiling, he nods. "I shall pick you up. There is a nice café where it is quiet to do homework."

"Whatever." I shrug again. Straightening out of my lazy sprawl, I rub my fingers idly on the bench. My skin catches on the rougher wood, and I pick at a splinter. "Thanks again, for helping me the other night."

I still don't remember everything that happened, but my fragmented memories are enough for me to piece together some of the story. I don't have to remember everything to know it was humiliating, but Henri hasn't said a single thing about it since I left his dorm that morning. If our roles had been reversed, I would have given him hell for weeks.

"You do not have to thank me for this—that," he corrects, waving a hand. "Anyone would have done so."

"Apparently not," I muse dryly. "I called seven people before I got to you."

This seems to stun him into silence for a few moments. I can practically feel his brain trying to think of something polite to say. He's probably never ignored a call in his life. If he had, it surely would have been mine.

"You deserve better friends," is what he eventually settles on. He's probably right.

"Whatever," I repeat, with another indifferent shrug. I'm better off alone—less people to let you down that way. He looks like he wants to say more, but is holding himself back. I can practically see the words crawling up his throat and knocking at his teeth. Rolling my eyes, I curl my fingers in the universal gesture of *give it to me*. "Just say it, Polo Shirt."

"I think you should be careful drinking so much alcohol, and I also think you should not be taking pills that others give you. Especially those people you were with. They are *not* people you should be friends with, Atlas," he says firmly, giving me the kind of stare that probably shouldn't be sexy but is. I struggle to remember why I used to think the way he said my name was annoying.

"They probably weren't my friends, dude. They were probably just people I was partying with."

"You do not remember still?" he hisses, incredulous. I laugh, surprised to have worked up so much emotion from him. Apparently, the cardboard man *does* have normal emotions.

"No, not really. I remember asking you to take my pants off, though, so that's great for me."

"It was nothing sexual," he assures, and I laugh again. He smiles tentatively, apparently happy that we're getting along so well.

"Sorry, the way you said sexual was just funny."

"Sexual," he repeats, in that fucking accent.

"Stop it, Henri."

"I had to throw away my trash can. I was worried about it being clean," he admits.

"I bet you were. Your room looked like an IKEA ad for a

serial killer's bedroom." He laughs softly, the sound dangerous and lovely in the midnight haze. Shivers crawl up my forearms at the sound. Frowning, I look down at my pocket. What the hell was in that cigarette?

"Yes. My mother was very strict about things being orderly," he admits. "But I, too, prefer it that way. The house I picked you up from was filthy."

He shoots me a look. I nod. "Sounds about right."

I'm wishing I had another cigarette, if only so I could have something to do with my hands. Trailing my fingers along the bench seat, I go in search of another sliver of wood I can pick at. Henri is quiet beside me, comfortable enough in his own skin to not need every silence filled with words. This is the most palatable interaction I've had with him yet. Maybe Nate was right, and he's not so bad after all.

"I tried to call my dad today," I tell him, voice sounding too loud in the dark. He looks over at me and smiles, like he thinks talking to parents is a good thing.

"Oh? That is nice."

"Might have been, if he'd answered. He never answers when I call." I shrug. "Busy guy and all."

"Oh," he repeats, frowning.

"I don't call him often. Or, ever really." Tiring of destroying my fingernails on the bench, I rest my hands in my lap and play with the ring on my finger. It's my mom's wedding band, because I'm pathetic and love her even though she never loved me.

"I do not speak often to my father, either," Henri says, drawing my eyes to his. "I am closest to my elder brother, Jakob. He is a sports agent. He lives in New York, for most of the time, but flies to Los Angeles a lot."

"Cool. No older brothers for me."

"You can share mine. He is sometimes a lot," Henri says, with absolutely no inflection at all. I laugh again, not sure whether that was even a joke, but finding it funny nonetheless. I have the same buzzy feeling in my head that I get when I smoke weed, like Henri's company tonight is an intoxicant. "Sometimes Jakob will send me money. 'Fun-time money' is how he calls it. We can study together over dinner, the next time he sends it, yes?"

"Sure, Hen, I'll help you blow Jakob's fun-time money," I tell him.

His head whips toward mine and his eyes widen. I didn't mean to drop a nickname so casually into the middle of the conversation, and there won't be any pretending I didn't say it, because he clearly clocked it. Looking away from him, I spread my knees and stretch my legs out. I need to go home and go to bed.

"I have an interview tomorrow afternoon," Henri says quietly, drawing my eyes back over to him. He has one ankle crossed over the opposite knee, and his khaki pants are stretched obscenely over his crotch and thighs. I definitely don't look. I don't even like him like that. "I am nervous."

"What's the interview for?" I ask his dick, because who the fuck am I kidding, I can't look away.

"It is for the local NHL team. It is a summer internship, so less involved with the team and more involved with things such as management and media. It would provide many good experiences and connections for when I am looking for a job after school."

Clearing my throat, I compromise by closing my eyes again and leaning my head back against the bench. I'm starting to see the appeal of khaki pants.

"Sounds boring as fuck," I tell him, and his chuckle zings

across my skin and sets my hair on end. I must have been body snatched. There is no other explanation for whatever the hell is going on right now. *You will not become attracted to Henri Vasel*, I tell myself sternly.

Standing, I stretch my arms over my head and bend backward, earning a satisfying crack in my spine. I peek at Henri and see him watching me, eyes on where my shirt has ridden up my stomach. I pull it back down. I do *not* have the abdomen of a hockey player, or that of any sort of athlete, actually.

"You better get some sleep before your big interview," I tell him, the words coming out a little harsher than before. I'm annoyed that I caught him checking me out, even though I'd been doing the same to him. Mostly, I'm annoyed that I liked it.

"Yes." He sighs, standing up. I take a step away from him so he doesn't brush against me. The entire sidewalk at his disposal, and he has to stand *that* close? "Do you live on campus? I can walk back with you."

"Fuck that." I wave a hand and step around him. "I'm not your girlfriend. Catch you in class."

THE WALL in my bedroom is shaking. One eye cracked open, I watch the lone picture frame reverberate and swing back and forth. Lifting my head off my pillow, I shout at my roommate.

"Nate! It's too early for this shit, go back to bed!"

"Come *here*," he yells back, and bangs his fist against the wall again. Growling in frustration, I throw my covers off and stalk over to his room. Stepping inside, I slam the door shut behind me and stand with hands on my hips, glowering at him. He's sitting up in his bed, back against the headboard and laptop balanced on his legs. His brown hair is wild from sleep and he's shirtless, which, at any other time of day, I'd appreciate.

"What do you want that is *so* important, it can't wait until a reasonable fucking hour?"

"You like dudes, right?" I stare at him. He clarifies: "Dick."

"I swear to God, I have never hated you more than I do in this moment."

He sighs, scrubbing his hands vigorously over his face and groaning.

"All right, *all right.* I'm having a minor identity crisis and I need the expert opinion of someone on the inside. Someone who won't fuck around and will just tell me like it is."

He gestures to me. My eyes narrow nearly to slits.

"And by someone on the inside, you mean the inside of someone's ass?" I clarify.

"Well." Nate shrugs.

"I'm going to get coffee. I'll be right back. Jesus fucking Christ," I mutter, leaving his room and walking downstairs in my boxers. Nobody else is awake, naturally, because it's way too early and no self-respecting college kid would be awake before six if they had a choice in the matter. I lean against the counter and close my eyes as the coffee percolates. The smell makes me feel marginally better, and I decide to bring Nate a mug, too. Nobody should have to go through an identity crisis without coffee.

"Here you go, jackass," I mumble, setting down a mug on his nightstand. He glances away from his computer screen.

"Thanks. So, here's the situation." He closes his laptop and leans forward, elbows on his knees. "I fucked a dude and now I'm pretty sure I'm gay."

Sitting down on the end of his bed, I close my eyes and take a sip of way-too-hot coffee. I can't believe this is my life right now.

"Fucking a dude is a pretty gay thing to do," I agree. Nate nods, vindicated.

"Three times," he says.

"This isn't an identity crisis. Sounds like you've got a pretty firm grasp."

"Listen, okay?" He waits for me to nod before continuing. I wish I had a fucking cigarette. "So, last year I was at a party, and there was this guy there I'd never seen before, and I was feeling some type of way, so I sucked his dick. But I was drinking, right? So, I just wrote it off as alcohol-induced gay insanity."

"Sounds believable," I mutter, taking a sip of coffee and wishing I'd put a shot of Baileys in.

"Right?" Nate agrees, not hearing the sarcasm. "But then I went to one of the baseball games and there he was in those tight pants and I just thought, 'huh.'"

He stops, staring at me and waiting as though he said something profound and is waiting for me to offer advice.

"Yeah, sounds super gay," I tell him. He makes an aggrieved noise and scrubs a hand over his face again.

"I asked for his number and we had phone sex and more blowjobs and talked all summer. Like, normal stuff, not sexting or anything. But both times we've hung out, I literally *could not* keep my hands to myself. So, that's where I'm at. Now, *help* me."

"I'm not sure what you want me to say. You've had more gay sex than I have, apparently."

Nate's eyes nearly bug out of his head at that.

"What the fuck do you mean I've had more gay sex than

you?" He practically shouts it, apparently on a mission to inform the entire household.

"I've never slept with a guy," I tell him and enjoy the way he nearly goes apoplectic.

"I thought you were bi?" he asks, sounding so offended I can't help but laugh.

"I am. I just haven't slept with any guys."

"Oh my *god*, how are you supposed to help me with this?"

I laugh again. I can't believe this is the conversation I'm having at 6 a.m.

"I honestly don't even know what you're needing help with. Sounds pretty clear that you like this baseball guy even when you're not drinking."

"I'm low-key obsessed with him," he admits. "And that's the problem. That first time? At the party? I wasn't drunk—I remember everything. And me putting his dick in my mouth was the hottest sexual experience of my life. Hotter than that time I slept with Jenny Goldstein freshman year."

I raise my mug in a cheers motion. Jenny Goldstein is a stunner.

"So, yeah, I think I might be bi, like you. Especially because I'm sort of noticing other guys, too, you know? Like, all over campus. There are a lot of hot guys around here. I'm probably not straight gay, is all I'm trying to say."

"Not so straight," I correct, and then hiss when he kicks me. "Sorry. Why am I needed for this, though? I repeat: this doesn't sound like an identity crisis."

"He won't let me go over to his place, or meet his friends, or like...go out on a date with me. I don't know what I'm doing wrong."

"Maybe he just likes it when you blow him, but he doesn't actually like you," I point out. Nate's face falls, green eyes widening and mouth opening on a small gasp. Goddamnit. "Just kidding. That's probably not it."

"Atlas."

"Listen, I'm just being realistic. Why the hell do you care, anyway? Sleep with him and move on, it's not as if any relationships we have will last."

"You are impossible." Groaning, he rests back against the wall and slides his laptop to the side. "Why are you so anti-love?"

"Love," I scoff. "Love is a concept developed by commercialism to sell greeting cards and shitty chocolate. You can't tell me you believe in true love—soulmates—all that crap?"

He shakes his head. "I don't know, but I think if those things don't exist, then that's pretty sad. I'd rather believe, and—"

"—be let down," I finish harshly.

"I need someone else to talk to. Your version of help is actually pretty unhelpful." He sighs dramatically, but cracks a smile when I flip him off. Nothing keeps Nate down for long.

"Isn't half of your hockey team queer? Why the hell are you coming to me with your questions?" I finish my coffee, place the mug on the floor, and flop backward onto his bed. Nate stretches out as well, feet pushing hard into my thighs. I scowl up at the ceiling but don't bother moving him. It is his bed after all.

"I mean a few of the guys, yeah. But I can't just walk into the locker room and announce I sucked my first cock."

"That's literally what you just did with me," I point out. He chuckles softly.

"So anyway. Where were you last night? I gave up waiting for you once it passed midnight."

"Just around. Hooked up with Raquel and then nothing."

I shrug, thinking about khaki pants, scruff, and big, meaty thighs. "I was just chilling on campus. Nothing special. Talked with Henri a bit."

"Vas, you mean?" He sits up, propping himself up on an elbow and jabbing me with his toe. "Fuck yes, you guys are friends now? I knew he'd get you."

"We're not friends."

"You so are. You just called him Henri and didn't sound like you were going to hurl."

"We're not friends," I repeat more forcefully.

"Whatever." His phone dings, and I watch his face as he picks it up and reads whatever is on the screen. A smile creeps across his cheeks and I roll my eyes.

"Don't sext when I'm in here," I tell him. He ignores me, thumbs flying over the screen of his phone. He's grinning like a fool and biting his lip. It might be cute, if it wasn't so disgusting.

"That's him," Nate tells me unnecessarily, dropping his phone back to the bed.

"Yeah. You're good, then?" I ask carefully. He doesn't seem like he's in a crisis, but he did also just come out to me. It's kind of a big deal.

"I'm good. I mean, freaking out and all, but I guess I'm good. It's funny, isn't it?" He laughs under his breath, slumped back against his pillows. "How can it be possible to think you're straight your entire life and then one day it's just *boom* —gay!"

I snort, shaking my head.

"Maybe you weren't straight, man. Not everyone figures out attraction right away. Maybe you'd been brainwashed by all the heteronormative bullshit we're forced to swallow our entire lives."

"Fuck 'em," Nate says, raising his hand and flipping off the ceiling. He drops it back down, mouth twisted as he thinks. "Actually, now that I think about it, I did have a lot of cowboy posters on my wall growing up. No cowgirls. "

"I'm going back to bed," I reply, chuckling as I picture Nate papering his walls with pictures of men in Wranglers. Groaning, I pull myself up and snatch my mug off the floor. Nate's smiling at his phone again. "Dude, seriously? Have some self-respect."

He raises his middle finger again, this time directing it at me. Stopping downstairs to refill my mug, I head back to my bedroom and crawl into bed. Sipping my coffee, I fiddle with my cellphone and think about, of all things, Henri. We're not friends, but that doesn't mean I can't be *friendly*. Before I can talk myself out of it, I pull up our text message thread and type out a message.

ATLAS

Good luck in your interview today.

9

Henri

I'M SITTING in my car in the parking lot of the practice rink for South Carolina's NHL team. Checking the time, I note that I've still got an hour before my interview and recline my seat a little bit, allowing my legs to stretch out. I didn't have to come so early, but I was nervous about traffic and finding my way. It's always better to be early rather than late.

Pulling my phone out, I look again at the message Atlas sent me this morning. *Good luck in your interview.* It was unexpectedly kind and so out of character for him, I wondered if he might be drunk at 6 a.m. I'd texted back a thank-you, but he hadn't responded. Even so, his was my favorite of the messages I'd received from my friends and brother, wishing me luck and telling me I'd do fine.

Carefully setting a timer, I prop my phone in the cup holder and grab the textbook I brought to pass the time. By the time my phone chimes forty minutes later, I've made little headway in the reading I'm supposed to get done. I know I've got a good grasp on the English language and that my problems mainly stem from low confidence, but it's a hurdle that only seems to get taller. The longer I'm in school, the harder the subject matter becomes, and the gap between the content and my understanding seems to lengthen. It seems rather unfair that the only language I struggle with is the one most people speak.

Checking my hair in the rearview mirror, I smile at myself and make sure there isn't anything in my teeth. I can't find anything overly offensive with my appearance, so I check the portfolio I brought to make sure everything is still inside. All is as it was the last five times I checked it. All of that done, there's nothing left but to leave the car and walk to the front of the building.

As I approach, the door opens and a man I recognize as Sam Jameson steps out, propping the door open with his hip and watching me. He's a nice-looking man, with warm brown eyes and an easy smile. I try to relax my shoulders, and extend my hand to shake his.

"Hello, sir. I am Henri Vasel."

"Sam Jameson," he replies, shaking my hand and gesturing me inside. The door locks behind us as it swings shut. "But please, call me Sam."

"Thank you, sir."

His lips twitch like he wants to grin, but he merely strides off down the hallway.

"Do you prefer to go by your last name, or Henri?"

"Oh." I pause, surprised to be asked. I'm so used to everyone calling me Vas. "Well, whichever you prefer! I am happy with however you like to speak to me, sir."

He chuckles softly and stops next to an open doorway, gesturing for me to precede him through. He puts a gentle hand on my upper back, the touch barely discernible through my shirt, and uses his free hand to indicate the chair in front of his desk.

"Have a seat, Henri. Can I get you anything to drink?"

"Oh no, I am fine, thank you so much." Sitting down, I rest my folder on my lap and link my fingers. "I should like to apologize if there are any mistakes in my English, sir. I will do my best."

"No need to apologize, and no need to call me sir. This is a casual interview, Henri. We're just going to be chatting. I'll tell you a little bit about what the program looks like, and what we're looking for, and you can tell me about yourself. Sound good?"

"Yes, si—Sam," I correct.

He hands me a packet that I glance at before tucking into the portfolio I brought. I will need to apply myself to reading it later, but for now I want to be sure and give him my full attention. He talks me through the internship, outlining each level of the organization I would be involved in. I start to get excited as he speaks, imagining myself in the role. I know I could succeed here, if given the chance.

Sam talks for a good ten minutes, before he stops and asks if I have any questions. I like the way his voice is smooth and calm, and the way his eyes crinkle at the corners when he smiles. He seems like a nice guy and I trust him immediately.

"You have some impressive letters of recommendation," Sam says, smiling at me in a way that makes his eyes seem impossibly warm, like melted chocolate. "Nico Mackenzie and Anthony Lawson have had nothing but good things to say about you, as I'm sure you know."

"They are too kind. I am appreciative of having the opportunity to learn from them."

"How's the season going?"

"It is early, but I am happy. It is fun to be playing with Max Kuemper. I will be having him sign a jersey before he leaves so that I have it before he is famous."

Sam laughs and I smile proudly. I'm not good at telling jokes, so I appreciate it when others pick up on them.

"He's impressive. I won't lie to you, though, I have the most fun watching the netminders. McIntire has a lot of promise. He's already showing improvement from last year."

"Oh yes, Micky will do well. Coach Mackenzie tells me you played at Harvard, sir. That is very exciting."

He waves a hand. "Thank you, but I was nowhere near as good as some of you college athletes these days. You're close with Carter Morgan, if I remember correctly?"

"Yes, he is a great friend. If I am getting this internship, I will be living with him and his boyfriend."

I flinch as soon as I say it. It isn't good etiquette to insinuate that you are making plans, as though you are sure you will get the thing you are interviewing for. Especially as it's me, and I know I have more connections here than most of the other applicants probably do. Sam doesn't correct me, just smiles.

"Zeke, right? I haven't met him yet, but I've heard quite a bit about him. I imagine he and I would probably get along well."

"Yes." I nod, thinking of the sign on the door that showed Sam's title. "You could talk about statistics and all the other math things. It would be like a secret language."

Sam laughs and I smile again. Two jokes and two laughs. I'm doing good today.

"Can you tell me a little bit about your degree path? I'm interested in the foreign language minor. It doesn't look like you've chosen a single language?"

I sit up a little straighter. Foreign language is the only part of my degree path I am 100% confident in.

"Yes, Sam, thank you. My main focus is media, but I am also taking foreign language classes. Because I am foreign student, there is a"—I pause, panicking as I lose the English word I wanted to use—"a...different rule? I am fluent in German, French, Russian, and Spanish. Instead of taking classes in all of these things, I am able to take a test."

I twist my fingers together on top of my folder. I didn't explain that right, but tripping over that word made the rest of the words more difficult. When I start to struggle, the best thing to do is to stay quiet.

"Wow," Sam says, shaking his head. "That's impressive. It's an incredible achievement to be able to speak two languages fluently, let alone five."

"Well, my English is not perfect."

"Neither is mine," he replies kindly. I flush a little bit at that. He seems to be a very gentle and welcoming person, and I hope more than ever that I will be offered this position. He reminds me of my brother. "Do you have any questions for me?"

"No, sir, I believe you covered them all. I will also read through the literature you provided me, as soon as I get home," I promise.

"No need to rush. My contact information is on there—you can reach out with any questions you might think of, okay?" He waits for me to nod before grinning. "Do you want to take a walk? I'll show you around; introduce you to a few people."

"I would enjoy this very much, thank you." Nodding, I stand up.

"You can leave your things here, if you want. We'll come back."

Gratefully, I leave my folder on my recently vacated chair and follow Sam out the door. We stroll the halls, sticking our heads into offices to say hello to people that I desperately try to commit to memory. *Sophia has scarlet hair,* I repeat to myself after meeting one of the women who manages the social media.

As we walk, Sam points out various things, hands tucked casually into his pockets. He is very relaxed, so I try to emulate that. I have been so nervous for this meeting, but it has been nothing but enjoyable.

"Sam," someone calls, and we turn around to see Corwin Sanhover walking toward us. Sam smiles widely.

"Hey, Cor. Video just finishing up?"

"Yeah, Troy will probably be waiting for you in your office." They share a private look that I politely pretend not to see. Sam puts a friendly hand on my shoulder.

"This is Henri Vasel, one of our applicants for the new internship program."

"I remember you well," Corwin says, holding his hand out to me to shake. "You've had an incredible couple of seasons since Max Kuemper joined the team. I enjoy watching the pair of you together."

I swell with pride at the words and wish I could have recorded that to play for Max.

"Thank you, sir. It is easy to play with Max, he makes us all better."

"Lawson speaks highly of you. Both of you," Corwin tells me. Again, I feel as though my heart has expanded to twice its normal size. My face burns with embarrassment.

"Thank you," is all I can think to say.

Sam and I continue through the halls, and I struggle to keep a smile off my face and my expression neutral. Not only did Corwin Sanhover remember me from training camp my freshman year, but he said he's been watching our games this season. He said I've had an incredible couple of seasons, as though I am a player worth paying attention to. My fingers itch to text Max.

"So, that's all the time we have unless you can think of any further questions?" Sam stops, turning to me. We are near the rink, so I watch the Zamboni make its rounds for a few moments before answering.

"Not yet, but I may think of some later."

We head back toward his office to grab my things, where Troy Nichols is indeed waiting. When he sees me, his face breaks out into a wide smile that has dimples poking to life in his cheeks. I'm not usually one to judge the way others look, but I think I like dimples. They are rather cute. I wonder what Atlas would look like with dimples.

"Vas, right?" Troy asks, holding out his hand. I have shaken the hands of two NHL stars today—incredible. "I came to help out at camp a couple years ago, remember? With Corwin?"

I stare at him, momentarily struck dumb by the realization that he is under the impression that I would ever forget that day.

"I remember. It was the best day of the summer for all of us."

Troy beams. "I didn't mean to interrupt the meeting. I can wait in the hall."

He takes a couple steps toward the door before Sam holds a hand out to stop him. "We were just finishing up. Give me a minute to pack up and we can walk out together."

"How's your season going?" Troy asks me eagerly. Bending to pick up my folder, I grasp it tightly between both my hands.

"Very well, thank you for asking. I will be missing Max when he is not with me next year." Realizing that this sounds like a complaint about the rest of my team, I rush to continue, "But we have many promising forwards. Many younger players that will do well."

Troy chats with me as Sam packs up his things, and together we leave the building. I am unsure of the etiquette here, as this feels particularly informal. I don't know whether I made the best impression, and already I am feeling nervous at the thought of letting Coach Mackenzie down.

"Thank you, sir, for meeting with me. I appreciate the time you have taken out of your schedule to do so," I tell Sam the moment he turns to me after we reach the outside of the building. He smiles.

"You'll hear from us in a couple of weeks, okay? Still a few interviews to conduct and then we'll be contacting all the applicants to let them know."

"I understand. Thank you," I repeat.

"I'm going to ask Nico if I can come back to practice one day," Troy announces. "So, hopefully we will be seeing each other again soon."

"Micky would be very happy to meet you," I tell him, thinking of our goalie's "lucky" Troy Nichols jersey. "You are his favorite."

When I get to my car, I sit in silence for a few moments. I always get a little nervous in situations like this, and coming down from them always makes me feel vaguely ill. From my car, I can see Troy and Sam crossing the parking lot together at a casual stroll, hands linked. The now familiar pang of jealousy burns in my stomach. I *really* want to know what that feels like.

When I get back to my dorm, I change out of my clothes and take a quick five-minute shower. Sitting down at my desk to get some work done, I set a timer on my phone for forty-five minutes. My mother told me that after forty-five minutes, I should be taking a break or moving on to a different subject matter; that after a certain amount of time studying the same thing, I will no longer be retaining it.

Unfortunately, when the timer goes off, I don't feel like I've retained much of anything at all. This English course is higher level and more intricate than my previous classes of the same subject. The reading assignments alone take me twice as long than they are probably taking other students, which makes me feel panicky. I am terrified of failing a course and letting my parents down.

Before I can switch my books and reset the timer, I notice there is a text message from Atlas.

ATLAS

how was the interview

I smile at my phone, a strange buzzy feeling in my chest when I look at his name on the screen, like I've swallowed a bee.

HENRI

Hello, Atlas, thank you for asking. The interview went well, I believe. I will not know for a few weeks.

I wait, but there is no indication that a reply is coming. It doesn't matter. The fact that he even remembered makes me feel good. For the first time all semester, I'm excited to go to communications class on Tuesday.

10

Atlas

I HOLD out for another two weeks before I eat the apple. The moment I reach for it, Henri's eyes practically bug out of his head and he bites his lip so hard I can see the indent of his teeth. He looks so happy, I nearly put it back on the desk. But I'm fucking *starving*, and it'll be hours before I'm able to go home and grab some food. So, Henri's weird friendship apple will just have to do.

"Thanks," I mumble, before taking a massive bite and using a full mouth as an excuse not to talk to him.

"No need," he says, waving off my thanks with a smile on his face. The smile remains for the entirety of class, like me eating his stupid apple made his day.

I can't seem to concentrate on the lecture at all, distracted by Henri's scruffy cheek and the smell of lemons. It's not important—I *know* it's not important—but I don't remember him smelling this way before, which means he changed something. Is lemon shampoo even a thing? Maybe I should lean over and get a good whiff of his damn polo shirt. He probably bought lemongrass detergent or some shit, and anyway, why do I care?

At one point during class, he fidgeted in his seat, and because my own legs were spread wide, his thigh bumped mine. Of course, he apologized and moved away, but my first thought was that I didn't want him to move away. I wanted that thick thigh to come right back and bump me again.

"I think I need to see a doctor," I say, shoving all my shit in my backpack after Dr. Robertson ends class. Henri looks at me, politely quizzical.

"Oh? Are you feeling ill? I shall walk you to the student health center."

"Not that kind of doctor. I think I need a fucking psych eval." Standing up, I sling my backpack over my shoulders and look down at Henri.

He's still seated, hands resting on his thighs and face tilted up so he can look at me. Blue eyes and heavy eyebrows several shades darker than his hair. From this angle, I'm looking down on his head and can see the way the longer strands curl together. He's fucking cute, like a little German puppy.

"Oh my god," I mutter, annoyed. *He's not cute, and you don't like him!* I think, disgusted with myself.

"If you wait a moment, I shall walk you to the health facility," he says, brow scrunched together in worry.

"It was a joke, dude. I don't need a doctor. I need to go outside and smoke." Also, find someone to bone, because apparently, I need to sweat Henri out of my system. He swivels his head, tracking me as I sneak behind his chair and down the aisle. My back prickles with the awareness of his eyes on me as I leave the lecture hall.

It's not as though I had a lobotomy and am suddenly writing Mr. Atlas Vasel on all my school notebooks, but I definitely feel *different* about him. I can't understand it—apparently, getting drunk and letting him take my pants off was enough to send my libido into a state of madness. I can't believe I've devolved into finding a man wearing khaki pants and polo shirts attractive. It's disgusting.

I pause suddenly outside of the building, ignoring the huffs of annoyance from the people who have to step around me. The thing is, Henri and I have another assignment we are supposed to do together, so it really wouldn't be strange if I asked if he wanted to hang out tonight. With my luck, both me and the homework assignment would get done. I turn around just as Henri's recognizable form exits the building. He sees me and smiles, walking over.

"Hello, Atlas," he greets me, like we didn't just come from the same fucking classroom.

"Want to do our assignment tonight? Just get it done?"

"Oh." His face falls a little bit, eyebrows coming together between his eyes in a way that should not be as appealing as it is. "I am unable to do so now. I am having a date."

Shoving my hands in my pockets, I rock back on my heels and smirk at him. "Another date, huh? Busy guy."

"Yes," he says, missing my sarcasm completely. "Shayla is studying French and I will sometimes assist her with her conjugations."

"So, that's what the kids are calling it these days," I muse. Henri's frown deepens as he tries to work out who the kids are and why they're saying that. Instead of asking, he just moves on.

"We are going to have dinner. But perhaps, if it is not too late, we could work on the assignment later? I could bring dinner from the restaurant for you. Do you like Italian?"

"Won't you be with this Shayla girl all night?"

More frowning. Christ, I wish he would stop doing that. A breeze blows a wave of lemon-scented air toward me, and I inhale involuntarily. Somehow, Henri smelling like goddamn Pledge makes perfect sense and is far sexier than it has any right to be. Maybe he scrubbed down his impossibly clean dorm room before class today.

"No, just dinner," he tells me, head tilted slightly to the side like a giant, quizzical bird. "It will not take all night."

"Okay, well, whatever. Text me if you want to do something later."

"I will, my friend."

"We're not friends."

"A little bit friends," he corrects, pinching his thumb and pointer finger together and holding them up. I sigh, shaking my head and turning away.

"Whatever. Have fun on your date. Use protection."

Walking away, I glance over my shoulder and see him watching me with another puzzled expression on his face.

When I get back to the house, I can immediately tell that it's empty except for Nate. There is a steady twang of country music shaking the house at a volume that no country song should ever be played at. Standing in the entryway, I listen to a man sing about his truck for a few moments before walking upstairs and letting myself into Nate's room without knocking. Predictably, he's stretched out on the floor, shirtless, performing some sort of abdominal exercise that looks like torture. He grunts as I walk in and take a seat on his bed.

He finishes his set and collapses onto the floor, head tipped back so he can look at me. I let my eyes trail a meandering path from his face to his toes. Nate's probably the hottest guy I've ever seen, so I might as well take advantage of the view while I've got it. It's crazy to me that a body like that was built on a farm and not a stripper pole.

"What do you want, perv?" he asks.

"Just enjoying the show," I shout back, trying to raise my voice enough to contend with the next country music star currently trying to blow out my eardrums. I point toward his Bluetooth speaker. "This is what gets you fired up to work out? Really?"

He presses a finger down on his phone, silencing the music. My ears ring from the sudden quiet.

"Buddy, I'm from the country," he tells me. Admittedly, it's a fair point.

"How's baseball guy?"

Nate rolls over onto his stomach, pillowing his cheek on his arm. There's a tattoo on the small of his back of a long-horn cow skull. He told me once he got the tramp stamp after losing a bet, but I'm not convinced. I'm pretty sure he's just a redneck. A hot one, but a redneck all the same. At the mention of baseball guy, his face flushes and he smiles.

"Good."

"Good? Really, that's all I get?"

"I mean, sort of good. Nothing's really changed. We haven't hooked up in a while, but we text every day and we had a really incredible date. But then I saw him at the coffee cart one day and sat with him for a bit, and when I touched his hand, he pulled his arm away from me." Nate shrugs and turns his face so the opposite cheek is resting down and I can no longer see his expression. "I think he's probably not into dating. Or maybe just dating me."

"Maybe," I agree. "Why does it matter to you so much?

Why not just be happy with banging in private and friends in public?"

I can hear it in Nate's voice as he talks—the longing. It makes me irrationally angry, the same way I get when people complain about their significant others. It makes no sense to me, the way people throw themselves into relationships. It's like purposely sticking your hand in a fire even though you know it will burn.

He sits up, bending one knee and stretching his other leg out in front of him. Scowling at me, he plants his hands on the floor behind him and leans back.

"Because I want to hold his fucking hand, Atlas. I want to kiss him after he wins a game. I want to bring him back to my uncle's ranch for a visit, and teach him to ride a horse. I want to see if this could actually go somewhere. I feel like...I feel like I'm *supposed* to know him. I saw him and it was this immediate attraction and I've never had that happen before. I don't want to just get laid, okay? I want to *date* him."

I still don't get it, but I know by the look on his face that he's prepared to argue if I push it. I settle for a disappointed headshake. He's giving this guy way too much power, and he's bound to get hurt. Judging by the look on his pretty face and the tone of his voice, he's *already* been fucking hurt.

"Maybe he already knows how to ride a horse," I point out, and Nate snorts.

"He doesn't. I asked and he said it's not safe to ride things that have a mind of their own."

I cast my eyes toward the ceiling dramatically. "That sentence is a veritable goldmine of gay jokes."

Nate chuckles and bends forward to stretch out his quad. I wish I had something more concrete to give him in the way of advice, but I can't even fake it. Relationships are a waste of time and energy. Happy endings are a fabrication used to sell novels and Disney movies—they don't exist in the real world.

"How are things with Vas?"

"What?" I ask, the single word coming out sounding snappish and defensive. Nate raises his eyebrows. "How should I know?"

"Aren't you guys partners in comm?"

"Oh, yeah, we are. It's fine. He's fine." Fine to look at, more like. Fuck my life.

"You can admit you like him. The sky won't fall, and I promise not to say I told you so."

"I don't like him. He's annoying and perfect and way too fucking nice. There is—quite literally—never a hair out of place on his head. It's all brown and soft-looking. Have you ever noticed how it's wavy but also sort of curly in the front? Pick a fucking lane! Also, I bet he uses some fancy-ass lemon-scented shampoo and conditioner. Separate too, not the cheap, all-in-one shit I get at the drug store. And his stupid scruffy face is so...*even*. I think he shaves with a slide rule." I hold my hands up, palms facing out like I'm warding something off. "He drives me *insane*."

"What I'm hearing is you're in love with him."

"What is it in the country air that made you so stupid?" I ask and Nate grins at me.

"You just talked about his hair for two minutes straight. I was sitting here listening and trying to picture his hair, but I can't because I've never noticed before. Want to know why I've never noticed before? Because I don't have a crush on him."

"Jesus fucking Christ."

"My guy has nice hair, too," he says wistfully. "Thick. Like, *really* thick. And just long enough to really get your fingers into, you know? God, he's cute."

"You're a little nauseating to be around, you know that, right?" I scrunch up my face in disgust. "Did baseball guy suck your brains out through your dick or something?"

"You should ask Vas out on a date. He's such a hard worker, he deserves a break." I give him such an incredulous look, he laughs. "He's here on a student visa, you know? The stakes are a little higher for him to get good grades and maintain his spot on the team. Especially since he wants to stay after he graduates, so he *needs* to cultivate relationships and maintain a high GPA so that he can get a job."

I stare at him, surprised that he knows so much about Henri. I'd assumed there wasn't much real talk in the locker room. Just a bunch of naked dudes, slapping each other's backs and talking about all the pussy they get.

"I don't date, and I'm not about to start with Henri," I tell him sternly. Sighing, I close my eyes and look up at the ceiling. God help me. "But, I would definitely fuck him if he asked me to."

"Ha!" Nate laughs. "I knew it. Absolutely incredible."

"Once," I say firmly. "I don't double-dip."

"You're missing out, bro." Nate straightens, reaching his arms over his head and stretching. Because I'm a red-blooded bisexual man, I enjoy the play of his muscles beneath his skin as he does it. I wonder if Henri has muscles like that. "Sex only gets better when you go back for more with the same person."

"Sure, Nicholas Sparks, whatever you say. You going to tell your teammates about the bi thing?"

"Yeah, I am. I already told one of them, actually. Also, Max—one of my linemates—is gay, and so is Coach Mackenzie. I don't even have to worry about the other guys being chill, I know they will be."

"Mm." I pick at a loose thread in his bedspread, aiming for nonchalance. "And Henri?"

I glance up at Nate to find him smirking at me. He shakes his head.

"Honestly, I have no idea. Vas is the guy you go to for advice, but he doesn't talk about himself a lot. I get the impression he might be demi, actually. Maybe ace."

"Really? Why?"

"Nothing in particular." He shrugs. "Just a feeling. Vas is quiet. The guys will all be talking about who they're with and what they're doing, and Vas will just be over in the corner listening. He's definitely not the kind to kiss and tell."

"Mm," I hum in agreement, succeeding in picking the thread out of the sheet. Nate reaches over and slaps my leg. "Ouch."

"You should ask him out if you want to."

"I don't want to."

"Sounds like you kind of want to."

"Sounds like you don't know me at all," I reply, but there's no heat in it. He's right. I do kind of want to.

Rolling his eyes, Nate rises up off the floor and starts rolling up his yoga mat. Again, I enjoy the ripple of muscles in his arms and back as he does it, and again I wonder if all the hockey guys look this good when they're shirtless. If Henri does.

"Whatever, man. Let me know if you want me to wingman for you with Vas. I'll put a good word in when we're naked together in the shower." He winks at me lewdly, before tucking his yoga mat away beside his desk.

"Please don't talk about—or even think about—me when

you're in the shower," I request, and he laughs. "And don't talk to Henri about me, dude, I was just curious about him. We're partners in comm, that's all it is."

"That's all it is," Nate mimics in a high-pitched, nasally voice that sounds nothing like me. "Famous last words, pal."

———————

HENRI TEXTS me at 8:42 to let me know that he is back at his dorm if I still want to work on the assignment. I wait five minutes before responding in the affirmative, embarrassed by how excited I am that he reached out like he'd said he would. I'm acting pathetic and there's no reason for it. Sure, Henri's attractive, but so are a lot of guys. What I really need to do is go out and find a guy to bang—get my first time over with and with someone who won't try and make it more than it is. Then, maybe I won't be so hard up that even annoying people look like attractive options.

When I knock on Henri's door, he opens it so quickly I wonder if he was standing on the other side waiting for me.

"You are here," he exclaims, grinning and stepping back to let me walk in.

"As always, you appear to have a firm grasp of the obvious," I retort.

"Thank you," Henri replies, letting the sarcasm just pass him by. "Have a seat, if you wish. I brought you spaghetti because this seems to be something everyone likes. Also, garlic toast."

He points to two aluminum containers sitting on the corner of his desk. The small room smells strongly of Italian seasoning and garlic, and I can no longer identify Henri's lemon scent from earlier. I try not to think too hard on the fact that I'm a little disappointed by that. Sitting down on his bed, I bypass the garlic toast and open up the spaghetti.

"Thanks, but you didn't have to bring me food. I have food at home."

"It was no trouble. Sometimes we must have a treat."

"Mm," I hum around a mouthful of noodles. The only treat I'm particularly interested in right now are his thighs. Fuck my life.

Henri sits down in the desk chair and scoots it close enough to me that I finally get a whiff of lemons. As he pulls out his notebook and a pen, I watch his hands. Are hockey players supposed to have hands like that? They don't look rough at all, but smooth and unblemished. Prominent veins snake their way over his wrist and up his forearm. He's like an anesthesiologist's wet dream.

"Would you like to start now or perhaps finish dinner, first?" Henri's smooth accent distracts me from wondering how soft his hands are. I think I need a solid slap in the face to knock some sense back into me. I can't believe I was just sitting here sexualizing his veins.

"Eat first. How did your date go?"

I'm not asking because I care, I'm asking because it's polite, I tell myself, even as I recognize that I care rather more than I should. I put a bite of spaghetti in my mouth before I do something insane like put his fingers there instead.

"It was enjoyable, thank you for asking."

He smiles at me, but doesn't seem overly concerned with expanding on that. Swallowing my half-chewed mouthful, I cough a little bit and Henri hands me a bottle of water like the gentleman he is. I don't understand this guy at all, and perhaps that's the draw of him all of a sudden. Maybe once I solve the puzzle, I won't want to play anymore.

We work on our project for a few hours. I brought my laptop, so I type everything out to save Henri the trouble of handwriting it. The room is filled with the quiet click of the keyboard and Henri's melodic accent. I blame the darkness outside, and the dim light of the room for how attractive the sound is.

"We have done good work this evening," he says, carefully cleaning up the containers my food was in and placing them in his new trash can. "We make a good team."

Instead of responding, I roll my eyes and stand up to stretch out my back. Henri stands as well, and I see a sliver of skin on his back where his shirt has ridden up, before he pulls it back down. My fingers itch to touch it.

"Do you ever hook up with guys?" I blurt out, allowing the madness to temporarily overtake me. Henri turns and looks at me, head cocked to the side. Fucking hell, I want to bone this irritating motherfucker so bad right now.

"I have never," he replies, which answers half of my question but not really the important part.

"Are you straight?"

He thinks about this, giving it the sort of speculation one might give a particularly difficult mathematics equation.

"I do not think so, but I am unsure," is what he ends up going with, which is exactly the sort of ridiculous shit I would expect him to spout off.

"You're not sure," I repeat, abandoning my laptop on his bed and taking a step closer to him. The room is lit by only a single lamp sitting on his desk; with shadows thrown across his face, his jaw and cheekbones look sharper. I wish he had his shirt off and I could see the light play over any curves there, as well. I bet there are quite a few.

I stop when I'm standing close enough to him to count his

eyelashes. He's taller than me, so I have to tip my head back to maintain eye contact. I'm not a very big guy, and I'm not comfortable with the thought of giving up control to someone else, which is why I've only pursued women thus far. It's hard to find a guy smaller than me.

Except with Henri, I don't feel that usual trepidation about being the weaker partner. He would, I realize, be the perfect person to experiment with. Someone I'm apparently physically attracted to, but have no possibility of falling in love with. Someone safe. I step a little closer to him, stopping once my chest brushes against his front.

"Want to find out?" I ask, and am again treated to another thoughtful silence. Evidently, he will not be one who becomes consumed by passion. I'm going to die of old age before I ever get the chance to see what he's hiding behind all the khaki.

"I am unsure of what you are asking," he admits. I roll my eyes, annoyed at having to spell it out. Flirting should *not* be this difficult.

"I want to kiss you. See if you taste like lemons."

This sends his eyebrows slanting downward as he frowns heavily, trying to figure out what I'm talking about. I can practically see him mentally tallying all the meals he's eaten today and coming to the conclusion that none of them contained lemons. I almost laugh—I've never met a more literal person in my life.

"Me? But I am not sure you like me."

"Honestly, I'm not sure either, but you're super hot and I think I need to do this so I can stop thinking about it and move on."

"You wanted to kiss me when you were drunk," he tells me. I nod. I'll kiss anything when I'm drunk.

"I'm sober now," I point out.

"Yes."

"And I still want to kiss you."

It's a question even though it isn't, and Henri gives it the same amount of thought he's given everything tonight. After a few moments of quiet pass, he whispers, "Yes."

My stomach jolts like I've just missed a step walking down a staircase. I hadn't come here intending to ask that, and I most definitely didn't expect him to agree. If everything goes according to plan, by this time tomorrow Henri Vasel will be kissed right out of my system.

I'm already close enough that I don't have to stretch far to reach him. He looks down at my hands as I put them on his waist, as though he's surprised I'm touching him. I wait for him to look back up at me, blue eyes meeting mine, before I move one hand to his neck. His breath hitches and he cocks his head to the side again, eyes bright in the dim of the room.

He stands perfectly still as I lean forward and press my mouth to his. The moment I do, his breathing stutters again, and he makes a soft gasping noise in the back of his throat. I pull him toward me until our chests are pressed together, and tilt my head, teasing the seam of his lips with my tongue to try and get him to open.

The smell of him is overwhelming, with my nose against his face, and his scruff scratches deliciously against the pad of my thumb. I want to kiss him hard enough to feel it against my lips. I want him to kiss me back.

Leaning back until I can see his face, I frown at him.

"What are you doing?"

"Kissing," he says, completely without guile. I raise an eyebrow at him.

"Really? Because I've kissed mannequins with more life

than you." I glance down at his arms, which are hanging loose by his sides. "You can touch me, if you want."

"Why are you kissing mannequins?" he asks quietly.

"I told you: I'll hit on anything when I'm drunk. Stop dodging the question. Why aren't you kissing me back? You can be honest—if the problem is me, just say it."

"It is not you," he whispers. "I am not sure what to do."

Frowning, I lean back a little more, trying to get his damn lemon-scented skin out of my nose so I can think.

"Henri, just kiss me back. It's not rocket science. Do whatever you usually do. Whatever feels right."

"I have never before."

I realize I'm still touching his damn face, thumb sliding back and forth idly over his scratchy jaw. Dropping my hand down to his shoulder where it's safer, I let go of where I'm also still holding his hip. I don't need to have my hands all over him if we're not making out, but I can't bring myself to break all points of contact just yet.

"Okay, I'm sorry, are you telling me you've *never kissed anyone before*?" He nods. "How the *fuck* is that possible? You're weird as shit, sure, but you also look like a fucking movie star."

I can see it on his face that he's about to say something literal and ridiculous. Putting my palm over his mouth, I give him a stern look.

"Are you a virgin?" He nods, lips warm on my hand. I curse under my breath and let him go, backing up a step. He licks his lips and my heart rate speeds up dangerously. "Are you serious? How? What about all these dates you've been going on?"

"I am sorry," he says, looking crestfallen. "Perhaps I

should have told you. But I thought I might like to kiss you and you did offer."

He looks so apologetic I can't help but laugh, even as a small seed of worry sprouts in my stomach. I just gave him his first kiss. Under no circumstances should I be providing anyone's first anything. I'm a plague, and a scourge. I'm the place love goes to die.

"It's fine, you don't have to be sorry," I tell him, rubbing a hand over my eyes.

"I have never been interested in kissing before, until I met you," he says, head tilted and eyes contemplative on mine. His gaze drops to my mouth. "But I like your hair, and I like talking to you even though you can be rude and think I'm strange. I like looking at you."

"Oh, well, sure. All of that makes sense." Shrugging, I offer him the smallest of smiles. I never smile, but I've also never kissed a guy, so I guess tonight is a night for trying new things. "You should always determine attraction based on hair."

Henri sighs. "I am hearing sarcasm."

"You've got good ears." Reaching up, I tug gently on a wavy lock of caramel hair. "You've got good hair, too. And... sorry about calling you weird. You're not, I'm just a dick."

Pulling away from him completely and taking a few steps away feels like I'm a planet trying to wrench itself out of orbit. He looks a little forlorn as I back away. If he had floppy ears, they'd be drooping to the floor. Again, he's giving off puppy vibes, and, again, I do *not* find it adorable.

"You are not wanting to do more kissing," he states glumly. I shake my head.

"I don't do serious relationships, or virgins. Or Germans."

He barks a startled laugh and grins at me. I don't grin

back, even though I want to. Even though I can feel it fighting to be free. Picking up my backpack and slinging it over my shoulder, I glance back at him. He hasn't moved from the spot where I kissed him, as though the bottom of his feet sprouted roots. *You need to leave*, I tell myself, as I open my mouth to find another reason to stay.

"Feel free to tell me to fuck right off if you don't want to answer this, but...are you ace?" When he just stares at me, I clarify. "Asexual."

"Oh." He pauses to think, and I wait patiently for once. I actually sort of appreciate that he doesn't just blurt out the first thing that comes to mind. I know his answer, whatever it is, will be sincere and well thought out. "Yes, I think I might be. I do not know how I would be sure."

I point over at his daily schedule, pinned to the wall.

"I'd say scheduling a time to jerk off is a pretty clear indicator."

Another chuckle, low and sexy in the dark room.

"I made a mistake in leaving that up, yes?" he asks, looking amused.

"Oh, yeah. I'm going to make fun of you for that all year."

He doesn't look annoyed. If anything he looks a little pleased. Half of his mouth is pulled up into a smirk and his eyes shine in the lamplight.

"I have never wanted to touch anyone like that, and I do not know that I would enjoy someone touching me," he admits quietly. "But I should like to try. I think, perhaps, it might depend on the person."

"Yeah," I agree, even though the person doesn't really matter much to me. I could sleep with anyone at all. The act means nothing to me. I don't have it in me to do the feelings part.

"I enjoyed kissing you," he adds, almost as an afterthought. "I wanted to."

I enjoyed it, too, I think, surprised at myself. I really shouldn't have enjoyed it. It was, as far as kisses go, one of the worst. And yet, if he asked me to, I'd drop my backpack on the floor and dive right back in for more.

Clearing my throat roughly, I turn to the door. "I'll see you in class, Henri."

"Goodnight, Atlas," he murmurs as the door closes behind me.

11

Henri

MAX IS UNCOMFORTABLE. He is fidgeting, fingers twisting together in his lap and lip caught between his teeth. He has not said a single word beyond thanking me for the ride. Pulling up to a stoplight, I keep my eyes on the light and try to reach him.

"It is nice for Coach Mackenzie and Coach Lawson to invite us over, yes?"

"Yeah," Max murmurs.

"Are you wishing you could have invited Luke?" I glance over at him before focusing back on the road. His face is turned toward me, and he's chewing his bottom lip so hard I worry he'll break the skin. "I am sure Coach Mackenzie would not have minded."

"A little bit, yeah. I uhm...actually, Vas, could you pull over for a second?"

Surprised, I sit forward and peer through the windshield. There is a gas station coming up. Putting my blinker on, I pull into the lot and put the car in park. Reaching for my wallet, I pull out some cash.

"Are you not feeling well? I will go inside and get you some water."

"No, that's okay. I'm fine. I just wanted to talk to you for a second?" He sounds so unsure, a tilt to each word as though he's questioning everything that comes out of his mouth.

"Of course, Max." Turning to face him, I settle my features into blandness and just wait. Silence, I have found, is the best way to get people to talk. Americans are very uncomfortable with silence, and will rush to fill it. Max closes his eyes and takes a deliberate, deep inhale.

"I've been seeing a therapist since the start of the year, and one thing Dr. K wants me to do is open up to my friends. He says I have trust issues and that the way to conquer those fears is by...well, by trusting people. And I trust you. I trust you more than anyone else other than Luke and Coach Mackenzie. You're a really good friend to me."

I stare at him, nervous now as to the nature of this conversation. Max looks pained, like each word is a fishhook in his throat.

"You do not have to tell me anything you do not wish to share, Max," I tell him quietly, hating to see him so upset.

"Thanks. I want to, though. It's important." Another deep breath, his chest expanding dramatically under his thin T-shirt. "I wasn't going to go to this today. I have trouble with big groups—parties—like this. Even though it'll just be the team there, I still don't...I just really don't like being around a lot of people. My first year here—that October—I went to a party with my roommate and..."

He trails off, turning away to look at the gas station

through the windshield. I give him a few moments before softly prompting, "And what, Max?"

"And someone put a roofie in my drink, and, well..."

My arm, which had been resting on the steering wheel, slips and the horn gives a quick report. I don't know all the street names that are used for drugs in this country, but I know *that* one. I know what it does and I know what it is primarily used for. I don't need for him to continue in order to guess what might have happened.

"Oh, no, Max. I am very sorry about this." Desperately, I try to think of anything I could say or do. I wish I could be like Zeke—he always knows the right thing.

"It's okay," he says quickly. "I'm not...I just wanted to explain why I don't hang out with the team very often. I wasn't going to go to this barbecue, but Dr. K said I should. It's my homework."

"We shall stick together. You and I will be together today, and everything will be well," I promise, feeling miserable and a little ill.

Max smiles and flattens his hands on his thighs, rubbing them back and forth as though he's drying his palms.

"Actually, that would be great. If you don't mind," he adds quietly.

"I do not mind!" I say a little desperately. "But I am thinking Coach Mackenzie would not want you to stress yourself. We can go home if you wish. I will tell Coach it is because of me that we did not go."

"You're right. Coach told me not to come if I wasn't comfortable. But I can't keep hiding, and it's just a backyard barbecue with friends. It'll be fine." He sounds like he's not stating a fact so much as trying to convince himself of the truth.

"Yes, it will be fine. And we shall stay together, you and I. I will be your Luke for the evening, except perhaps with less jokes and kissing."

Max chuckles and I relax into my seat a little bit. I want to reach back in time and smack myself for not being a better person; for not trying to talk to him when I had noticed something was off. I feel awful. I'm a terrible friend.

"I am very sorry," I repeat. This time it isn't English failing me, but words in general. I don't understand how this could happen. How someone could hurt Max, who is sweet and quiet and never makes any trouble.

"Vas, please don't feel bad. I just wanted to explain, that's all."

"It is very hard not to feel badly when your friend tells you something like this." Max smiles a little and I try my best to return it. I almost wish he had asked me to turn around and drive us back to his apartment. Suddenly, I am not feeling much like socialization myself.

"I wouldn't have told you what happened back then, even if you'd asked," he says quietly, eyes intent on my face. "So don't go feeling guilty. You and Carter being my friends was help enough. I don't know what I would have done if you guys hadn't done that. I would have been alone on the team and felt a hell of a lot worse than I already did."

"That is kind. Thank you for telling me, Max. I promise I will not abuse your confidence, and I promise I will stay with you at Coach's barbecue."

"Thanks. We'd better get going so we aren't late."

The car is silent once more as I drive, but it's a more comfortable silence. I did not grow up with a particularly affectionate family, and I have mostly used that model of behavior in my adult life. But now I am wishing I had given

Max a few more hugs, and Carter as well. Perhaps there are a lot of people in my life who might benefit from a little show of affection, and I have been letting them down. I think of Atlas, as I so often seem to do these days, and add him to the list of people who probably need a few extra hugs. When we pull up to Coach Mackenzie's house, and park behind some-one's truck, I turn to Max.

"I think I might hug you, if that is all right."

He smiles. "That's all right."

Nate pulls up right as I'm letting Max go. He walks up grinning, and slings an arm over each of our shoulders, squeezing us to his sides in a single-armed hug.

"Hey, guys."

"Hello, Nate." I smile at him. He is an easy guy to be around, and one of my favorites on the team. He is always in the thick of things, making the rounds in the locker room and talking to everyone. At one practice, he somehow convinced Micky to lend him his pads and stick so he could try being a goalie. He might give Coach Mackenzie an aneurism, but he'll have the rest of us laughing in the process.

"I am so fucking hungry. Haven't eaten all day in prepara-tion," he says, dropping his arms and rubbing a hand over his stomach.

Coach Mackenzie instructed us to come straight to the back and not bother knocking, so we skirt around the edge of the house. As nonchalantly as I can, I step behind Nate and put myself on Max's right side, so there is no longer a body between us. I am going to stick to him like glue today.

Judging by the amount of people milling around, we are some of the last to arrive. Smoke is rising from a massive grill over on a large deck, and there are tables set up and already strewn with food. Nate groans dramatically, making Max chuckle.

"How many servings do you think I can eat before it's considered rude to fill my plate again?" he asks.

"I think you can have as much as you want," Max answers, with a small, knowing smile.

Nate sets off toward the food, and I look around the backyard. Even though the grill is smoking, there doesn't seem to be anyone maintaining it right now, nor can I see Coach Mackenzie. Micky and a few of the defensemen are to the side, setting up some sort of game with a wooden board and hand bags. I squint at them, trying to see better.

"Cornhole," Max says quietly.

"Pardon me?"

"The game." He gestures to Micky, who tosses one of the bags and hits the board with an audible *thunk*. "It's called cornhole."

"Oh. Perhaps because there is corn inside of the bags? Or do you eat corn when you play? What are the circles representing—different points?"

Laughing, Max turns to gaze around the yard. "I'll teach you how to play later. Want to try and find Coach?"

We find Anthony Lawson first, or rather, he finds us. With a smile, he gives Max a long hug that I approve of, before moving to me and hugging me as well. Surprised, it takes me a moment to return it.

"Hello, Coach Lawson, how are we doing today?" I ask, feeling the vibration of his laughter against my chest. He steps back and claps a hand on my shoulder.

"Vas, buddy, you can drop the 'coach.' That was three years ago. I'm not your coach anymore, I'm just your friend."

I try not to look too pleased at that, and fear that I fail. I'm saved from having to formulate a response by the appearance of Coach Mackenzie, who walks up next to Max and puts a gentle hand on his shoulder. Lawson beams at the sight of him, as though he hasn't seen him in days.

"Max. Vasel. Glad to see you could make it. Have you eaten yet?"

"Not yet, sir. We just got here. Sorry, we were a little late," Max replies, glancing at me. "My fault."

"We're just happy you came." Lawson waves the apology away easily. "Go get something to eat, and come find me if you need anything."

Max and I grab plates and find an open spot on the deck to settle. It's a beautiful day, warm and sunny; perfect for a backyard barbecue. Suddenly inspired, I pull out my cellphone and take a picture of my teammates scattered around —some playing games, others sitting on the grass or chairs, eating. I text it to Atlas, who responds almost immediately with a single word: *gross.*

Smiling, I put my phone away. Across from where Max and I are seated, Nate is chatting to Lawson with a pleased, excited look on his face. Beside me, Max sighs and leans back on his hands.

"Time for bed," he mutters after we finish eating, making me chuckle. I glance over at the food table, which is still relatively full even after being attacked by a hockey team.

"Coach Mackenzie is going to be eating leftovers for a long time, I think."

Max snorts, eyes closed and face tipped upward into the sun. I'm just opening my mouth to ask him how he's feeling when a soft, small voice interrupts me.

"Who are you?"

Max and I turn around to find a small child standing

behind us. He's got a head of unruly curls and glasses held in place by a strap around the back of his head. He looks between Max and me, squinting suspiciously.

"Goodness," I say, glancing at Max. Does one of our teammates have a kid? "Where did you come from?"

"Hi, I'm Max." Max smiles and points at me. "And this is my friend Henri."

"I'm Caleb. You guys are being loud."

At the cornhole game, someone chooses this moment to let out a scream of frustration that is closely followed by laughter from the team that apparently just won. I nod solemnly.

"Yes," I agree with Caleb. "My apologies."

He thinks about this for a second, quietly chewing on his lip and looking between us. Apparently coming to a decision, he turns to Max. "Do you like to color?"

"I do," Max replies. "How about you, Vas—Henri?"

"I think I should like to color, yes."

"All right," Caleb holds out a hand to Max, waiting for us to climb to our feet before leading us inside. Before we can step through the back door, he turns and regards us seriously. I have never met a child so stern. "You can't make a mess. If you make a mess, Uncle Nico might get hurt."

"We will not make a mess. I promise." I glance over at Max, unsure what to think of this warning, but he doesn't meet my eye.

Content with this vow, Caleb brings us inside and leads us to the dining room table. It's littered with markers and crayons; an entire stack of finished coloring pages next to a sloppier pile of blank ones. Caleb crawls back up into his chair, adjusts his glasses, and waits for us to sit down. He turns to Max, whom he seems to like best.

"What do you want to color?"

"How about you choose something for us?" Max gestures to me, and Caleb's eyes light up as he reaches for the stack of papers.

He pokes his tongue out as he shuffles through. Eventually, he finds what he's looking for. Max is given what appears to be a dragon, while I am handed a cranky-looking owl holding a coffee mug in its talons. Max huffs a soft laugh and holds his coloring sheet out for me to see. It is in fact a dragon—a dragon holding a baseball bat and wearing an ill-fitting uniform top.

"Fitting," Max notes.

"You can give it to Luke!" I tell him happily.

Caleb carefully rolls all the markers and crayons into the center of the table, within easy reach of everyone. I wait for him to choose a color before I pluck up one of my own. We work in silence for a bit, nothing but the scratch of markers over paper and the occasional sigh from Caleb. I focus on my owl, carefully remaining inside the lines. When I start coloring the face, I smile to myself. The expression reminds me of Atlas.

"You're doing a good job," Caleb tells me, leaning over the table and peering at my paper.

"Thank you. You are as well. Are you making that for yourself?"

"No, this is for Uncle Win. He likes it when I make him pictures. I can write his name now, without help," he tells me proudly. "If you show me what order to do your letters in, I bet I could do your name, too."

"Oh, certainly." I carefully write my name in big, block letters, before adding Max's below that. "Here is mine, and here is Max."

"Cool," Caleb says, grabbing the paper, but getting distracted by the opening of the back door. His eyes widen behind his glasses and he scrambles off his chair to waylay Nate. "Don't make a mess!" he shouts desperately.

"Nate, Caleb would like everyone entering the house to know that it must remain clean and you are not to make a mess," I explain, biting back a laugh at the look on Nate's face. I leave out the part about Coach Mackenzie hurting himself if a mess is made. I'll have to think on that one later.

"Sure thing, little man," Nate says easily, ruffling his hair. "I'm just here to use the bathroom."

"Okay. It's over there." Caleb points down the hallway and climbs back up into his seat. "But don't make a mess."

Max bites his lip to keep from laughing and bends his head over his baseball-playing dragon. Nate strolls off down the hallway, apparently taking in stride the fact that we are sitting inside coloring with a kid instead of engaging in the party. When the back door opens again, Caleb's head snaps up so fast it's a miracle he doesn't hurt his neck. He practically levitates off of his chair and runs for the door.

"Uncle Nico!"

Max and I turn to find Coach Mackenzie regarding us through squinted eyes, mouth pulled up in a small smile. Caleb throws his arms around Coach's leg, peering up at him as Coach rests a gentle hand atop his curls.

"How are things going in here, Caleb?" he asks.

"Good. Nobody is making a mess, I promise. I told them."

Coach Mackenzie sighs and addresses Max and me.

"Anthony might have been a little too exuberant in explaining why things have to be put back in their place."

"No worries," Max replies, smiling softly. I don't say anything, because I haven't quite puzzled out what they're talking about. Caleb pulls Coach's attention back down to him, tripping over his words as he excitedly talks. Coach Mackenzie threads his fingers through the boy's hair, listening intently as he speaks and smiling tenderly as Caleb tells him all about Max coloring with him.

When Caleb's talked himself out, he makes his way back over to the table, trailed by Coach Mackenzie. He peeks over my shoulder.

"Solid work, Vas," he compliments me, nodding down at my owl and making Max laugh. "Are you two okay in here? You don't have to feel obligated to babysit."

"I'm pretty big," Caleb puts in, head bent over his paper once more. "I don't need a babysitter."

"Oh, we are okay, sir." I glance over at Max to verify this is true. "It is not every day we get to color with our good friend Caleb."

"All right. Caleb here is staying with us for a few weeks. He's Anthony's nephew."

"I figured," Max says, pointing to Caleb's curly hair, which is a near perfect replica of Anthony Lawson's. As though summoned, the back door opens once more and Lawson steps through. Caleb shouts gleefully and Lawson returns it, lifting him up and tossing him into the air.

"Anthony, your shoulder," Coach Mackenzie says in exasperation. "Are you *trying* to reinjure yourself?"

"He loves me," Lawson says conspiratorially to Max and me.

Coach Mackenzie mumbles, "I do. I really, really do," under his breath in a resigned sort of way, walking away to the kitchen. Hefting a giggling Caleb under his arm, Lawson drops us a wink and follows him.

"I love them," Max says, the moment they leave the room.

"Yes," I agree. "You are good with kids, Max. Do you think someday you will have any?"

A slight flush colors his cheeks as he nods. "Yeah. I'd like kids, one day. I think...I think Luke would be a really good dad."

"He would, and so would you." He blushes a little deeper, but looks pleased.

I glance down at my half-colored owl, thinking about frowning faces and first kisses. Snapping a photo of it with my phone, I send it to Atlas without any context. Again, he replies with alacrity.

ATLAS

what the fuck is that

HENRI

It is a grumpy owl that looks a little like you.

ATLAS

jesus fucking christ did you color that

HENRI

Yes! I will bring it to class for you.

ATLAS

I don't want it

HENRI

To Atlas, Love Henri

ATLAS

please don't

Laughing softly, I tuck my phone away in my pocket and carefully finish coloring the owl. When it's time to leave, I fold it up and tuck it away safely to give to Atlas on Tuesday. Waiting until we're settled in my car and Max is bucked in safely, I maneuver us out of Coach's driveway and carefully bring up the subject that's been sitting at the forefront of my mind all evening.

"Why do you think Coach Mackenzie might hurt himself if the house isn't neat?" I ask Max, hoping this doesn't come across as nosy. I don't want to gossip about my coach, but I am wondering now if there might be something wrong. If there's something wrong, there might be something I can do to help.

"Oh," Max says carefully, pausing and glancing over at me. "Well, I think it's because he is...he can't see very well."

"I thought that was it!" I tap the steering wheel, feeling vindicated. "I am always thinking Coach Mackenzie needs glasses, when he squints at me as though he cannot see me."

"You know how Coach's career ended, right? The accident? Well—and so, I don't know all the details—but he told me he's been legally blind since then. He can see, but he can't see *well*. He can't drive or anything, because of it."

For the second time today, my heart feels like it's being squeezed in someone's fist. For nearly four years I've played hockey for SCU under Coach Mackenzie, and not once in that time have I had a conversation with him about his own career. I've never thought of myself as an incredibly selfish person before, but obviously, I am.

"Oh my." I breathe out hard. "I am feeling terrible about this."

"I only know because I had a panic attack at his house last year and he told me, Vas. He hasn't told the team, because I don't think he wants anyone to know. I wouldn't...I wouldn't say anything about it. Jesus, I probably shouldn't have even told you—I didn't even think."

"I will not tell," I promise quickly. "You can trust me."

"I know," he agrees quietly. I shake out my hand, fingers aching from how tightly I was clenching the steering wheel. Anxiety sits heavy in my stomach. We do not behave at practice in a manner that is safe for someone with bad vision.

"Sometimes at practice, we are leaving pucks and things on the ice," I say a tad desperately, mentally tallying all the ways I've endangered Coach Mackenzie's life these past few years. "I have bumped into him before, Max, when I was not watching where I was going!"

"Vas!" Max turns in his seat so he's facing me. "He wouldn't be on the ice with us if he couldn't handle it. I'm sure you've noticed that he's not as hands-on as the other coaches—he mostly stays off to the side and watches? He's not going to do anything that's beyond his limitations. He knows himself better than we do."

"Yes, true," I concede, still not feeling great about this development. I'm going to start staying behind after every practice to help clean up. Something else Max said makes me pause. "You are having panic attacks?"

"Oh, well...not often, no. I had a couple last year, but none recently."

"Goodness," I mumble sadly. "You will tell me, yes? If there is something I can do? I want to help, but I do not know how."

"Yeah, I'll tell you if I need anything. Thank you."

Max requests I drop him off at Luke's house. I idle in the street, watching as he goes inside and wishing I could go inside for a little bit as well. Luke has an almost uncanny ability of making people feel good—like he's the human embodiment of a hug. He's so joyful and friendly, and I think I could use some of that right now. But if I go up and knock on the door, I'll be interrupting Max and Luke. They wouldn't mind, or ask me to leave, but I hate feeling like a burden and I don't want to infringe on their time together.

Pulling away from the curb, I drive back to campus. Too soon, I'm parking in my usual spot at my dorm and looking forlornly up at the building. I am a mostly solitary creature; usually after a day like this, with so much time spent with others, I'd be ready to have some time alone. But not today. Today, lonesomeness and gloom settle over me like a shroud, and I feel like being alone is the exact opposite of what I need.

Instead of turning around and driving back to Luke's house, or perhaps going in search of Zeke, I text Atlas as I walk into the building.

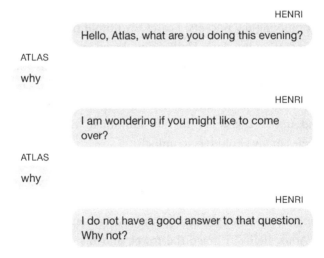

HENRI

Hello, Atlas, what are you doing this evening?

ATLAS

why

HENRI

I am wondering if you might like to come over?

ATLAS

why

HENRI

I do not have a good answer to that question. Why not?

There is no response from Atlas as I walk through the halls and up the stairs to my floor. I doubt he will come over. We do not have an assignment that needs doing together, and we are not the kind of friends who spend time together outside of class. We *could* be, though, if he wasn't quite so

stubborn. Atlas remains a bit of a mystery to me. His frosti-
ness has melted toward me after that drunken night when he
called me for help, and has gotten even better recently after
he kissed me, but he's still holding back. I get the impression
that he likes me, but he doesn't *want* to like me.

He doesn't smile, and rarely laughs. I will occasionally
catch him staring at me, but these times are very few and very
far between. He replies to my texts, but never initiates the
contact, and he certainly never invites me places unless we
have an assignment that needs to be done. I'm unexplainably
drawn to him, skin buzzing and stomach awash with nervous
energy whenever we're together.

I've thought about the press of his lips against mine every
day since it happened.

Emptying my pockets, I carefully unfold the owl drawing
and rest it on my desk. Undressing, I step into the bathroom
to take a quick shower that ends up being twice as long as
planned. The hot water feels heavenly, though, and it's been a
surprisingly difficult day. I finish washing in two minutes, but
stand under the water for an additional five, willing the
muscles in my shoulders to unlock.

It's not until I am drying my hair that I hear the knocking
on my door. Surprised, I wrap the towel around my waist and
go to answer it. I'm even more surprised when I open the
door and find Atlas glowering mutinously at me.

"Atlas, hello." I grasp the towel, and his eyes fall to my
hand, before crawling slowly up my chest and back to my
eyes.

"Jesus Christ," he mutters, scowling. I step back to let him
in, closing the door gently behind him. He's wearing dark
jeans and a dark long-sleeved T-shirt. It looks nice on him.

"You look nice," I tell him, which makes him scowl with

renewed vigor. "I was in the shower. I hope you were not standing out there knocking for too long. Give me just a moment, and I will get dressed."

I grab what I need from my wardrobe, holding it to my stomach one-handed and keeping a firm grasp of the towel with the other. As I close the bathroom door behind me, I hear Atlas mutter, "Don't get dressed on my account."

I dress quickly and do my best with my wet hair. My face is still flushed from the heat of the shower, and my shirt is sticking to my damp skin. I don't look put together at all, but it can't be helped. Probably, Atlas will not care.

Leaving the bathroom, I walk back into my room to find him reclined on my mattress, legs stretched out in front of himself and hands resting on his abdomen. His shoes are off —thank God—but left next to the bed. I grab them and tuck them next to mine by the door. When I turn back around, Atlas is watching me.

"I am glad you are here," I tell him, reaching for my desk chair and meaning to slide it closer.

"You can sit here," Atlas says, patting a hand on my bed. I pause, looking at him. The last time he invited me to join him on a bed, he'd been drinking. Reading this from my expression, he rolls his eyes in a practiced motion and crosses his arms. "Dude, I'm sober. Just come over here and sit the fuck down."

Carefully trying not to jostle him, I slide onto the mattress next to him. He hadn't bothered scooting over, so I have to settle with his leg pressed against my own so that I do not fall off the edge and onto the floor. Both of us are wearing pants, but I'm convinced I can feel the heat of his skin through the layers. Or perhaps it is just warm in here. I'm wishing I hadn't taken quite as hot of a shower as I did. The leftover warmth and Atlas' presence is going to cause me to overheat.

"It is hot in here," I comment.

"I'm fine," Atlas retorts, and I sigh. "How was your team barbecue?"

I glance over at him, surprised. I don't recall telling him about Coach Mackenzie's barbecue. "It was good, thank you for asking. I did not realize I had mentioned it to you."

"You didn't. Nate said he had a team thing, and then you sent me that picture today." He pauses, notes my confused expression and explains. "Nate Basset. He's my roommate."

"Is that so? How lovely. Nate is quite a lot of fun."

"He's fucking insane," Atlas replies. Unsure of whether he means this as a good or bad thing, I don't comment. He adjusts his leg, jostling mine. "So, what's up? Why'd you want me to come over?"

"I do not know," I admit, shrugging. My shoulder bumps his. We are *very* close together. "Why did you come?"

"Touché, Henri. Touché." He moves his leg again, pressing more firmly against mine. I wonder if he's doing it on purpose. I move my arm and our skin connects, sending a fresh round of jitters through my system. I'll never be able to tell if his actions are flirtatious, or if they're meant to indicate that he likes me.

"I wonder, Atlas, whether you might want to try more kissing," I say, and startle a laugh out of him. The sound is so rare, I can't help but smile at him. He uncrosses his arms to rub a hand over his face.

"Only you," he mumbles under his breath. That doesn't sound like a "no" to me, so I wait him out. "Did you seriously text me for a booty call?"

"Certainly not!" I protest, offended. "But you are sitting

very close to me, and you make me feel...strange. I don't want to pressure you, but I think I'd enjoy more kissing. With you," I clarify, in case he's confused. I really don't want to kiss anyone else.

"What do you mean you feel strange?"

I think about this for a moment. It's a hard thing to describe. If only he spoke German. I press a hand to my stomach.

"I feel...shaky? Like I am stepping off of a boat onto land. And also, a little bit like there are electrical currents in my skin, or bees in my chest."

He hums softly, fingers picking at a loose seam on the pocket of his jeans. "It's not a good idea to get involved with me. I don't do relationships. Not ever."

I ponder that. It's not a surprise—Atlas is abrasive and rude, and I've never heard him speak about the same girl twice. But I think my curiosity toward him is actually attraction, and I just didn't recognize it. I've never felt attracted to someone before, and I'm a little worried that I might never feel it again. It's such a *good* feeling, that I don't want to let it go just yet.

"I do not think we would need to be in a relationship," I point out. His head whips around and he looks at me, startled.

"You can't be serious," he says, humor and surprise evident in his voice. "You? *You* want to be friends with benefits?"

"Well...no," I admit. "I would enjoy being friends, and I enjoyed kissing you. I think it would be nice to have both."

Truthfully, what I really want is intimacy without the expectation of sex, but I think intimacy might be a word that would send him hurtling for the door. Atlas slides down the bed until his head is on my pillow, crossing his ankles and drawing my attention to his feet. He's wearing mismatched socks. I look away, because that will drive me crazy if I stare at them for too long. When I look down at his face, his dark eyes are already on mine.

"I don't know. Still seems like a bad idea. I don't want you to fall in love with me."

"Goodness," I murmur, earning another soft huff of laughter from Atlas. "I think the likelihood of this is very low. I...I am thinking I am not one who falls in love easily."

"Mm," he hums, but lifts a hand and places it gently on my thigh. I stare down at that hand—pale, narrow fingers and veins visible beneath his creamy skin. "So."

"So," I repeat.

"This is your booty call. You tell me."

12

Atlas

HAVING a conversation with Henri takes twice the amount of time it would take with anyone else. He doesn't say a single thing without thinking about it first. I wait him out, already used to this in the weeks we've known one another. When his fingertips brush across the top of my hand and up my arm, I know he's come to a decision.

"Maybe we could try kissing again," he says.

"Come down here," I tell him, and wait as he immediately slides down until he's lying flat beside me.

Rolling up onto my side, I prop my head up on a hand and look down at him. He looks a little less perfect than usual: hair sloppy and damp, cheeks flushed, and shirt crinkled. I like it. I like it better than the perfectly coifed and polo-shirted version. *This is a terrible idea. This is the worst fucking idea you've ever had*, my brain screams at me as I reach a hand out and touch gentle fingertips to Henri's cheek. The scruff is nice. The scruff is *really* nice.

He doesn't move as I trace my fingers along the line of his jaw, but keeps his eyes on my face. I'm not planning on going after anything below the neck, but I'm not sure he'd stop me if I tried. The way he's watching me is almost clinical, like he's cataloguing each thing I do and his own reaction to it. Same, Henri, same.

"Don't just lie there without moving," I instruct him, pressing my thumb to his bottom lip so he knows what I'm talking about. "Keep your mouth relaxed, and don't worry about using your tongue unless you're feeling it."

Instead of laughing—which any other sane person would after hearing those instructions—Henri nods solemnly and says, "I understand."

As though to prove he's a good student, the moment I lean down to touch my mouth to his, he opens. I keep my hand relaxed on the side of his face, fingers cupped around his ear. I'm trying to keep it gentle and let Henri lead, but kissing him is apparently some sort of magical dick-raiser, because I can already feel myself getting hard. This isn't even a good kiss, for fuck's sake.

Scooting my hips back so he won't feel it if my semi turns into a full-on boner, I melt into the kiss a little bit, trying to let him lead while also moving things along. I told him not to worry about using his tongue, but damn if I don't want to use mine. I want to know what every inch of his mouth tastes like.

After a few minutes, I pull back enough to look at his face. He hasn't once moved his hands from where they're linked together on his stomach, nor has he made a single sound. I honestly can't tell if he's enjoying himself or not. Luckily, Henri's particular brand of honesty doesn't leave much to the imagination.

"I like this," he says, and smiles up at me. My stomach makes a strange swooping sensation, not unlike what it was doing when I was last here and wasted. Goddamn this guy for being so goddamn cute.

"I honestly wouldn't have been able to tell if you hadn't told me," I admit. "Most of the time when someone is into it, there are hands and noises involved."

"I wouldn't mind touching you," he says baldly, eyes tracking over my face and down my neck. "But I don't need you to touch me, if you are not wanting to. What noises?"

"Well, you know...sex noises." I almost laugh at the absurdity of the situation—me explaining sex noises to a virgin while I teach him how to kiss. "Moaning and stuff."

"Oh. You were not making noises," he points out.

"Fair. But I'm also trying to focus on going slow and not eating your face. Also, I don't need sex noises to prove I'm into this, my dick is doing that for me."

I watch as his gaze lands on my crotch and ping-pongs back to my face. A slow, satisfied smile crawls across his face.

"You like me," he says cheerfully.

"No, I don't like you. I like kissing and hot guys," I correct, but it does nothing to wipe the smile off of his face. He can tell I'm lying. His own dick has remained dormant, I notice, but I'm not surprised. I don't consider myself an expert on asexuality, but I've got a pretty good read on Henri at this point. A few minutes of lip-lock isn't going to be enough to raise his flag.

He shrugs, still looking mighty pleased with himself. "I am thinking you like me a little bit."

"I am thinking you're getting a little ahead of yourself for someone who kisses like a fourteen-year-old," I counter, making him laugh.

"I will get better with practice. I am very teachable—Coach Mackenzie has told me so."

"Oh my god." I shake my head, unable to hold back a small chuckle. This guy. This fucking guy. "All right, Henri. Let's keep practicing."

I GIVE myself a stern talking-to on my way home from Henri's. I actually am starting to like the guy, despite desperately trying not to. He's just so damn eager and ready to please. I bet he'd be a damn dream in bed—pliable and willing. *Do not go there, Atlas. Fucking is where you need to draw the line,* I mentally chide myself. This guy needs to stay firmly in the friend zone, and it's my job to keep him there. Sleeping with virgins is an emotional mess, and I don't do emotions or messes.

By the time I get back to the house, it's barely past ten and I'm starving. Per usual, the only edible things in the kitchen are junk or frozen foods. I opt for the junk and bring a half-eaten bag of chips up to my room.

When I get to the top of the stairs, I'm just deciding to poke my head into Nate's room when my phone rings. Thinking it might be Henri, I pull it out of my pocket with more excitement than I'd care to admit. The name on the screen isn't Henri, though. It's Dad, which goes to show that anybody who plants an expectation, reaps a massive disappointment.

I consider sending it straight to voicemail or ignoring the call completely, but I still love my dad and miss him, even though it makes me the biggest idiot on planet Earth.

"Hey." I pick up on what would probably have been the

last ring, and try hard to modulate my tone. Dad hates it when I sound *petulant*. Whatever the hell that means.

"Hey. Just calling to check up on things. How are classes?"

"Fine. I really like my ceramics class." I squeeze the phone tightly in my fingers, pressing it hard to my ear as I step into my room and close the door behind me.

"That doesn't sound like something you can make a career of," Dad responds immediately, and I have the sudden urge to put my pillow against my face and scream.

"I guess not."

"How about anything else? You're taking a couple computer classes, right?"

Right, Dad, because all Asians are good at math and should work in tech, I think acidly. "Yeah."

"And? Do you like it?"

"Not really," I answer, unable to keep the petulance from my voice. Oh well, I tried. "I don't want a job at a desk, Dad. You know that."

His huff of impatience is so familiar to me, I almost laugh. Sitting down on the floor, I put my back to the bed, tip my head against the mattress, and close my eyes. I can't number the times I've told my dad that I don't want to do work similar to his, and each time has gone ignored. I don't know why he expects a different answer every time he calls, like he's expecting a different son to answer the phone or perhaps hoping that I've gotten a lobotomy and changed my entire personality. I have the sudden, gut-clenching desire to still be in Henri's dorm.

Ridiculous, Atlas. You're being ridiculous.

"Well, you're going to have to decide what to do sooner rather than later. You're going to run out of general study classes, and what then? Sell ceramics?" He chuckles at his own joke, and I think I might hate my father.

"Yeah, maybe," I retort, because I love riling him up and also because people *do* make ceramics and sell them for a living.

"Your mom also wanted to know whether you were planning on coming home for Christmas break? We're painting the house. If you're going to stay at school, we'll tackle the guest bedroom over Christmas," he continues, ignoring what I said.

My mouth tastes sour at the mention of my room being the guest bedroom, and my stepmother being my mom. He knows I hate it when he calls her that. He *knows* it. Just once, I'd like him to listen to what I say and not use it as ammunition against me.

"I'm staying here." I hadn't actually thought about my plans for break yet, but if he's giving me an out, I'm damn well going to take it.

Propping my phone between my shoulder and ear, I stand up and open my tiny window. Lighting up a cigarette, I take a deep inhale, leaning my head against the wall and closing my eyes. Henri's voice in my head telling me smoking is bad for me makes me smile.

Dad gives up on trying to entice me into family talk, which means we've officially run the gamut of things we can chat about.

"I'll put some more money in your checking account. Send me a text if you need anything else."

"Sure. Thanks," I mutter. I can't wait for the day when I can earn my own money and cease being a leech on a family that I don't belong in. A family that doesn't want me.

"Have a good rest of the week," Dad says, already sounding distracted.

"Say hi to the boys from me," I request quickly, not wanting him to hang up before I get the words out. It's not my stepbrothers' fault that I've got a fucked-up relationship with my dad and their mom.

"See you," he says before disconnecting the call, making me wonder if he heard me at all. Whatever. I'll just text the boys myself to make sure the message is received.

Finishing off my cigarette, I'm just going to put my phone down when I notice a text message from Henri that came through while I was on the phone with Dad.

> **HENRI**
>
> Thank you for coming over. I enjoy spending time with you. You forgot to take your owl picture, but I shall bring it to class for you.

No matter how hard I try and fight it, I can't help but smile. I hate people that smile at their cellphones like idiots. I hate that Henri is turning me into one of those idiots. This is exactly how it starts; pretty soon I'll be too attached to him to survive it when he inevitably leaves me.

> **ATLAS**
>
> i left it on purpose because i don't want it

> **HENRI**
>
> But I worked so hard!

> **ATLAS**
>
> if you give that to me i'll just throw it away

> **HENRI**
>
>

ATLAS

oh my god i can't with you right now

bye henri i'll see you in class

Dropping my phone onto my bed, I gather my shower kit and my pajamas, going across the hall to the bathroom I share with Nate and one other roommate. It's not until I'm standing under the water that I realize what he did. Without meaning to, Henri hijacked my bad mood and distracted me enough to have me grinning at my phone and forgetting all about my dad.

Next time I see him, I'll give him another lesson in kissing to show my appreciation.

13

Henri

NATE IS FIRED UP—HALF-NAKED, standing on the bench in front of his stall, and telling a ribald story that I lost the ability to follow five minutes ago. He has the rest of the team laughing—even Max, who rarely joins in on locker room shenanigans, is chuckling—and I'm wondering if Coach Mackenzie is allowing him to continue only because he knows how badly we need to be pumped up.

It's a big game tonight, and if we pull off a win, that means we'll likely be going into the holiday break seated as the number one team. Everyone is feeling the pressure, but none more so than McIntire. He's pale, knee bouncing and eyes locked on Nate as he talks, but a vacant expression on his face that gives away the fact that he's not really paying attention.

Max and I are already dressed out, so I carefully walk over to where Micky is sitting and slide in next to him.

"Hello, my friend," I say just loud enough for him to hear me over Nate's wild voice.

"Hey," he replies, low enough that I can't hear his voice at all, but have to read the word off his lips. Micky's problem is nerves. He is a good netminder, but struggles with getting out of his own way.

"You are excellent goalie," I tell him. His eyes meet mine in surprise. I'm not one to give pep talks—usually leaving that up to our captain—but I fear that if I don't say something, Micky might faint from performance anxiety. "And we have your back, yes? It is not all on you to defend the net and win the game."

"I know that," he says, but bites his lip. "Sometimes it feels like that though, you know? Sometimes it feels like it's my fault when we lose. And I really don't want to lose tonight."

"It is my job to score goals, yes? Is it not also my fault if we lose, because I did not score enough goals? And Max? His fault, too?"

Micky gapes at me. "I never looked at it that way."

I pat his padded leg as Nate finishes his story, and finally climbs down from the bench amid a round of applause. He's grinning as he turns to his stall to finish getting dressed.

"We shall do our best tonight, you and I. That is all we can do, yes? And if we lose, it will be a team effort, just the same as it would be if we win."

"Right," Micky agrees, nodding. "Thanks, Vas. Thank you. That...I just get so nervous, you know? It's stupid."

"No, no, is not stupid. We are all a little nervous. These things are normal." Coach Mackenzie walks into the locker room, and snaps something at Nate that has the guys closest to him snickering. He gives us two minutes before we need to be on the ice. Across from where I am now sitting with our goalie, I see Max stand up and shake out his legs. "It is a good night for hockey, Micky. Let us go have some fun."

And we do. Max makes the opposing team look like junior league players, and after his second goal in the first period, I even feel a little badly for their goalie. It's not his fault Max is a league beyond the rest of us.

Instead of chasing a hattie, though, Max sends the puck to me and our linemates more often than he keeps it. When Nate scores his first goal of the game off of a suicide pass from him, I swear I can see tears in his eyes when he takes a seat next to me on the bench. Coach Mackenzie pats him on the shoulder as he passes behind us and I worry he might faint.

"Did you see that?" Nate asks me.

"I did." Grinning, I slap a gloved hand on his leg. "Nice goal."

During my next shift, we get stuck between shift changes and I am pushing ninety seconds on the ice when Micky loses sight of the puck as a shot is made. It partially deflects off of his skate, but he has to spin around and make a secondary save before the puck can cross the goal line behind him. Desperately, he sends it to me and I try to squeeze a little more gas out of my exhausted legs. Somehow, I carry it coast to coast and sail it bar down over the goalie's right shoulder. My teammates on the bench jump up, screaming and banging their sticks on the boards, cheering for Micky as much as me. It is not often a netminder gets a primary assist.

Max doesn't get his hat trick, but we put up an impressive six points and win the game. When it's my turn to hug McIntire in the lineup, I put my face as close as I can to the cage on his helmet so that he can hear me over the din of the arena.

"You are so talented of a goaltender, you start doing our job too, eh?"

He laughs, arms tight around my shoulders in a hug that would be painful if we didn't have our gear on. We skate to the bench together, and the roar that goes up when Micky enters the locker room makes me fear for our eardrums. Max is waiting for me next to our lockers, eyes bright and smile painfully wide on his sweaty face.

"You should have gone for your hattie," I tell him, but he shakes his head and looks across the room toward Nate.

"Nah. I hog the puck too often. He needed that."

"You do not hog the puck, Max." I laugh, pulling my sweater over my head and running a hand through my wet hair. "We give you the puck most often because you are best player and goal scorer."

Embarrassed, he shakes his head and turns away from me to get undressed. I know it makes Max uncomfortable to be the center of attention, but I also want to make sure he is confident in himself and his abilities. Next year he will be playing in the NHL. He will no longer be the best player on the ice, but a rookie. I only have a short while left to talk him up and build up his confidence, and I mean to make the most of it.

———

WHEN I WALK into our last day of communications class before winter break, Atlas is already in his seat. He so rarely beats me to class, I can't help but give him a little grief for it.

"You are missing me so much, you come early today?" He glares at me as I set a to-go cup of coffee on his desk, but there is no force behind it. He drinks black coffee, which I learned after pulling the information out of him the same way one might pull a tooth. I try to bring him one every class, as well as a nutritional snack. I do not think Atlas takes very good care of himself, and I worry about his health.

He rolls his eyes, but doesn't comment beyond a mumbled "thank you" for the coffee. When I produce a red apple and hold it out to him, his lips twitch as though he wants to smile. Turning it over in his hand, he leans back in his chair and takes a bite.

"Do you go home for the holidays?" he asks. "To Germany?"

"No, I will be staying here. Last year I spent Christmas with my brother and that was very nice, but not this year. What about you?"

"Staying here," he replies, lips twisting unpleasantly as though there's a sour taste in his mouth.

"Perhaps you and I can have plans," I offer carefully. Atlas is always very firm with me about the boundaries of our relationship, and I don't want to push that by asking him to spend Christmas with me. A strange expression crosses his face, but it's gone before I can make sense of it.

"Yeah, maybe," he responds noncommittally.

Knowing that I won't get anything more out of him, I bend to retrieve my notebook from my bag. Atlas clears his throat and fidgets.

"I brought this for you," he says, and slides something over to my desk.

Abandoning my bag, I look at the object. It's badly wrapped in tissue paper, whatever it is, and is oddly shaped. When I touch a finger to the paper, I have a momentary sensation of lightheadedness. Atlas brought me a gift.

Carefully, I pick it up. It's weightier than I was expecting. Tearing the paper off, I glance over to see Atlas staring resolutely at my hands and looking like he's sincerely regretting this bit of kindness. I figure out it's a coffee mug before I've got it fully unwrapped, but it's not until it's completely uncovered that I realize what I'm looking at.

The mug is an impossibly vivid shade of green—darker on the base before slowly brightening toward the mouth. Turning it around in my hands, I notice there is a small drawing carved next to the handle. This time, the lightheadedness feels a little bit like falling, and I have to press my feet hard into the floor to center myself. It's a drawing of an apple.

"You made this," I say, turning it over carefully and seeing an artist's mark on the bottom.

"Yeah." Atlas shrugs as though it's no big deal, and he hasn't just given me the most thoughtful gift I've ever received. "Do you get it? It's because you always bring me red apples, but you prefer—"

"The green ones," I whisper, clenching my hands tight around the mug and finally looking over at him.

He's got his arms crossed over his chest defensively, and has his usual surly expression on. For the first time in my life, I want to kiss someone in a public place.

"It's just a mug," he says warily, apparently reading some of my thoughts on my face. I shake my head. No, it is not just a mug.

"You are very talented," I tell him, tracing a finger over the glaze. "I am thinking ceramics class is your favorite for a reason."

This sets off a renewed round of scowling, which means I've embarrassed him. He shrugs, casually trying to let my compliment roll off his back. It is not surprising to me that Atlas is not good at accepting compliments. Carefully, I set it down in the middle of my desk and stare at it.

"Thank you, Atlas," I say quietly. "Thank you very much."

He fidgets, uncomfortable. Before he can deflect or say something snarky, I put a hand on his thigh below the desk. He stills, but doesn't shove me off or yell at me.

"It's just a mug," he repeats desperately, as though if he says it enough times, it will make it true. I shake my head again, but don't argue. He's letting me touch him in a public place, and he's just given me a gift. I should be happy with these developments and not push him for more. If I make him uncomfortable, he will run away from me and I will lose all the ground I've gained these past few weeks.

The classroom has slowly filled up around us, the volume in the room steadily rising. Regretfully, I have to move away from Atlas to finish gathering my things out of my bag. I give his leg a small squeeze, before bending over and pulling out my notebook. I rewrap the mug in the tissue paper the way an archeologist might handle a precious artifact. I can feel Atlas' gaze on me as I do; can practically feel the words *it's just a mug* trying to claw their way out of his throat for a third time.

He watches as I get it settled in my bag, and prepare myself for the lecture. I notice we're sitting closer today than we usually do, elbows and knees knocking gently together when one of us moves. Neither of us moves away or mentions it. In fact, I make it my mission to cross the line between our desks as often as possible—foot pressed against Atlas' and forearms brushing. It's the most enjoyable Creative Communications class we've had to date. They seem to only get better and better.

When class ends, Atlas doesn't sprint for the door the way he usually does, but hovers beside me as I pack up my things. I take extra care to make sure the mug is secure and will not get broken. Instead of swinging my bag onto my shoulder, I lift it gently and nestle it into my side. When I turn to Atlas and smile, he mutters *finally* under his breath and leads the way from the classroom.

The air is brisk when we get outside, and I take a nice deep inhale. It smells like rain. Feeling inspired, I look at Atlas as we walk. His head is tilted downward giving me a view of his dark hair, shiny in the weak afternoon light.

"Atlas?" He grunts, which in Atlas-speak means *why are you bothering me?* "Are you free this evening?"

"Sure." He shrugs, kicking at a loose rock on the ground and sending it skittering over the sidewalk. "Want me to come over and blow you?"

I stumble over a perfectly flat piece of ground, and feel my face flush.

"Goodness," I reply. Atlas looks over at me, smirking. "Thank you for the offer, but I was actually going to see if you would like to come to the game this evening? It is our last home match. It shall be a lot of fun."

He looks at me like I've recommended the murder of puppies as a pleasurable pastime. "Are you serious?"

"Certainly. I have a ticket for you, if you would like. But no pressure! I know you have many friends and things to do. I know you are not a hockey fan. Please do not feel obligated to come."

He stops dead in the middle of the sidewalk, forcing me to come to a halt and turn around. He's clutching the straps of his backpack tight in his fists, eyes squinted at me and mouth turned down in a frown. This is not an angry-Atlas face, though. This is the confused-Atlas face.

"Why?"

"Because we are friends and I am thinking it might be fun!" I don't tell him it's also because I want him to see me play. I want to score a goal and look up to find him in the stands. I want to share something with him that isn't homework and platonic kissing. "You might enjoy it, Atlas. And Nate will be playing—you like Nate, yes?"

He rolls his eyes. "Yes, I like Nate."

"So, you will come?" I shouldn't keep needling him like this. I should take my green apple mug and be happy with what I have.

"Okay," Atlas says, sounding as though he's just agreed to a chemical castration. "Fine. I'll come, but only this *one* time. I'm not your groupie."

I don't know what a groupie is, so I merely agree. "No. No groupies here."

After sending him the virtual ticket, I carefully explain where he'll be going and how the seating works. He listens to my speech in silence, glowering at me, before snapping that he's not an idiot and he knows how stadium seating works. I watch him walk off in the opposite direction of my dorm, a happy warmth suffusing through my limbs.

Atlas is coming to my game.

14

Atlas

I HATE HOCKEY GAMES. All sporting events, really, but I've just decided that I hate hockey most of all. The hallways are *packed*, and I've already stepped in three sticky spots even though the doors to the stadium have only been open for an hour. Annoyed, and quickly losing patience, I stop trying to weave my way through the crowd and instead start shouldering my way through. I don't make any friends, but I am finally able to get to my seat.

Flopping down gracelessly, I accidentally bump the leg of the guy sprawled in the seat next to mine.

"Sorry," I grunt, and move away from him.

"Atlas, right?"

I look over at him, narrowing my eyes. Dark hair and skin a shade of brown I could never in my wildest dreams hope to achieve. He's got an open, friendly sort of face that makes me instantly wary of him. I've never seen or talked to this guy before in my life.

"Who's asking?" I reply rudely, which makes him smirk at me.

"I'm Luke. Vas is a friend of mine. He mentioned you might be coming to the game."

Clenching my fingers around the armrests in annoyance, I turn away from him and look out at the ice. I don't like that Henri has been talking about me to his friends. I hope to hell he hasn't told them what we've been doing in his fucking dorm.

The teams are skating around down below, one on each half of the ice but not mingling yet. I assume that means the game hasn't started, so I look back at my companion and notice he's wearing a jersey.

"Who's number eight?"

"Max Kuemper. Current leader of the division in points, and hottest guy on the team. Also, mine, so don't fuck around unless you want to find out," he says, so smoothly it comes out practiced. I can't help but laugh.

"Noted," I reply. "What number is Henri?"

I'm sort of hoping he's the goalie, because I can already tell they're the easiest player to keep an eye on. I can hardly see the numbers and names from here—I have no idea how Luke manages to follow his Max Kuemper.

"Twenty-nine. He's right there." I follow his finger to where Henri is standing bent over and playing around with a hockey puck. It looks like he's passing to himself, but doing it so fast I can hardly see the little rubber disc. Luke turns toward me, propping his head in his hand and grinning at me. I don't trust that grin. That grin spells trouble. "We've got a little bit before the game starts."

"I shouldn't have come so early."

His lips twitch up into a smirk. "So, you and Vas, huh? Cute."

"There is no us and we're not cute." I glare at him, but it doesn't seem to have any effect other than to make him smile wider. "We have a class together."

"Aw."

"How firm are the seating assignments?" I ask, frowning down at the mobile ticket on my phone. "I'm going to move."

"Sorry, you're stuck with me for the next two hours," Luke replies happily. "No switching seats. They are *very* serious about that."

I feel like he's fucking with me, but since this is my first game, there is no way of me knowing. Tucking my phone back into my pocket, I decide to employ my old standby: silence. I'll just ignore Luke and hope that he finds someone else to annoy.

"Vas was pretty excited you were going to come. Texted me that I should be nice to you because you guys are good *friends*." The careful emphasis he places on the word makes me clench my jaw. I'm staring so hard at the ice, my eyes ache. "I'm happy to hear he's got such a good *friend* outside of hockey. Vas is just the best, isn't he? Nice guy. Tall. And don't even get me started on those thighs. Hockey thighs—am I right?"

"Hey," I snap, turning toward him and already forgetting my vow of silence. "How about you keep your eyes on Max Kuemper's thighs and off Henri's, got it? Unless you want to—what was it?—fuck around and find out?"

"Mm," Luke hums, looking pleased with my outburst. "Defensive, are we?"

Okay, Luke, you little shit, I see what you're trying to do.

"Henri told you, didn't he," I say, not really a question, but not really a statement either.

"Not in so many words. But you just did—the way you got all puffed up just now when you thought I was hitting on him."

"We're not together," I correct him firmly, trying to derail this train before it runs away. "We're just friends. Seriously, that's all it is. You will never see me wearing his jersey."

I cast a disdainful look down at the number eight on Luke's shoulder. He doesn't seem affected by the dig, merely shrugging and looking down at the ice. I watch his eyes ping-pong around until they find Max Kuemper. Apparently happy that he's still there, Luke looks back at me.

"Cool. Like I said, I'm glad Vas has a good friend outside of hockey. I just hope that friend knows what they're doing, and that they don't accidentally cause him any trouble, you know?" Luke's voice is calm—friendly—even though the words carry just a hint of a threat. I can't help but respect him for it.

"I'm only going to say this once, and then we aren't going to talk about it anymore: Henri and I aren't together. We're friends who occasionally fool around—nothing more. I haven't made it a secret that I don't want to be in a relation-ship. He knows what this is."

"Cool, cool," Luke says again, tone insufferably casual.

By now the game has started, and he's no longer looking at me. His eyes are firmly on the ice. I pay attention to the game as much as I'm able, but, quite frankly, I have no fucking idea what's going on. I barely even manage to keep an eye out for Henri's twenty-nine, and he's not always on the ice either, which makes it even more difficult to keep track of him. Luckily, it seems like Henri and Max Kuemper play together usually, so I can tell when they're on the ice by the way Luke sits up straighter in his seat.

A sharp intake of breath from my seatmate has me narrowing my eyes at the game. Everyone else is cheering, but Luke is shaking his head.

"What?"

He glances over at me, surprised, and gestures to the game. "Vas just got boarded."

I have no idea what being boarded means, but I did see someone get hit into the wall. Apparently, that was number twenty-nine. Fucking hell this is hard to keep track of.

"Okay," I say slowly. Again, Luke glances at me, throwing me a look that is clearly meant to imply what an idiot I am.

"Vas had surgery on his knee over the summer. A bad hit could set him back or get him benched for the season."

"Oh." I squirm in my seat a little bit, uncomfortable with the sudden realization that I don't actually know Henri all that well. I've kept him at arm's length with my elbows locked, unwilling to share anything personal with him and desperate to keep him far enough away that he can't hurt me.

"Maybe you guys should chat a little bit, in between all the fucking," Luke suggests mildly, flopping backward in his seat and slinging an arm over the back.

"You know," I muse, "I don't think I like you all that much."

He laughs. I actually do like him a little bit, but over my dead body will I ever say those words out loud. I don't even bother correcting him about the fucking thing, even though Henri and I haven't done more than kiss, and even that has been very rare. Let him think what he wants.

We make it through the first two periods of the game without any further chitchat beyond Luke asking if I want anything from the concession stand. When second intermission rolls around, I've developed a slight headache from the noise and lights of the arena, and my eyes hurt from the strain of trying to watch both Henri and the puck.

"Do you come to every game?" I ask Luke, who's got his arms raised above his head as he stretches out his back.

"Nah, I can't make them all. I play baseball and the schedules don't always coordinate. But I try to make as many as I can. You should come more often—it's fun, right?"

"It's fine," I hedge. It's fun, I suppose, but not fun enough for me to come back for every game. This is a *lot*.

"You and Vas hanging out over break?"

"Maybe." Sighing, because I already know where he's going with that question, I tack on, "And before you bring up how spending holidays together is something boyfriends would do, let me reiterate that Henri and I are not together. I'm not looking for a boyfriend now or ever."

Luke snorts. "And you think I was? I didn't go looking for a boyfriend or a relationship, but Maxy found me anyway. Might as well stop fighting it, buddy."

"We're just friends and that is all we'll ever be."

"And yet, here you are to support him at a sporting event we both know you don't like or enjoy."

"Didn't anyone ever teach you it's rude to be nosy?"

"I missed a few lessons in manners. Just like you," Luke adds dryly. It startles a laugh out of me, and he grins. Fuck it all, I like this guy. Damn Henri for having cool friends.

I stand up as soon as the game ends, meaning to sprint out of here as fast as my legs will carry me. I feel like I need a bottle of water, a cigarette, and eight hours locked in a dark, quiet room—preferably in that order. Luke unfolds himself lazily and stretches again, smiling down at the ice with a goofy expression I hope never graces my face. He turns to me, slinging a heavy arm over my shoulders. I shrug it off, pushing him away.

"You coming down to the locker rooms?" he asks, completely unperturbed.

"No."

"Come on. Come say hi—you'll make Vas' night."

I'm all set to refuse again, but apparently Luke works some sort of spell on me because fifteen minutes later I find myself standing at the end of the hallway that leads to the team lockers, unsure how I got here. Arms crossed tight over my chest, I do my best to blend in with the wall behind me and shoot daggers at Luke with my eyes. He ignores me in favor of texting someone on his phone and whistling under his breath.

15

Henri

LUKE

There's a feral alley cat waiting for you in the hallway.

DISTRACTED, I stand half undressed and stare down at my phone in confusion. I am very fond of Luke, but sometimes his jokes go over my head. This is one of those times. Looking up, I wait for Max's reddish-brown head to pop out of the collar of his shirt.

"Max, are you able to translate this for me?"

I give him the phone, watching as his brow scrunches up and his lips move as he reads.

"Uhm. I got nothing on that one. Come on, let's get changed, and go out and ask him. He should be waiting for me outside."

Putting my phone down, I do my best to keep pace with Max, who is prone to dressing unusually fast. By the time we are leaving the locker room, I am actually a little out of breath again. There aren't any messages from Atlas, and I do my best not to be too disappointed by that. He'd said he would try to come to the game, but he hadn't actually fully committed. Max's small huff of laughter pulls my eyes away from my phone.

"Feral alley cat," he says, up-nodding toward the end of the hallway where Luke is waiting. I follow his line of sight and see Atlas standing across from Luke and doing his best to blend into the darkly painted wall behind him. Given his black jacket and dark hair, he is doing quite an admirable job of it. I can't control the bloom of joy in my chest at the sight of him, or the smile that is birthed because of it.

"Hello, you," Luke says to Max, pulling him into a hug.

Max melts into it, bag thumping to the ground as he drops it to wrap his arms around his boyfriend's waist. Something that feels strangely like jealously burns through me at the sight. I want that. I want that so badly. Swallowing this down, I turn to find Atlas, whom I also want, watching them with the expression of someone suffering from a stomach cramp.

"Hello, Atlas." I walk up to him, stopping as close as I dare. My fingers brush his, but I don't try to initiate any further contact. He'll only push me away.

"Hey," he replies, clearing his throat and giving me an obvious once-over. "Nice suit."

I smile. "Thank you. I am happy you are here, thank you for coming."

"It's no big deal." He shrugs this off, just like he tries to shrug off everything he does that might be considered a kindness. I decide that tonight I am too tired to let him get away with it.

"It is a big deal to me. I do not have family here, nor many friends that are not already on the team. Nobody comes to watch me play, Atlas. So, thank you. I wish I could explain better, but you are not so skilled at speaking German."

He smiles at me—quick and barely there, but I catch it all the same. When he runs a hand through his black hair, scattering the lights reflecting on it, I catch that too. I wonder if anyone has ever told him he is beautiful before.

"I saw that goal you scored," he tells me. "Oh, and how's your knee?"

"My knee?" I look down at my knees, which, to my knowledge, Atlas has never seen before. I always have my pants on when he is around. "Fine, thank you. How are your knees?"

He huffs an impatient breath and fights against the smile I know wants to come out. I don't even mind if he's smiling at my expense. I just like to see it on his face.

"My knees didn't have surgery over the summer," he says snippily.

"Oh, I see." I glance over at Luke, guessing that he is the culprit for Atlas learning this little tidbit. "It is fine. I feel a little sore, but that is to be expected after a game. I will ice it when I get back home."

"Let's go, then." Atlas waves a hand, and without waiting for me, turns to walk toward the exit. I follow, tugged along in his wake like he commands a gravitational pull.

"See you, Vas!" Luke calls, voice echoing in the concrete hallway.

Atlas is scowling as he holds the door for me and we start walking toward the dorms. I could drive, but I usually enjoy the short walk to the rink to clear my head and warm up my muscles. I'm even more glad I didn't drive now that Atlas is here with me. The walk back will take three times as long as driving would have.

"What's the deal with that Luke guy?" he asks.

"Deal?"

"He seemed to know a lot of information about us fooling around. He also seemed to think we were dating."

"I did not tell anyone that I like to kiss you, if that is what you are meaning," I say patiently. "But Luke is...how can I say it? Emotionally intelligent? He is good at understanding people. He is also in love and I think perhaps this changes the way he sees other couples."

Atlas snorts and shakes his head. "In love. In college? Come on—he has to know that relationship won't last."

I sigh, adjusting my bag to sit higher on my shoulder. "Atlas, you must be very tired from being so distrustful."

Grabbing my arm, he pulls me to a stop. I face him, standing so close that I can see the light from the lamps that line the sidewalk reflecting in his dark eyes. He leaves his hand on my arm and I curse the presence of my suit jacket. I wish I could feel his skin against my own.

"I'm not a cynic, I'm a realist," he corrects.

"In this, you are wrong. Max and Luke are strong, and happy. They will get married. They will have babies one day, and perhaps I will get to be a godparent if I am lucky. Many things may change, but they will have each other, always. I know this. *That* is real."

Atlas doesn't answer. Mouth pinched, he shakes his head and drops his hand from my arm. He looks disappointed, like I've let him down in some fundamental way. When he takes a step away from me, I know I've lost him for the night.

"I'd better head home," he says.

"Okay. Thank you for coming." He's already walking away,

shoulders rigid beneath his black jacket. Before he gets too far away, he spins around to face me and walks backward.

"Don't forget to ice your knee," he calls.

———

I DO NOT HEAR from Atlas the first three days of break. Then, on the fourth day, not only do I hear from him, but I get an invitation to his house. I've never been to his house before—we always meet up in my dorm—and it feels momentous that he is inviting me over. I take special care with my appearance, making sure my hair is lying properly and getting rid of the two-day beard I had been cultivating. I even fight the urge to wear something nice, and instead put on a pair of sweatpants and a hockey shirt.

Atlas, I know, will be very proud of me for bypassing the polo shirts.

Before heading to Atlas', I stop at a local grocery store and wander the aisles a bit. I am not sure what, if anything, I should be bringing, but it feels wrong to show up empty-handed. Suddenly inspired, I gather the ingredients for old-fashioned stollen. Atlas lives in a house, which means he has access to a full kitchen and I can make him something home-made instead of bringing store bought.

When I pull up to his house, I take note of the empty driveway. He hadn't told me whether any of his roommates were staying here for the holidays. Eyeing my bags of groceries, I do a mental tally of how many people I could potentially feed with the recipe I have in mind. Deciding that if it comes down to it, I can just go without eating, I get out of the car, gather my bags, and walk up to the front door.

Atlas opens it and I lose several beats of my heart. He's

wearing a loose pair of black sweatpants and a shirt that says *Glazed and Confused* with a picture of a pottery wheel. His feet are bare and his hair is a little spikier than I've seen it. He smells like cinnamon.

"You are very handsome," I tell him, unable to control my tongue. His eyes widen a little bit. I love how dark his eyelashes are, and how he always looks like he's wearing eyeliner. If he ever does wear eyeliner, I will probably die.

"So are you when you aren't wearing a polo shirt," he replies, lips twitching like he wants to smile. I beam. I knew he'd notice.

He steps back to let me inside, watching as I deposit my shopping bags carefully on the floor and shrug out of my jacket. He takes it from me and throws it over an overflowing coatrack in the foyer. That done, we stand there, awkwardly staring at one another. Three days without contact suddenly seems like an insurmountable distance.

"Fuck it," Atlas murmurs, and puts a hand against my cheek before leaning up and kissing me.

He has impossibly soft lips. I noticed the first time he kissed me, and I've noticed every time since. They are probably the only soft thing about him. Sighing, I lean into him and let myself fall into the sensation. Carefully, I put my hand high on his hip, spreading my fingers wide and enjoying the heat of his body through the thin shirt.

"You're a good student," he murmurs, pulling back only far enough to whisper against my lips.

"Thank you," I mutter back. "I have a good teacher."

His laugh is little more than a huff of air against my mouth, but I can feel it all the way to my toes. Still with one hand on his hip, I mimic the way he's touching my cheek and put my other hand against his face. Gently, I pull him back in and kiss him.

When he steps closer to me and his stomach brushes mine, I feel the first spiky tendrils of heat in my pelvis. Surprised, I groan, and feel Atlas' fingers curl more firmly around the back of my neck. Of all the times we've made out in my dorm room, not once have I gotten an erection. Evidently, today is the day that changes.

"Atlas." I lean my head back just far enough to see his face. "I apologize, but I am getting hard."

He laughs. The sort of full-belly laugh I'm accustomed to hearing from Luke, and have never heard from Atlas. Leaning his forehead against my shoulder, he drops his hand away from my face.

"Only you," he mutters, before straightening up and stepping back. "Do you want to keep going and see where that leads?" He gestures to my crotch and I have to fight the urge to cover myself with a hand. "Or were you planning something else?"

He looks pointedly at the groceries.

"Oh, yes. I am going to make you stollen, if you are agreeable?"

"Sure, Henri. Whatever the fuck that is." He snatches up a couple of the bags and walks away. Grabbing the rest, I follow him. He leads me to the kitchen and drops the bags on the counter in a way that makes me flinch. Luckily, there is nothing breakable in the pair that he was carrying. Hopping up on the island, he kicks his feet and watches as I put the rest down with infinitely more care.

"I was not sure what you had in mind when you texted, but if you are hungry, I thought perhaps I could make you stollen. It is a German dish. I think you may like it."

"I didn't have anything in mind," he says, shrugging. "Just thought we could hang out. Maybe watch a Christmas movie, and I could blow you if you wanted."

"You watch Christmas movies?" I ask, because this is easily the strangest thing about what he's just said.

"Sometimes. I like *The Grinch* with Jim Carrey." He eyes me. "Want to make this stollen shit, watch the movie, and then get back to the blowjob? Or maybe I could eat your ass."

"Sometimes I think you are only saying things to make me embarrassed," I tell him, pulling ingredients from the bags and lining them up on the counter next to where he is sitting.

"Nope, not this time. I've never eaten anyone out before— well, not a dude, anyway—but I have a feeling you've got the cleanest butt around, so." He raises his eyebrows suggestively. I don't argue, because, yes, I do make sure I shower thoroughly.

"I am not sure, Atlas. I don't know what I want to do," I tell him honestly. I've never had fantasies about anyone giving me pleasure like that. Never had fantasies about sex at all, before meeting Atlas. Now, all of my ideas usually center around how I would go about making Atlas feel good. There have been a few nights recently where I wondered what it would be like to give *him* a blowjob.

"Okay. No worries," he says. I smile at him. He's prickly and argumentative almost all the time, but he never pushes me to do things. For weeks all we've done is kiss, and not once has he tried to hurry me along or made me feel badly about moving slow. About not feeling aroused or wanting to have sex.

It takes me a bit to find everything I need in the kitchen. Nothing seems to be kept where it should be, nor do they have the full array of utensils, but I make do. All the while I am puttering around, Atlas doesn't move from his perch on the counter. Every now and then he'll inquire about what I'm looking for and attempt to point me in the right direction, but mostly he sits in silence and watches. I take care to do as many things right next to him as I can, touching his leg and feeling his toes brush against me.

"Okay, we must let this rise for three quarters of an hour and then it shall go in the oven," I tell Atlas. He nods, hopping down from the counter and skirting around the edge of the island.

"Movie time," he says.

I follow him into the living room, which is a lot cleaner than I would have expected from a house of college students. He pats the back of the couch and I take the hint, sitting in that seat and watching as he gets the movie queued up. Instead of sitting down with space between us, as I expected him to, he flops down so close to me, he's practically in my lap. Automatically, I put an arm out to steady him and he moves in even closer.

"Do you want me to put German subtitles on?" he asks. I stare at him, shocked by the offer. Misreading my silence, he gestures to the TV and continues. "I just mean, maybe you prefer German to English and it would be nice to watch the movie that way. I know you can understand the movie in English, I wasn't—"

"I know what you meant," I say quietly, pressure sitting heavy in my chest at the offer. It's a strange thing to explain to people, how much one misses speaking their native language when they are in a different country—a different flavor of homesickness that is often more potent for me, as I struggle with English. Not a day goes by, when I am here, that I do not wish for more opportunities to talk to someone in German. "Yes, please, thank you, Atlas. That is thoughtful of you to offer."

His cheeks are tinged with pink as he turns his face away and fiddles with the remote, turning on the subtitles. I swallow down any further comments about how that little bit of kindness makes me feel, knowing how uncomfortable it would make him. Instead, I put my arm around him as he settles back against me, giving him a small squeeze.

We're side by side with legs and hips pressed together. A few minutes in, he relaxes his head, cheek resting against my shoulder and arm draped across my thigh. I am not sure if he realizes it, but we are absolutely cuddling right now.

We mostly stay silent through the movie, but every now and then Atlas chuckles dryly. It makes me smile every time. After forty-five minutes have passed, I sigh regretfully and loosen my hold on him.

"I must go put the bread in the oven," I tell him as I extricate myself. "Stay there, I will be right back."

I move a little faster than I usually would, worried that he'll be seated on the opposite side of the room once I get back, and there will be no possibility of further snuggling. Luckily, he's right where I left him. Retaking my seat and sliding as close to him as I can, I set a timer on my phone and rest it on the coffee table.

"About half of an hour," I tell Atlas, who simply restarts the movie in silence. This time, when he lays his head on my shoulder, I rest my cheek against the top of his head. Apparently, his lips are not the *only* soft thing about him.

"Can you imagine how uncomfortable all that makeup would be," he murmurs, eyes on the screen. "And the prosthetics."

I eye Jim Carrey's furry green face and nod. "Indeed. I would not be liking it, I think. Atlas?"

"Mm?"

"You smell like a cinnamon roll."

He snorts, adjusting his head, which rubs his hair across my face and sends my pulse skittering in paroxysms of joy.

"All the body washes and shampoos at the store are holiday scented. I think it's meant to smell like Christmas, not a pastry."

When the timer goes off, I leave him once more on the couch and head into the kitchen to finish the bread. I'm surprised when Atlas trails after me, hopping back up on the counter and watching as I prepare the toppings.

"That smells fucking bomb," he compliments. I smile at him and he returns it, very slightly.

"We shall have to let it cool for a little while, before we put the glaze on."

"Oh yeah?" he asks, fisting a hand into the front of my shirt and tugging me to stand between his spread legs. I look up into his face, hands on the counter bracketing his hips. "What shall we do while we wait?"

16

Atlas

SOMETIMES WHEN I'M kissing Henri, I question whether or not he's into it. He's so careful and quiet, and not once has he gotten even semi-hard. If he didn't tell me constantly, I'd honestly wonder whether he was attracted to me at all. But today, when I gave him one of the least filthy kisses I've given anyone, he's suddenly half-hard and gasping against my mouth.

I tried to play it cool, but inside I was anything but. I feel like someone catapulted me into the ozone, dizzy and shaky as I float back down to Earth. I wasn't kidding about eating him out or sucking his dick—right now, I'm not sure I've ever wanted anyone as badly as I want Henri Vasel.

We kiss in the kitchen while his bread thing cools off, and this time I decide to let my hands roam a bit. Cupping my palms around his neck, I scratch the pads of my thumbs over the stubble on his jaw for a few seconds. Sliding them down to his shoulders, I take a few moments to appreciate just how stacked this guy is. I cannot wait to get him naked one day.

"How do you feel about taking this shirt off?" I ask him, nibbling gently at his bottom lip and earning a lovely intake of breath.

"It is not safe to be unclothed in the kitchen," he answers seriously. His hands are resting on my thighs, fingers spread wide to cover the most real estate. My dick is extremely aware of the location of those hands and the way he's standing between my legs.

"Okay," I allow, because he's probably not wrong about that. "Do you want to go upstairs? To my room?"

He licks his lips, which is far more indecent than it has any right being. I half expect him to demure and say we need to finish baking first, but Henri surprises me by stepping back and holding out a hand to me.

"Yes," he says firmly. Putting my palm into his, I hop off the counter. He doesn't let go of my hand once my feet are on the floor, and I have to resist the urge to physically pull away. I don't hold hands. Holding hands is something couples do.

Although I don't usually snuggle on the couch, either. Or invite hook-ups over and let them bake for me. I don't usually hook up with the same person more than once, and certainly not someone who won't actually engage in the hooking-up part. I need to cut this off. I need to stop letting Henri's soft accent and wavy hair turn me into an idiot.

But, not today. Today is the day before Christmas, and for once in my life I want to do something for no other reason than that it will make me happy. I want to not fear the future, or be miserable, for one fucking day. Today I want Henri. Tomorrow I'll go back to reality.

I tug him up the stairs by the hand and lead him to my

tiny room at the end of the hall. Reaching in and flicking on the light, I step aside and let his hand slide from mine as he enters and looks around. The room is barely bigger than the pantry in the kitchen, and with Henri's wide shoulders and long legs taking up space, it feels even smaller.

"I like your room," he says, turning to me and smiling.

Following him inside, I close the door behind me. We're the only ones here and there's no chance of my roommates coming home, but it feels strange to have the door standing open when I mean to have Henri naked within the next five minutes.

"Thanks." I pat the wall I share with Nate. "Nate's room is on the other side of this wall."

"That is nice." He thinks about it for a second. "Although, Nate does play his music quite loud."

"That he does," I agree. "Country, too. It's hell on earth around here, some days."

Checking that my cellphone is on silent, I set it on the dresser before sliding my sweatpants down and off. Leaving them in a heap on the floor, I tug my shirt off and drop it as well. I don't look at Henri until I sit on the side of my mattress and face him, feeling more self-conscious than I ever have before. The "freshman fifteen" were more like twenty for me, and I can't remember the last time I set foot in a gym. Soft would be a generous way to describe me.

I don't say anything for a minute, and neither does Henri. He stands there, in the middle of my room, staring at me with an inscrutable expression on his face. Before the silence becomes too much, he bends over and pulls off his socks before tucking them into the pockets of his sweatpants. Grasping the hem of his shirt, he pulls it up over his head. I keep my eyes on him, watching each sliver of skin that comes into view and feeling heat curl in my chest. This isn't the first time I've seen him without a shirt on, but given I'm half-naked, it *feels* different.

"Jesus," I mumble, looking at the light dusting of chest hair over his pecs. I hadn't noticed that before—how did I not notice that before? I want to rub my face on it.

"No, only Henri," he quips, and then grins as though waiting to see if I get the joke. My mouth is too dry to give more than a half-hearted chuckle, but it seems to please him because he starts pulling down his sweatpants.

When he finishes undressing and is standing in front of me in his boxers, I don't know whether to send up a prayer of thanks or to cry. He's devastating. In no universe should a guy who looks like that be interested in a guy like me. My brain is screaming so loudly at me that we are incompatible, I miss what he says.

"What?"

"I wonder if it would be okay for me to join you on the bed? I am a little embarrassed to have you staring at me," he admits sheepishly. The admission makes me lose some of the tension I'd picked up as he undressed.

"Sure, yeah, of course." He sits down next to me, thigh brushing mine, skin to skin. The contact obliterates my brain-to-mouth filter. "You don't have to be embarrassed, though. You look like you were fucking airbrushed. I've seen *Men's Health* cover models with less definition than you."

"Thank you, Atlas. That is a nice thing to say, although a little strange."

I laugh, bringing one knee up on the bed and turning to face him more directly. This means I've lost contact with his leg, so I rest my hand there instead. The brush of coarse hair against my palm is oddly sexy. I've always liked how soft and smooth girls' skin was, but I can see why this has its merits. I've never been so glad to be bisexual than I am at this moment. He stares down at my hand, and I'm just wondering if he wants me to remove it when he puts his on top, completely dwarfing mine.

"Atlas," he repeats. I honestly don't know how I could ever have thought the way he said my name was annoying. He says it so often, and each time is like a little treat for my ears. *Ah-tlas*—it's fucking sensual.

"Yeah?"

"I think you were probably making a joke earlier about the blowjob, but I would like to do that." He trails his fingers gently over the prominent vein in my arm, stopping when he reaches my elbow.

"Okay, cool." I grab my pillow and go to stand up, meaning to crouch down between his spread legs. I've never done this before, but I'm counting on years of porn, daydreams, and raw enthusiasm to help me. He stops me with a hand tight on my forearm.

"But I am not sure..."

"That's okay," I rush to say. "I've never done this before, either. Even playing field."

He nods gratefully. The truth is, I wouldn't say it's a totally even playing field. He's a virgin, and while I've never been with a guy before, I've had a lot of experience with women. Sex means nothing to me, and I know for a fact it will mean something to him. Looking down at the pillow still clutched in my hands, I toss it back to the bed.

"New plan. You lie down." Bending over, I pat the head of the bed. It takes him a solid minute of staring at my hand before he decides to comply. Sliding back, he crosses his ankles and rests his hands on his stomach. He's looking up at me as I'm staring down at him, and I feel another brick crumble away from my carefully built wall.

Shit.

Slowly, he raises one hand to trail his fingertips gently over my leg, just below the hem of my boxers. I want to climb onto the bed and get his dick into my mouth, but I can't seem to move. His soft blue eyes are pinning me in place, tingles zipping across my skin in the wake of his fingers.

"You are so pretty," he mutters, accent thicker than it was five minutes ago. "Like a sculpture."

"So pale, I look like marble," I say dryly.

"Do not joke, Atlas. I am being romantic," he scolds. I snort a laugh, and move his hand away gently. Bending over, I rest my own fingers on the smooth skin just above the waistband of his boxers.

"Can I take these off?"

I never know just how carefully I need to tread with him. He's painfully honest, so I don't think he'd just lie there and let me do something to him that he didn't like, but he's also completely inexperienced. He doesn't even like watching porn. The odds of him not knowing the steps of this process are pretty high.

"Yes. Thank you."

I snort, tucking my fingers into the band and drawing the fabric down his legs. He lifts his hips to help, and I'm not proud of the way my mouth waters like I'm the Pavlov's dog of dicks. My first view of him confirms that he's just as perfect everywhere as his face suggests. Tossing his to the side, I pull my own boxers off and fling them behind me.

"Manscaper," I note, planting a knee on the bed and rubbing my thumb over his hip bone. He huffs a laugh.

"It is the polite thing to do," he tells me.

"Had this in mind, did you? Blowjobs and bread for the holidays?"

"You are too much," he jokes, smiling widely. I look away, unable to face that much affection aimed in my direction.

I look back at where his dick is lying soft against his leg, any trace of earlier arousal gone. Leaning down, I kiss his stomach right above his belly button. Henri's breath hitches, so I do it again. And again. When I reach his pecs, I put a hand on that patch of chest hair.

"Tell me if you want to stop," I instruct firmly. "If you change your mind, or...or you decide you're no longer in the mood, you have to let me know, okay?"

"I will," he promises.

"All right. Cool. Don't judge me on my dick-sucking prowess—I'm new here."

He laughs, but cuts off sharply when I lean down and put my mouth on his neck, sucking gently.

17

Henri

ATLAS JUST LICKED MY NECK. A couple of months ago, I would have found the thought of that slightly abhorrent, but today I am very much seeing the appeal. Slowly, I tilt my face to the side to try and wordlessly get him to nibble elsewhere. He's not making any noise, just gently kissing along the lines of my tendons and bones as though creating a map of my body with his lips. It feels good. It feels *really* good.

Carefully, I put my hand to the back of his head. He makes a small noise of approval, so I slide my fingers through the silky dark strands of his hair. I don't want to hold his head down, but now that I've got contact, I don't want to lose it.

My skin buzzes as Atlas slides a hand down my flank—ribs to thigh—and his chest brushes my stomach. He's treading a very clear path toward my only half-hard dick, and I feel a momentary flutter of panic. I have a hard time becoming aroused, and there is no guarantee that it will happen no matter how much I like Atlas and what he's doing.

I will be incredibly embarrassed if my body doesn't cooperate.

"Atlas," I mutter, meaning to apologize for my uncooperative dick. When he lifts his head, I let my hand slide from his hair and back to the bed.

"You done?" he asks, and it takes me a second to work through what he's asking. Warmth, which has nothing to do with the temperature of the room, saturates my body.

"Oh, no. I was only wanting to tell you that I might not..." I gesture vaguely at my waist. He looks down and back up at me.

"Get hard?" he clarifies, and I nod.

"I am sorry."

His face scrunches up like he's got something distasteful in his mouth, and scoots up far enough to drop a kiss on my lips.

"Fuck that," he says. "Don't be sorry. I'm hard enough for both of us."

"That is not the way anatomy works, Atlas," I tell him seriously, hoping to tease out a laugh as well as another kiss. I get both, so I smile against his mouth and relax further into the bed.

When he trails gentle fingertips over my cock, it feels no different than when I do it myself. But it *is* different. If I tuck my chin, I can see the top of Atlas' shiny head, and the pale slope of his shoulders as he continues kissing my stomach. He wraps his fingers more firmly around me, thumb teasing the tip before sliding away to explore elsewhere.

When his fingers dip lower to my balls, I spread my legs a little wider to give him more room. He doesn't sit all the way up, but speaks against my skin, breath tickling the inside of my thigh.

"Can I suck you?" he asks, which makes me blush furiously.

"If you'd like."

He laughs, and I gasp at the puff of warm air against my balls. Every cell in my body is waking up and tingling in awareness. My nerves feel so delicate, it's as though they've been sandpapered, and my skin has never been so sensitive. As his hand strokes slowly over my length, I have the strangest desire to thank him.

By the time he wraps tentative lips around me, I'm wondering why I ever worried about being aroused. In fact, I am now worried that I will be having the opposite problem.

"Atlas," I mumble, startled by how scratchy my voice sounds. "Atlas, I am going to come very quickly."

He laughs, and because he does it with his mouth on my dick, I feel it in my pelvis. Biting my lip, I tangle one hand in the sheets and reach the other for his head. I have never touched anything as soft as Atlas' hair.

I'm trying very hard to be quiet and not make any embarrassing noises, so I hear it very clearly when Atlas gags. Pulling away, he reaches up to wipe the back of one hand over his mouth while slowly continuing to jack me with the other. Before I can ask if he's okay, he grins at me. It's an impish sort of grin, particularly when paired with his flushed cheeks and bright eyes.

"Let's try that again, shall we?" he asks, before leaning over and sucking me so deep I hit the back of his throat.

I come so quickly, it takes even me by surprise. Atlas makes a startled noise and jerks his head back, but immediately hollows his cheeks and slides back down, sucking in earnest. Eyes squeezed closed, I press myself into the mattress in a fight against my body to thrust upward. I have never felt so out of control of myself as I do in this moment.

Atlas sits up, but doesn't take his hand away. Instead, he idly strokes me as I soften, his other hand resting on my thigh. When I open my eyes and meet his, he smiles at me.

"Okay?" he asks.

"I am very sorry. I did not mean to ejaculate so quickly."

"Oh my god, don't say *ejaculate*," he scolds me, mimicking my accent. I grin. He doesn't seem mad, and is joking and smiling. Blowjob Atlas is apparently a happy Atlas.

"Shall I?" I ask, gesturing vaguely in the direction of his waist while maintaining polite eye contact.

"Oh, no." He snorts. "I was too worked up to wait. Jacked myself the whole time. I already came—all over your leg, in fact."

I sit up, surprised. There is most certainly cum on my leg, and I didn't even notice.

"I can grab a towel, if you want," Atlas offers, stepping off the bed and pulling his underwear back on. "Or you could take a shower. Whatever you want."

"Do you think you might come over here and kiss me?" I ask, and am immediately worried by the look that crosses Atlas' face. I hope we did not trade blowjobs for kissing. If I am only to pick one, I will choose kissing every time. But just as soon as the shadow was there, it's gone, and he is putting a hand on my cheek and pressing his mouth to mine.

"Thank you," I say as he pulls away. "And now, I do think I would like a towel."

I'm not overly fond of being dirty, and the cum is already starting to dry and pull on my leg hair. I also feel like I need a few moments alone to collect myself. Having sex is probably not meant to be a world-shattering experience, but it is feeling that way for me. I do not want Atlas to see something in my eyes that might frighten him away.

"Bathroom is across the hall," he tells me. "Help yourself to whatever."

I only take a few minutes in the bathroom, eager to keep riding this wave of good cheer from Atlas. When I walk back into his bedroom, he's sitting against his headboard waiting for me. Still clad only in his boxers, there is so much smooth, pale skin on display that I stop and enjoy the view for a minute. He notices and it makes him scowl.

"What?"

"I like to look at you. You are very beautiful. I am not sure if you know this."

"You don't have to do that." He scoots over so there is room for me to sit beside him on the bed. "Give me compliments like that. We're just fucking around. I don't need you to pour honey in my ear."

I stare at him mutely. I have no idea what that is supposed to mean.

"I am not sure about the honey," I tell him slowly, sliding up a little closer to him in bed and touching my fingertips to his rib cage. He has lovely skin. "Although, it might be good to have with the stollen, yes? And I like complimenting you. It is the truth."

"Pouring honey in someone's ear is an idiom for sweet-talking," he explains.

"Oh yes, this makes sense." I trail my fingertips down the inside of his forearm, enjoying the way goose bumps follow after. "But I think I shall continue with the honey talk. I like it when you make this face."

I touch his cheek and he rolls his eyes, as I knew he

would. Slowly—giving him a chance to move away—I lean in and kiss him.

"I am thinking the stollen is ready," I tell him, before coming back in for another kiss. "We should put shirts on and go eat. After that, perhaps we can come back here?"

"You angling for round two?"

"Well," I say seriously, holding out a hand to help him off the bed, "I believe we shall get better each time. Just like the kissing, yes? We must practice."

He snorts a laugh as he bends over to grab his shirt.

"All right, Henri," he mumbles softly, sounding as though I've made him sad. "Sounds good to me."

MY PHONE RINGS less than five minutes after I receive a notification from my banking app that a deposit has been made. Tucking my pen into the textbook to save my place, I close the cover and bring the phone to my ear.

"Jakob," I greet my brother with a smile. "Guten Abend."

"Bruderherz," he replies fondly. "Kein Deutsch mehr. Wir haben darüber gesprochen. Du musst dein Englisch verbessern."

I sigh. He's right. Jakob picked up English quickly—speaking it with the ease of a native. Even his accent disappears when he's on the phone with clients.

"Yes, you are right."

"Of course I am. Big brothers know best," he says stoutly. "Did you get the money I sent you? I don't trust the banks here. I put in five hundred, but if that is not enough, I can always transfer more."

"Jakob, I do not need so much." Scuffing my foot along

the floor, I shake my head even though he can't see it. I rarely spend the money he sends me, but it doesn't stop him from sending it. My brother lives in fear of me needing help but being caught up in the red tape of wiring money from my parents in Germany to me in South Carolina.

"Nonsense. Everyone needs money. Buy some new clothes—I know how you are, Bruderherz."

"My clothes are fine," I say weakly, glancing at my wardrobe and immediately thinking of Atlas. He would probably faint if I ever showed up to class *not* wearing a polo shirt.

"Well, it's your money. Spend it however you wish. How are things going otherwise? Did you hear back about that internship?"

"Things are well. I am struggling with some of the English classes—I am not so smart as you." Jakob makes a disgruntled noise, but doesn't interrupt. He is my staunchest supporter and doesn't like it when I say things about myself he doesn't agree with. "I did get the internship, though. I am thinking Coach Mackenzie is why."

"Bullshit," he scoffs. "You got the internship because you are incredibly smart, talented, and hardworking. Also, devastatingly handsome."

I laugh happily. "I am looking exactly like you. You are putting honey in your own ear, I am thinking."

Jakob scoffs, but I can hear his smile in the noise. I am lucky to have a brother like him. We never wanted for anything growing up, with two hardworking and successful parents, and we spent so much time together that the age gap never mattered much. We were brothers and best friends, and that bond has only gotten stronger in adulthood.

"That was pretty good. I've never heard you use a saying like that before," he notes. I practically puff up with pride at the words. Atlas is apparently teaching me more than sex things.

"Yes, I am learning that from my friend Atlas. He tells me I pour honey in his ear when I call him beautiful."

Jakob chuckles a little. "Well, I'm not sure friends often use that word choice. Unless—is this Atlas a special kind of friend?"

"Yes." I worry my bottom lip between my teeth. I've never talked to my brother about this sort of thing before. Will he care that Atlas is a man? "Is that okay?"

"Bruderherz, stop. Of course that's fine. Mama will give you a sex talk when you tell her, though. Be warned. She won't care how old you are. When I got married, I even got *pamphlets*. I know everything there is to know about child-birth, Henri."

"Goodness. I do not think I want pamphlets for sex."

"I hate to break this to you, but it doesn't matter what you want. My advice would be to avoid any packages she sends you after you tell her about your Atlas. God only knows what sort of medical literature might be in there."

Sighing, I bite my lip again and spin my chair in an idle circle. "Atlas is not mine, Jakob. We are only friends."

"Ah." He makes a stern, disbelieving noise in the back of his throat. I can practically see him waving a hand through the air, scattering my words. "You are so young. Give it time. Friends is a good place for a relationship to start. Now, let's talk about this internship. None of my clients play for South Carolina, but I know your coach—"

Opening my French notebook to a fresh page, I jot down notes as I listen to him talk. My mother is whom you would go to for questions concerning your health, and my father knows everything there is to know about foreign affairs and policies, but the sports world belongs to Jakob. We talk for an hour, before he has to go and meet up with a new potential client. Before we hang up, he reminds me once more to check my bank account and to do something fun with it.

"Take Atlas to dinner," he recommends, which makes me feel like I was walking down a staircase and missed the last two steps.

"Yes," I mumble. "That is a good idea. I shall do that."

True to my word, I log in to my account and see a fresh deposit of five hundred waiting for me. Also, because I told Jakob I would, I text Atlas to see if he would want to grab something to eat. I type out the message and delete it several times. No matter how I write the words, I can't make it sound less date-like.

HENRI

Hello, Atlas. I am thinking I will go get dinner off campus. If you are hungry, you could join me.

ATLAS

no dates

Sighing, I rub a hand over my face. I should have known he'd be too clever for that. I should have waited and asked him in person. He's easier to convince when I can smile at him and ply him with my accent. He pretends not to like it, but I know that he does.

HENRI

Just one will not hurt, yes?

ATLAS

what restaurant

HENRI

> Your choice, of course.

ATLAS

seafood?

HENRI

> Shall I pick you up in an hour?

ATLAS

k

not a date tho

Smiling, I put my phone down and replace all my school things where they belong. I'm already showered, so there's nothing to do but change clothes and wait. I text Carter while I do so, asking if he has any recommendations for good seafood restaurants locally. Carter loves taking Zeke out to dinner. He'll know all the good spots.

CARTER

You could go to the one we went to together. The Pearl. Or, if you don't mind a drive, you could try Maiden Catch. I'll send you the location. It's on the water. Low-key. You can sit outside on the deck. Zeke said he'd eat there every day if he could.

HENRI

> That is perfect, thank you. My brother is wanting me to have fun.

CARTER

Are you going alone? Ask Zeke to go with you. I'm in fucking Indiana.

HENRI

> I am going with Atlas, my friend from communications class. He likes seafood.

CARTER

Wait a second, Zeke told me that guy was a
dick. Fuck that guy.

HENRI

Oh no, he is not so bad. And yes, I think I
will.

CARTER

I can't believe you just made that joke.

I laugh out loud in my empty room, picturing Carter
glaring down at his phone. It's time to go pick up Atlas,
though, so I don't respond. When I pull up to Atlas' place,
he's sitting outside on the front step smoking a cigarette.
Burning it out on the concrete when he sees my car, he
stands and walks toward me. He's wearing a pair of dark
jeans and a black T-shirt. With his pale complexion and dark
hair, the black clothes make him look striking and a little bit
dangerous.

In comparison, I fear that I may look like a door-to-door
salesman with my khaki pants and green polo shirt. I know
Atlas prefers it when I wear more casual clothing, but I
certainly can't wear sweatpants to a restaurant.

"Hello, Atlas," I greet him when he slides into the car. He
grunts, clicking his seat belt into place. "You look handsome
in black."

He sighs and trails his fingers over my thigh. "I'm going to
have a ceremonial burning of all your khaki. Sacrifice them
to the fashion gods."

"You are funny," I tell him. He takes his hand off my leg,
which makes me sad. Putting the car in drive, I check the
map app on my phone and get us on the road. Glancing over
at Atlas, I decide I should probably remind him exactly what

this is, in case he's already forgotten. "You should keep your hand on my leg, because this is a date, yes?"

He shoots me an acidic look, and I smile cheerfully back. We're a few miles down the road before I feel the weight of his palm on me once more. Pleased, I smile, but keep my eyes on the road and my own hands on the wheel.

It's a nice night—perhaps a little on the cooler side, but still similar enough to the rainy winter weather I'm used to in Germany—so we opt to utilize the outside seating at the restaurant. Lights are strung up overhead, and the outdoor heating lamps are burning bright. As we're led to a table next to the railing, Atlas curls his fingers over the wood and looks down into the dark water. I thank the hostess and turn back to Atlas, nervous.

"Is this okay?"

"Yeah," he says, straightening and walking over to me. He touches my cheek and leans up to drop a quick kiss to my mouth. Shocked, it takes a few seconds for me to follow him to the table and sit down. I cannot believe he just did that. Usually, I can't even get him to smile at me in public, let alone *kiss* me.

The table we're at is a little too big for only two people, which means there's a choice as far as seating goes. Instead of sitting across from him, I take the corner seat, right next to where Atlas sat down. This way, if he gets it in his head to kiss me again, he won't have to reach too far. When we take a look at the menus, Atlas' eyebrows shoot up his forehead, and his eyes widen. He lets out a low whistle.

"This is expensive," he mutters, eyes flicking upward to mine.

"Yes, I thought it might be. Carter recommended it to me," I muse, leaning down and starting the arduous task of reading so many strange English words. "But that is okay. I will like spending money on you."

He taps his finger against the wood of the table, eyes narrowed as he tries to decide whether he wants to argue or not. Below the table, I hook my ankle over his.

"What is this, do you think?" I put a finger on the word and hold my menu out for him to read.

"Cremini—it's a mushroom."

"Cremini," I repeat, but must say it wrong because Atlas' mouth twitches like he wants to smile.

We go through the menu together, and several times I get him to laugh at the way we try to pronounce some of these unpronounceable words. I should have just asked Carter what to order—he would have known. But this is fun, and Atlas is relaxed; the lights hanging above us shimmer on his hair and the water laps gently against the deck below us. I'd sit here all night with him.

Our waiter is a tall, fit-looking man with a tattoo of a snake curling up his forearm. He introduces himself as Ty, before taking Atlas' order. When it's my turn, he comes to stand by me, leaning on the table close enough that I can smell his cologne.

"Nice night," Ty comments mildly, scratching down my order and grinning at me. "Where are you from? Can't say I've heard an accent like that around here before."

"I am from Germany, but am going to school at the university."

"Yeah?" Ty steps a little closer, pen tapping against the palm of his other hand. He's staring at me very intently, which makes me wonder if I need to use the men's room and check my appearance. "Well, this place closes down around ten most nights, if you're still around—"

Atlas' fingers on my wrist distract me. When I look over at him, his grip is tight on my arm and he's staring venomously at our waiter.

"No," he interrupts him firmly, and then doesn't take his eyes off of Ty until he leaves with a promise to bring our food out soon.

"What is wrong?" I ask him. I haven't moved my hand, and neither has he. His hold feels almost proprietary. Atlas' eyes track Ty across the patio and back into the main restaurant before meeting mine.

"He was asking you out."

"Oh, no, Atlas, I do not think so." I shake my head, making him scowl at me. His fingers tense incrementally on my wrist. I wonder if he's even aware he's doing it.

"Yes," he says firmly, "he was. He was telling you what time he gets off of work in case you wanted to hang around. He was hitting on you."

I shake my head again. People do not come on to me like that. Probably, Ty was just being friendly. He works for tips, after all. I imagine he chats with all his customers the same way.

"I think he was only doing his job."

"Oh? And that's why he didn't say a single word to me, but felt the need to comment on your adorable accent and let you know what time he gets off of work?"

I perk up at that. "My accent is adorable, yes?"

"Henri," Atlas huffs, annoyed.

"Aye, okay, perhaps you are right. But that seems very rude to me, to do that when I am on a date."

"He's handsome."

"Not so handsome as you," I tell him truthfully. "Probably,

he will spit in our food now, yes? Because you were giving him mean looks."

Atlas snorts, sitting back in his chair. I half expect him to let go of my arm, and am surprised when he uses his grip to pull my hand into his lap. When he threads his fingers through mine, I nearly fall out of my chair.

"Can't even blame him for trying," he says about our waiter. "You're so damn nice, would you even have said no if he asked you out?"

"I am only wanting to be here with you, Bärchen. I will be saying no to everyone who is not Atlas."

He squints his eyes at me, and I take the opportunity to trail the pad of my thumb over his knuckles. Atlas has very smooth hands, without any of the rough calluses that pepper my palms.

"Bärchen?"

"It is...little bear? Kleiner Bär. Because you are cute, and a little bit mean, yes?"

He shakes his head, but doesn't tell me not to call him that. I smooth my thumb over his hand again, enjoying the fact that he's letting me get away with such an obvious display of affection.

"Are you excited about starting the internship in a few months?" he asks.

"Yes. Also, nervous, but that is to be expected. I am not wanting to let down Coach Mackenzie, who wrote a nice letter about me."

"You won't let him down. You're the hardest worker in any room, don't even pretend otherwise. They're going to try and offer you a job at the end of the summer, just wait and see."

Uncomfortable with the sudden surge of support, I shift a little in my chair. I am not one who seeks attention, and Atlas isn't usually one to give me any. He notices my discomfort and smirks.

"And now you know how I feel when you call me beautiful," he says.

"That is the truth."

He's saved from answering by the reappearance of Ty carrying our food. Atlas' eyes snap toward him and narrow dangerously when he comes to my side to serve us. I watch him, amused with this new side of him. Even though it's unnecessary, I'm not unhappy to see him so jealous. Thanking Ty, I wait for him to be out of earshot again before squeezing Atlas' hand to bring his eyes back to mine.

"I am not interested in other people, in this way," I tell him. "I am not attracted."

"But you're interested in me that way," he muses. I nod. "Wow, you've got terrible judgement."

Laughing, I pick up my fork and look down at my plate, trying to figure out a way I can eat one-handed. If I cannot manage it, I will just go hungry. I do not want to let go of Atlas' hand. I worry if I do, I'll never get it back again.

Seeing my dilemma, he squeezes my fingers before gently extracting his hand from mine. He must see the disappointment in my face because he chuckles softly.

"Eat your food," he says testily, before muttering, "I'll hold your hand later."

The evening becomes steadily darker as we eat, the temperature dropping with the light. I make Atlas smile no less than four times, and after he finishes his food, he puts his hand on my leg the same way he did in the car. I'm unsure whether this is for Ty's benefit or my own, but I feel as though I've won either way. He watches as I slowly eat my dinner, probably picking up on the fact that I am in no rush for the evening to end.

"Thanks for this," he says, apropos of nothing. Frowning, he fiddles with his fork, clinking it gently against the side of his plate. "I, uh…it was my birthday, yesterday."

"What?" I ask, abandoning my last piece of fish and looking at him incredulously. I must have misheard him.

"Yeah." He shrugs. "I didn't do anything. It's not a big deal. Nobody even remembered."

"Atlas, what are you saying?"

"My dad and his family—I guess they forgot. My stepmom is usually the one who keeps track of that sort of thing, because my dad just can't be bothered, but." Another shrug. Atlas is such a good liar, I cannot decide whether the nonchalance is real or practiced.

"I am sorry," I say on an exhale, feeling rotten even though I didn't know until now it was his birthday.

"It's okay. You must have some sort of sixth sense, since you asked me to dinner the day after."

"No, I was only being selfish. Also, my brother said I must have some fun."

He quirks an eyebrow at me. "Oh? I'm fun?"

"Yes," I agree solemnly, and then try for a joke. "Especially when we are not wearing any clothes."

Chuckling, he pats my leg. "Well, let's pay the check and go back to your place. It's my birthday, and I mean to cash in on that."

18

Atlas

LOSING my mind wasn't so much a gradual thing for me. Rather, it was a full-tilt sprint off the edge of a cliff. Agreeing to go on a date was my first strike, and from there the evening has only gotten worse and worse. Holding hands, sharing food, and smiling more than I can ever remember smiling in my life. Hell, we were damn near playing footsie underneath the table. I've loosened my grip so much, my control has been obliterated.

I don't do this sort of thing. I don't choose people when I know they'll never choose me back. Love and pain go hand in hand—invite one inside, the other comes along. I bar the door to both and good riddance. I was doing fine before a big, goofy, floppy-haired German brought me an apple.

Now, Henri is driving us back to his dorm after I gave him a goddamn sob story about my family forgetting my birthday. I swear there is something wrong with me. I don't need to pump the brakes so much as *slam* on them.

Henri drives us back to the dorms with a small smile on his face, and his fingers tangled with mine. The boundaries I worked so carefully to establish have been destroyed in a single evening, and I have no idea how to bring us back to stable ground. I'm not done with this—with Henri—and even though I know it's a foolish mistake, I can't help but let myself be a little selfish. I need to break things off, but it doesn't have to be tonight. Tomorrow. I'll talk to him tomorrow.

Once we're parked in front of Henri's dorm, we walk silently together up the stairs. When we get inside his room, I stop him from turning on the overhead light and instead click on the lamp he keeps on his desk. Turning around, I see Henri standing in the middle of his room, watching me.

I always let him lead when we're together, mindful of how easy it would be to push him too far, too fast; to coerce him into doing something he's not in the mood for, or doesn't like. Regardless of the joke he told at the restaurant, we've only had our clothes off one time together. Mostly, he tends toward not being into it, and thankfully, he hasn't yet had a problem telling me that.

Stepping close to him, and tilting my face upward to keep my eyes on his, I dip my fingers into the pocket of his khaki pants.

"Do you trust me?"

"Yes," he answers automatically.

"Can I touch you?" He nods. I jostle my hand that's still tucked into his pocket, making it clear I'm talking about below the waist. "Here?"

"Yes."

Already, my dick is chubbing up at the mere proximity of him and being in a room with a bed. It's possible I'm a little bit of a slut for Henri Vasel. Glancing down, I notice he's not having the same issue just yet. He rarely has a physical reaction when we're kissing.

"I will do what you want me to do," he whispers. I shake my head immediately. Blind obedience is the opposite of what I want.

"No, Henri, not that. Let's just see where things go? If you aren't feeling it, you'll tell me and we'll stop."

He nods again and reaches up to the collar of his shirt to pull it off. I step back, letting him go through the motions of undressing and putting everything in its proper place. When I shed my own clothes, I leave them in a pile on his desk chair, figuring that's a middle ground between his own neurotic cleanliness and my more casual kind.

Because he's far more methodical about it, I'm undressed way before Henri. Crawling onto his bed, I tuck an arm behind my head and just watch him as I wait. The low lighting was a good call. It gives us just enough to see by, while also throwing shadows across every dip and curve on his body. And boy are there a lot.

Until now, I'd never given much thought to what my preferred type of guy might be. I've always known I was bisexual, but had never actually found myself in a position comfortable enough to act on it. Women, for me, were safe. Men, on the other hand, felt less so. Particularly as I am well below average height, and pretty weak after years lacking in physical fitness. Henri, with his wide shoulders and thick thighs, probably wouldn't have been my first choice if I was just going off of body type alone. He's too big, too strong—too much man.

But the reality of Henri is different. He's tall and built, yes, but he's also gentle and kind. Of all the options in the world, he is the safest.

"If your clothes are in a pile like this, they will get wrinkles," he tells me, finally finished with undressing and walking over to join me naked on the bed. I glance over at my clothes, sitting on his desk chair.

"And what a tragedy that will be," I respond dryly, eliciting a soft chuckle.

The bed creaks as he lies down next to me. At Christmas, Henri let me have my way with him; tonight, I want the same thing. Putting my palm flat on his chest, I carefully brush my hand over the smattering of hair across his pecs. Why that is so hot, I can't even explain to myself. Henri's heart beats a steady, slow rhythm beneath my palm—not a trace of nerves in sight.

I just touch him for a bit, slowly testing the waters and trying to tease reactions out of him. His hands stay flat on the bed, fingers clenching and unclenching steadily until I realize he's waiting for permission.

"You can touch me," I tell him. I should be annoyed at always having to provide approval, but mostly I find it endearing. I like that he waits for consent, instead of just assuming he's got it.

"Oh, good," he murmurs, and immediately reaches up to thread his long fingers through my hair.

I go back to what I was doing before: leaving my fingerprints on every inch of his body. When I move so that I'm situated above him, I lean down to kiss him slow. Heat simmers between us as Henri runs the tips of his fingers down my back, the light touch trailing shivers down my spine. We kiss until I feel the first stirring of Henri getting hard against me, and then kiss some more—a bit more urgently—as I wrap a gentle hand around him. Pulling my mouth away from his in case he wants to talk, I slide my lips across the scruff of his jaw and allow him a second to decide if he wants me to stop.

"Atlas," he says, and I remove my hand from him immediately, sliding my palm up his stomach until I can rest it on his chest.

"Henri."

I wait, face still resting alongside his, nose brushing his ear. His hands gently cup my ribs, before ghosting over my shoulder blades. He doesn't say anything else, but I don't immediately go back to jacking him off. Instead, I detour back to what I know he loves—kissing.

Slow as molasses, I move down his body, smiling when he brushes his fingers through my hair. He jolts when I lick his navel, my mouth having found its way down to his belly. I laugh against him.

"Ticklish," I muse, peeking up at him through my lashes. He teases a hand through my hair again, fingers playing with the strands.

"Apparently so," he agrees softly.

I glance up at him again. He doesn't sound quite right. Sitting up, so that I'm kneeling next to his hip, I brush my hand over his hip bones and up to his chest. He looks at me and I raise an eyebrow at him, watching as his cheeks flush pink.

"I am sorry," he tells me.

"What's wrong?" I'd noticed he wasn't getting hard, but that doesn't mean much where he's concerned. Unlike me, who can pop a boner practically on command.

"Nothing is wrong," he says quickly. "I would like for you to enjoy yourself."

I frown at that. Not exactly the turn of phrase I was hoping for. It's easy for me to enjoy myself having sex—I'm not worried about me. I want *him* to enjoy himself.

"Well, I don't like that," I muse. My hand is still on his stomach, so I give a few gentle strokes with my thumb, watching his face closely. He looks embarrassed, a little bit shy, and something else I can't quite pinpoint

"I am sorry, Atlas," he repeats. "But I do not think I want to do this."

I yank my hand off him so fast, my wrist pops. He sits up, putting his face close enough to mine for me to finally figure out the expression: shame.

"You're supposed to *tell me* that," I hiss, feeling unreasonably angry all of a sudden. Jesus Christ, was he just going to lie there and let me have my way with him? I open my mouth to tell him I don't want to fuck a sex doll, but snap my jaw closed just as fast. No. I need to remember who it is I'm with right now. He's the king of people-pleasers, but he's also honest. I'd been hoping the latter would trump everything else.

"It is your birthday," he says, as though this is a valid explanation. I shake my head in mute disbelief.

"You promised to tell me if you wanted to stop," I remind him.

"I did not mind! I like it when you touch me. I wanted you to do..." He flutters his fingers in the direction of his waist, apparently unable to put into words exactly which direction things had been headed. Maybe he didn't even know, which gives me yet another thing to worry about. Ignoring that internal voice that wants to remind me this was a mistake, I slide a little closer to Henri and put a hand on his upraised knee.

He looks at me, a pair of curls catching on his eyelashes as he blinks. Discomfort sits heavy in my stomach—I hate this sort of thing. When I do hook-ups, they're quick and dirty and there is none of this emotional shit. I don't have to talk. Henri smiles, apparently happy with my silent scrutiny of his face, and reaches out to trace a finger under my eye.

"I am very fond of this," he tells me softly. "The way you are looking like you're wearing eye makeup."

I blow out a hard breath. That's the problem with hook-ups, though. None of those people are Henri. *God, what have I done*, I think sadly, trying once more to get rid of the gloom that constantly tries to pull me under.

"Shall we—perhaps maybe we could do a little more kissing," he asks tentatively, fingertips stroking down my neck. "If you wish."

I snort a laugh. He's delusional if he thinks there is ever a time when I don't want him. I've never been the kind of person who would forgo an orgasm in exchange for fucking *kissing*, and yet I'm happily going to agree to just that. Kissing Henri feels better than anything ever has.

"I am in so much damn trouble," I mumble, before cutting off his reply with my lips.

Carefully, I put a hand to the center of his chest and press him back to the bed. He goes easily, automatically spreading his legs so I can fit myself against him. My dick, having softened during our intermission, begins to perk back up. *You will not hump him*, I tell myself firmly, as every brush of his skin against mine has my groin burning with unreleased pressure.

I slide my fingers into his hair, licking deep into his mouth like I'm trying to fuck him with my tongue. Henri, who's always remarkably self-contained, groans so deeply in his chest I swear I can feel it in my bones. It feels like invisible fingers plucked a guitar string inside me, my body reverberating with the echoes.

By the time we stop, I feel almost lightheaded—floaty, as though the oxygen has all been sucked out of the room. Having a difficult time thinking around how painfully hard I am, I sit back on my heels. Henri drags his forearm across his eyes, muttering in German, before sitting up and reaching for me. He pulls me in by the back of my neck, pressing his mouth to mine in an almost frantic kiss. I splay my fingers across his abdomen, close my eyes, and try to let go of control.

"You good?" I ask, confident now that he won't bullshit me after our earlier conversation.

"Yes," he answers immediately, without pausing to think for once. Tightening his grip, he brings me in again for another kiss, this one soft and barely more than a brush of lips. I should pull away. I shouldn't let this evening spin further out of control. But I'm so fucking tired of fighting this, and he's right here, and he wants me. *You can have this one thing,* I think to myself.

"I need to use the bathroom," I tell him, fisting my hands in the sheet to keep from reaching for my dick. I have never needed to come so badly as I do right now.

"Okay. But then you shall come back here, yes?" He pats the bed, eyes wide and beseeching. *Say no, Atlas. You don't spend the night with other people,* I remind myself.

"Sure," I agree, like the fool I apparently am. He smiles and watches as I slide off the bed. If he knows I'm going into the bathroom to jack off and not take a piss, he doesn't let on.

I take care of myself in seconds, probably breaking land-speed records with how fast I come the moment I put a hand on my dick. Washing my hands, I splash a little water on my face as well, trying to cool myself off.

We switch off once I leave the bathroom, Henri brushing a hand across mine and smiling as he passes. I try to return it, but don't manage more than a half-hearted grimace. My emotions are teetering unsteadily between happiness and doom, and the ongoing battle is exhausting.

Sitting back on the bed, I scrub my hands over my face. This isn't a friends-who-fool-around situation any longer—it's a relationship. I tried so hard to avoid one, I'd somehow missed all the signs and ended up in one by mistake. I'm unsure exactly how it happened, but I like Henri Vasel. I fucking *like* him. I like his cute, floppy hair, and his adorable accent. I like the way he talks like an actor in a period drama, and how selfless he is. Most of all, I like the way he likes me back: genuine and unconditionally. Despite all my efforts to push him away, here he is. I can't even pretend I'm not happy about it.

But I am worried.

I'm worried about when he inevitably decides this is too much work; when he finds someone worthy of him. Because that is the crux of the matter—I'm just not good enough for someone like Henri Vasel. He deserves better than the scraps of affection I'm able to pluck out of my loveless heart. I have never been—nor will I ever be—someone's first choice. He's going to break my fucking heart, and because I knew better, it'll be nobody's fault but my own.

He walks back into the room and I jolt, shaking my head and trying to bring myself back. Right now is not the time for an existential crisis about my inability to love or accept love in return. Not when Henri is looking at me like that: blue eyes soft and warm, a pleased smile tugging at the corners of his mouth as he crawls in beside me and kisses my bare shoulder. Again, my entire body thrums with pleasure. I'm a tuning fork vibrating at his frequency.

"Hello, Bärchen," he says, and my stomach swoops dangerously.

"Hey," I whisper back.

"I am thinking you should stay here this night," he tells me. "It is too late, and too cold to be going back outside, yes?"

Snorting, I slide down in the bed until I'm lying flat and pull the sheets up around me. Watching me burrow in, Henri's eyes light up and he does the same—tucking himself in and reaching over to fit the sheet more firmly around me. Again, my stomach performs an acrobatic maneuver. I want to tell him not to do things like that—not to treat me so tenderly—while at the same time being desperate for it to continue.

We end up on our sides, facing each other with as much distance between us as the small bed will allow. The lamp is still on behind Henri, sending shadows slashing across his angular face. Not even the dramatic lighting could disguise how happy he looks, though, eyes bright and face crinkled as he smiles helplessly at me. Relaxing down into his pillow, I smile back, but can't seem to hold on to it. I feel impossibly sad, all of a sudden. Dragged under by the weight of inevitable heartbreak.

"We're going to hurt each other, Henri," I tell him quietly. "This isn't going to work."

He ponders that for a moment, fingers gently tracing the line of my collarbone. "You might be right, but you might also be wrong, yes? Sometimes, things work out."

"Not for me."

Another pause, this one going on so long that I doubt he's

going to reply at all. He's still touching me, almost mimicking the way I did earlier to him. Reaching out, I thread my fingers into his thick, wavy hair and slide my hand along his scalp. His hair, where it falls over his forehead, has a curl to it. I play with the strands for a second, enjoying the way the curl holds its shape, before sliding my fingers back along his scalp. Soft and lemon-scented—two things I will now always associate with Henri.

He sighs, eyelids fluttering closed as I knead gently at his scalp. I keep at it, enjoying the way he just melted into the mattress at the touch. If he were a cat, he'd be arching his back and purring.

"You are happy now?" he asks quietly.

I should lie to him. Crack a joke. I'm only setting myself up for pain if I tell the truth now. I pause.

"Yes," I whisper back. His eyes open. I circle my thumb in the soft hair behind his ear.

"Perhaps it is your turn to be happy, after so many years of sad."

"I wasn't sad," I argue, but the words are flat and hold no weight. It's exhausting, keeping my elbows locked and feet planted; everyone held at arm's length. I almost laugh as Luke's words from months ago float unbidden to the forefront of my mind: *I didn't go looking for a relationship, but one found me anyway.* Apparently, Luke owes me an "I told you so."

"Maybe a little bit sad," Henri teases, scooting a little closer and leaning his head into my touch. I knead a little harder, rubbing at his scalp and eliciting a small groan. "But now you are happy, because you have me."

"Jesus—kiss one man and suddenly you're full of yourself, huh?" He laughs, his face close enough to mine that his breath puffs across my cheeks. "I'm serious, Henri. This won't last. You're too good for me."

"I wish you would not talk this way."

"What, tell the truth?"

"This is not the truth, Atlas," he says, voice suddenly losing the sleepy, satisfied quality of minutes ago. "The truth is you are just right for me. You are worrying too much about the future, I think."

Not believing him, but also not wanting to ruin the night by arguing, I stay silent. Love is conditional. Nobody, not even Henri, can love someone selflessly forever. Eventually, he'll leave, too. Everyone does. People change and it's not always for the better.

"Let us go to sleep, Atlas. Perhaps in the morning you will realize that I am right, yes?"

Snorting, I give his hair another stroke before dropping my hand back to the bed. Sliding back from him as far as the small bed will allow, I watch as Henri reaches over and turns off the lamp. The dorm plunges into black, with barely a sliver of moonlight illuminating the room through the window. I wait to see if Henri decides he wants to try his luck and snuggle, but he settles on the other side of the bed and I can breathe a little easier.

Closing my eyes, I try not to think too hard about the fact that this is the first night I'll be spending in someone else's bed.

"Happy birthday, Atlas," Henri murmurs into the dark, and I squeeze my eyes shut against the sudden pain in my chest. Nothing good can come of feeling this good.

19

Henri

I LOVE CREATIVE COMMUNICATIONS CLASS. I love sitting next to Atlas and accidentally-on-purpose brushing his hand with my fingers. I love leaning over and catching a whiff of spice and cigarette smoke. I particularly love it when his dark eyes meet mine and his lips curve up into the barest hint of a smile. I am certain he doesn't know he's doing it, which is why I'll never say anything about it—if he knew how much I loved that look, he'd be sure to stop.

"Hello, Bärchen," I greet him warmly as I slide into my seat. "How are we today?"

"Fine. You?" He sets a small gift bag on my desk, smirking.

Atlas and I have developed something of an inside joke where apples are concerned. It started out as a genuine concern for his health, and has slowly manifested into a game between us to see who can find the most ridiculous apple-themed item. Last week, I was thrilled to find a horrendously ugly apple-patterned tie, and he has yet to beat me. Before that, Atlas brought me a set of children's barrettes that were different types of apples. I have quite the stash of apple gifts from Atlas, and I cherish them rather more than I probably should for what is essentially a load of junk.

"And what is this?" I ask.

"Open it and find out," he says smugly. Clearly, he believes he's found something better than the tie.

Pulling open the bag, I peek inside. It looks like some sort of fabric—silky, like pajamas. Furrowing my brow, I reach in and pull it out, only to stuff it back out of sight under the table. Atlas snorts with laughter.

"Atlas!" I scold, feeling my face heat with embarrassment. "You cannot give me underwear in class, this is not appropriate!"

"Apples, though," is all he says between chuckles. "Satin, too, did you notice?"

"Atlas," I repeat, desperately trying to keep my expression stern. It's very hard not to smile when he's obviously so pleased with himself.

"Wear them tonight, yeah? I need a picture. Maybe you could pose for me."

Sighing, I turn around in my seat and try to gauge the nearest person and whether or not they just saw me flinging boxers around. Nobody appears scandalized, so I quickly transfer them to my bag. When I turn back to him, Atlas is still looking ridiculously proud of himself.

"Okay," I say on a sigh, "that is pretty good. I suppose you are winning, for now."

He looks smug as Dr. Robertson walks into the room. I immediately face forward, pen poised over my notebook and ready to take notes. Beside me, Atlas has his laptop ready. We make a good team, him and I. Although handwriting things does help me retain the information, it is a great deal slower and I occasionally miss pieces of the lecture. With Atlas typing his notes and giving them to me later, I'm able to fill in the blanks.

When class is dismissed later, I carefully finish up my last line of text before turning to Atlas. He's watching me—again, with that cute smile on his face—and waiting for me to finish.

"Are you free for this Saturday?" I ask him. He shrugs.

"I can be."

The way Atlas makes plans is a little bit anxiety-inducing. He doesn't so much make plans, as stroll casually into them. While I prefer to have everything structured and planned in advance so I know precisely what my days look like, Atlas prefers to agree to things spur of the moment. Similarly, he has no problem discarding plans when something better comes along. In this case, I am hoping that is me.

"I was thinking we might have a date," I tell him, sliding my books into my bag. "My friend Zeke has given me an idea, and I do not have a hockey game."

"Oh?"

"Are you free?" I press, not wanting to give away too much information before he actually agrees to going. He scowls at me, because he knows exactly what I'm doing.

"Sure," he grunts.

"Excellent! I shall pick you up around four, yes? And we will go and enjoy some glow-in-the-dark miniature golfing."

"Actually, I'm not free," Atlas corrects quickly

"Yes, you are. Four o'clock on Saturday, I shall be there to pick you up." Leaning forward, I give him a quick kiss to the top of his dark head. He sighs as though I am testing his patience, and stands to follow me out of the lecture hall. I hold the door for him and he scowls as he walks past me and out of the building.

"We're not dating," he reminds me, although the words lack any conviction at all. "We're just fucking."

"With feelings," I add cheerfully.

"No feelings."

"A few feelings." I nudge him with my elbow, grinning. He rolls his eyes but still smiles back.

"Fine. I'll go mini golfing, but I'm not happy about it," he tells me crossly, though there is still no heat behind it.

"All right, Bärchen. It is a date." I kiss the top of his head again, because Atlas is starved for affection and I am happy to provide it. He sighs gustily and leans into me, arm wrapped loosely around my waist in a half-hug.

ATLAS PRETENDS he is not having fun with the mini golf, but he is. The room is dark, with the only illumination coming from the brightly painted, glow-in-the-dark course structures. Atlas, with his dark hair and pale skin looks even more striking than usual. I ask a nice woman to take our photograph as we are waiting at a hole, and although he grumbles a little bit, he leans into me and smiles at the camera.

"Look at this." I show him the picture, grinning down at it.

"How are you even real," he mutters. "It looks like I'm standing next to a celebrity."

This is my first experience with mini golf, and it is a tad humbling. Having been gifted with more athletic acuity than most people, I had assumed this would be easy for me. That is, until Atlas never scores higher than a two and I seem to average a four on every hole.

"You are quite good at this, yes?" I comment. Atlas shrugs.

"My youngest half brother likes to do stuff like this." He looks down at his feet, scuffing the tip of his Converse against the turf.

"Oh? And how old is he? How many brothers?" I try to temper the excitement in my voice, but it's difficult. Learning about Atlas in any capacity is ridiculously hard. He doesn't like to talk at all, let alone about himself. He once told me he didn't have any older brothers, and I'd foolishly taken that to mean no siblings at all.

"Two. Ethan is five years younger than me, and Ryan is ten years younger."

"Wow! And how old are you, then?" I ask, making Atlas laugh.

"Twenty-two. Ryan just turned twelve. He still likes to do stuff like this"—Atlas gestures around, encompassing the golf course—"but Ethan is sometimes too cool for it."

"Like you," I tease, and he shoots me a wry look. "Jakob is nine years older than me, so I am having a big age gap like you."

"Yeah. Even though he's a lot younger, Ryan and I get along fine. For now," Atlas adds, shrugging and attempting nonchalance. "Soon enough he won't want to hang out with me, though. Neither of them will."

"I do not think this is true," I say lightly. "I am always trailing after my brother growing up, no matter how old I am. Big brothers are always the hero, yes?"

"Maybe," he allows, chin still angled downward so I can't see his expression.

I touch a fingertip to the back of his hand, resting on the

handle of his golf club. It's our turn at the hole, so Atlas is able to avoid further conversation by taking his shot. He sinks his ball in three this time. Plucking it out, he smirks at me.

"Might be time for you to post a comeback," he teases. Sighing, I shake my head and bend over to place my ball on the turf. I don't think a comeback will be happening tonight. Indeed, this ends up being my worst hole yet, which makes Atlas smile as he jots down a six on the scorecard.

"Good thing the hockey net is so big," he notes casually. I give him a small jab with my elbow, but he sidesteps me, grinning.

Atlas ends up winning, which will likely earn me a little chirping when I tell Carter and Zeke. According to Zeke, Carter "destroyed him." Atlas, smirking, hands me the scorecard as we pass a trash can on my side as we head out the door. Instead of tossing it, I tuck it into my pocket. Proof, for the future, that perfect days do exist.

"Are we going back to your dorm?" Atlas asks, clipping his seat belt and turning to face me.

"Sure, if that is what you wish." Smiling over at him, I see him nod and turn his head to watch out the window. He sits in silence for the majority of the ride, and it's not until we reach campus that he looks over at me.

"That was fun," he admits grudgingly.

"Yes," I agree, smiling widely at him. "Although next time I will be sure to pick an activity that I excel at, I think. It is hard to be impressive while losing at a game most children can do."

Snorting, he pushes open his door and rounds the hood of the car to wait for me. The dorm is a little more rowdy tonight than usual—music thumps through the hallways, and raised voices carry through the doors left wide in open invitation. I wonder for a moment if Atlas will want to join the party, but he only trails after me silently until we reach my door.

Inside, he moves about my space with the practiced efficiency of someone who has been here many times. It makes my chest feel tight to see it—Atlas comfortable in my room, and with me. He catches me watching him and narrows his eyes at me.

"What?"

"Nothing, nothing." I wave a hand, not wanting to embarrass him. He lifts his shirt over his head, loosely folding it and laying it on my desk chair the way he does every time he spends the night. Bending over to slip his pants off, he glances up at me.

"Are you sleeping in that?" he asks.

"No, but I think I shall wait until you finish. I am enjoying watching."

Chuckling, he slips off a sock, balls it up and tosses it at me. Catching it, I walk over and hold out a hand for the other before folding them together and putting them with the rest of his clothes. When I turn back around, Atlas is standing in his boxers and watching me.

"All right," he says, gesturing to me. "My turn to watch."

Atlas sits on the edge of my bed, leaned back on his hands, as I take my clothes off and put them away. Usually, I'd be using this time to get some studying in, or watching whatever NHL games were on; maybe working through some of the physical therapy exercises I can manage in my dorm room. But ever since Atlas and I have tentatively dipped our toes into dating, he's been spending quite a bit of time here, and my carefully structured life is no longer so rigid.

I join him on the edge of my bed, and smile when his

hand immediately rises and fingers trail down my spine. He's waiting for me to tell him what I want or don't want. Atlas—who seems to always be ready and willing—is forever up for anything. I, on the other hand, am very seldom in the mood. Mostly, I just want to be around him. Sitting quietly for a few moments, I enjoy the gentle slide of his fingertips over my back.

"Can we sleep?" I ask him. I'm always nervous about requesting that he stay the night, particularly when most nights I don't want to do anything sexual. He's so skittish about relationships, I feel the need to step lightly around him. One wrong move will have him springing for the door.

"Sure," he agrees, dropping his hand and reaching around us to pull the sheets back. Relieved, I slide into the bed to the spot closest to the wall and wait for him to join me. I stare hard at his face, looking for any annoyance or disappointment, but find none. I turn him down quite often, and I do not want him to be mad. He looks relaxed, fortunately.

"Thank you," I mutter, as he settles himself in next to me, clicking off the lamp. He lies on his side, one arm tucked under the pillow cushioning his cheek. "I am sorry, I know you were wanting to—"

"Don't do that," he says crossly. "Don't apologize for not wanting to fuck. You're allowed to say no, Henri."

"But what about you—"

"Don't," he repeats. "I don't like that you feel bad about that. I don't want you to ever feel obligated to have sex with me or anyone else, okay? That's not cool. Nobody should make you feel that way."

"Okay," I agree, a little surprised at his vehemence. He sounds angry. I can't see his face, but even in the dark I know he's wearing a frown. "I am just not wanting to let you down. I want you to like me."

He sighs, and I feel his breath on my face. His fingers find the side of my head and slide soothingly into my hair. I try not to moan, but it's a close thing. Of all the things I like doing with Atlas, my favorite is when he touches me in this way—loving and gentle.

"I like you," he says, in the same tone of voice one might use to describe a root canal they received. Another sigh. "I shouldn't, but I do."

And here we go with this again. I hate it when Atlas talks like this. Like he's not good enough, and is just waiting for me to find someone better. I do not understand how someone so smart could be so blind. How could I want someone else when Atlas is in the world?

I wonder, for a moment, whether now is the time to bring up the summer. The end of the school year has been looming in the periphery, bringing with it both an exciting new chapter for me, but also a great deal of uncertainty. For the first time since starting school here, I won't be going home to Germany for the summer months. Atlas, of course, hasn't said anything about his own plans, and the ambiguity is beginning to feel damning. It feels like his silence means the end.

I need to bring it up—I *know* that I do—but talking about these things with Atlas sets him on edge. I can easily imagine the way his eyes would fill with panic if I asked him to visit me here over the summer. He's as skittish as a wild animal, prone to running when someone makes an abrupt movement around him. So I've kept quiet and let my anxiety fester, and now here we are: a handful of weeks before the end of the semester and time is up.

"Atlas?" I whisper.

"Mm," he grunts back, already half-asleep.

"I need to talk to you."

"Now?" He huffs, fingers gently pushing my hair back in a way that makes my heart hurt and my eyes burn.

"Not now," I mutter, even though I long to say *yes, please, let's talk now.* "Go to sleep, Bärchen. I can wait until morning."

But the morning comes and goes in a haze of lazy cuddles and soft kisses, and Atlas is gone home by the time I remember that I wanted to talk to him.

20

Atlas

I AM, to put things delicately, freaking the fuck out. There is something strange about the way time is moving right now— barreling forward like a sprinter off the starting line. How could it be possible that tomorrow is the last day campus is open, but Christmas had been only yesterday?

I can tell it's bothering Henri, too, particularly since his hockey season ended and his calendar has had a great deal more free time. Free time which he mostly spends with me, and mostly spends worrying his bottom lip between his teeth, looking nervous. Several times in the past few weeks he's tried to start a conversation with me, and even without letting him get on with it, I knew exactly what kind of conversation it was going to be. Each time, I'd distracted him and each time he'd looked a little more crestfallen.

And then, to top everything off, I'd received a call last week from my dad, explaining that he'd "had a scheduling mishap" and would no longer be able to pick me up from the airport when I flew home. Reading between the lines, I was able to deduce that he'd forgotten his promise from months ago when he booked my ticket. He had, as per usual, forgotten *me*. It was a not-so-gentle reminder that distance from Henri would not do me any favors. He'd be here in South Carolina, and I'd be back in D.C., and eventually he'd forget why he ever put in the effort for me in the first place.

Unable to stand the way my insides feel as though they're being shaken about, I light up a cigarette and stand next to my window. My phone rings, and I glance down to see my dad's name on the display. I am really not in the fucking mood, and his calls never provide anything but distress. Even so, he's my dad and I can't very well ignore him. Something could be wrong with my brothers.

Filling my lungs with as much nicotine as I can manage, I answer the call with trepidation and a hefty dose of resignation. Two phone calls in less than two weeks is not a good sign.

"Hey, Dad."

"Atlas. I need to talk to you."

Obviously, I refrain from saying. Closing my eyes, I angle the phone away from my mouth and take another drag of my cigarette. If Dad notices the sounds of me smoking, he doesn't comment.

"Okay. About me coming home?"

"Sort of. I heard from your mother."

My elbow bangs against the wall as the words hit me like a lightning bolt. Instinctively, I know he's not talking about my stepmother despite him always referring to her as my mom. The tone strongly suggests he's talking about my *mom*.

"What?" I whisper, and hate myself for the tiny spark of

hope that flares in my chest. I'm too old to care if she wants me. Too old to need her.

He huffs in annoyance. "I've been sending her emails periodically through the years, updating her on her son. Not that she ever replied," he adds testily, even as the words are like a knife in my chest. "The emails were never returned as non-deliverable, though, so I kept at it. This is the first time she's sent one to me."

I open my mouth but words don't make an appearance. I'm stuck on the fact that he's been emailing her about me for years—*years*—and she's never replied. I've always known she didn't care about me, but being slapped in the face with it randomly feels like a bucket of ice water dumped over my head. I knew I shouldn't have answered this call.

"What did she say?" I finally manage to ask.

"Well, I'd told her when you started college that you were in your first year at South Carolina U. As I said, this is the first I've heard back, but apparently she is living in Florida."

My hand shakes violently as I bring the cigarette to my mouth. Unfortunately, not even nicotine can save me from the high-speed wreck I fear this conversation is heading toward. My nerves, which have already been brittle with the end of the school year looming, feel raw and exposed.

"She remarried years ago, and apparently has a two-year-old. Her husband works in *fishing*." Dad snorts, and I can easily picture the contempt on his face. "That's not why I'm calling, though. Apparently, she's decided that now the time is ripe to reconnect. She asked me to pass along her phone number in case you wanted to give her a call."

Me, give her a call. Even now, it would be me coming to her when she's the one who left in the first place. My chest hurts so badly, I fear I might be having a heart attack.

"She knew I was going to school in South Carolina?" I clarify. "You told her when I started?"

"Yes. No reply, naturally." Another disdainful sound. He hates being ignored in any capacity.

She's been in Florida this whole time, I realize. Only a couple states away from where I've been going to school, and she couldn't even be bothered to reach out, let alone try and visit. My own mother, and I was nothing more than an email to be ignored and a son to replace. I will myself to feel angry, but can't manage more than a sort of panic-induced numbness. The sort of feeling you have when you're experiencing a terrible day, and one bad thing happens after another, so you just learn to accept it.

"So, the ball is in your court now," Dad continues, casually throwing grenades without waiting to see if any have landed. "I told her I'd pass along the message. Do with it what you will."

"I don't..."

"Anyway, we'll see you tomorrow, or whenever you get home. I'll text you your mother's phone number." He's already done with the conversation. Message passed along, time to get on with his day.

"Dad, wait—" I pull the phone away from my ear and look at the screen. He's already hung up.

Exercising what I consider to be an incredible amount of self-control, I lay my phone gently on the bed instead of smashing it against the wall. It pings with a message, but I ignore it the same way I intend to ignore my mom's new phone number. I'm not going to call her up and beg her to love me—if Dad had waited more than five fucking seconds, I would have told him to not even bother sending it over.

The doorbell rings, making my already galloping heart

jump. *Henri*. I'd forgotten that we'd made plans for today. Forgotten, that in my fucking delusional state, I'd allowed him to get too close. Thank you, Dad, for the reality check.

Panic eats at my insides until I'm almost sick with it. So much so, in fact, that when I answer the door of my shared house and see Henri's handsome face on the other side, my vision tunnels dangerously. The lizard part of my brain is screaming at me to run. Self-preservation is my default state, and today Henri is a threat. *Breathe*, I remind myself, and work to unclench my fingers from the doorhandle.

"Hello, Atlas," Henri greets me, smiling like he always does, his face open and warm the way it always is when he speaks to me. I want to cry, just now, at the unfairness of it all. Of being presented with someone so perfect, and knowing he deserves someone much better than me. Of knowing that every good thing comes with an expiration, and today the piper needs to be paid.

"Hey," I mumble, wishing like fucking hell that he wasn't here. "Come on in."

Shoving the door wide, I watch as he carefully wipes his feet on the mat, before turning and leading him upstairs. Nate and I are the only two still here. I send up a silent, desperate prayer that he has his headphones in and doesn't have his ear pressed to our shared wall.

"What is wrong?" Henri asks, the moment we get to my room and I shut my door. "You are looking sad."

"Nothing," I mutter back, desperately trying to think through my panic-disordered mind.

I need time alone to think. I need him to leave. I need him to stop being able to read me like a book, like he's trying to do now. He angles his head and looks at me quizzically, as though he can tell I'm lying but can't think why. As it usually does, defensiveness comes to my rescue and turns my words hard and unyielding.

"What do you want?" I snap.

Henri's eyes pop wide, and I can hardly blame him. It's been a long time since I've spoken to him like that. I hate myself so much in this moment, I can barely stand it.

He deliberates for a second, before carefully touching the back of my neck and kissing my lips in a silent hello. I don't kiss him back; don't even move until he removes his hand.

"I am wondering if we might talk about the summer," he says, sitting down on my bed and nervously running his hands back and forth on his thighs. If he noticed that I didn't return the kiss, he doesn't let on.

"Nothing to talk about." I shrug with a casualness I do not feel. "I'm going home to D.C., and you're staying here for your internship."

"Right," he agrees slowly, "but I will have weekends off, and I was wondering if you might like to come visit? I have already asked Carter and Zeke, and they are happy to let you stay with us. With me."

My heart beats frantically against my rib cage, alarm sending my pulse skittering dangerously. I'm going to faint.

"I don't think that's going to work," I tell him, and watch as his face falls. "I mean...we might as well end things now, on our own terms. School is over, Henri. What's the point?"

"The point?" he repeats, accent a little thicker the way it gets when he's tired or nervous.

"I don't want to pretend for half the summer, only for us to decide that we should break up. We weren't even really together in the first place," I tell him harshly, hating each word as I say them, but unable to stop. "We never had a conversation about being *together*. If we had, I would have told you no."

Henri pushes himself to standing, facing me from across the room. I'm not the only one panicking now. His eyes are wide and fearful, hurt already recognizable on his features. He holds up a hand, palm facing me, as though needing me to stop or slow down.

"Wait, *wait*. I do not...why are you saying this? We are not breaking up," he says firmly. "If you do not want to visit over the summer, that is fine, but there is no reason to—"

"We aren't going to be in the same state for *three months*, Henri."

"And so?"

So you will realize how much better things were before I was there, I want to scream at him. But it won't work. Not with Henri, who is both stubborn and a people-pleaser. He'll tell me I'm wrong until he's blue in the face.

"I *want* to break up." Straightening my spine and squaring my shoulders, I practically spit the words at him. He flinches back, cheeks coloring and eyes wide. He look like I've hit him.

"I do not understand," he says quietly. "You are not making sense."

"I want to break up," I repeat, enunciating each word carefully as though he's hard of hearing and stupid. "This shit got out of control—I told you at the start that we were just fooling around. It was never supposed to be more than that."

"But it was."

"Not for me," I lie, and have to clench my hands into fists, nails digging painfully into my palms, to fight the sudden burn in my chest. Henri stares at me silently, chest rising and falling beneath his polo shirt.

"You are lying," he says.

"What the fuck do you think is going to happen?" I explode. "You don't *live* here, Henri! You've got one more year of school, and what then? What happens if you don't get a job here? Or you can't extend your visa?"

"This is all...it's all..." He makes a frustrated noise in the back of his throat and runs a hand through his hair. Unable to come up with the word, he abandons that thread and tries again. "You are saying things that may never happen. You are ruining something right now, and using the future as an excuse."

"This"—I gesture between us—"is why I *told* you I don't do relationships. I fucking *told* you, Henri. I'm not going to sit around and wait for you to get your fill of me and leave."

Mutely, he shakes his head at me. He looks stricken, and I want so badly to pull him into my arms and apologize that I have to take a step backward. *Leave. Please leave,* I beg silently. I don't want to waver on this, and the longer he stands there, the less firm I become. I know I'm doing the right thing to protect myself, but it's hard to remember that fact when Henri's standing in front of me looking close to tears.

"Atlas," he whispers.

"No." I shake my head. "I want you out. I want you to leave."

At an impasse, we stare at each other. I can see the struggle on Henri's face, as he wars with the desire to do as I ask and the desire to fight for what he wants. I know him well enough to see the argument in his eyes, even if he's struggling to put it into words. He's not good with confrontation—by putting him on the spot, I've made sure this is a fight I'll win.

I've made him uncomfortable enough that he can't think of a way to argue back in English. *Way to go, Atlas, you piece of shit.*

"This is it?" he asks, voice breaking over the words. I nod sharply, unable to trust myself to speak any more. Resolutely, I stare at the wall over his left shoulder so I don't have to look at his face. "Atlas—"

"Just *go*, Henri." I'm not looking at him, so I don't see his reaction to the words. Nor do I see him leave the room.

I don't hear the front door slam, because of course Henri is too polite to do so. Even so, I can feel the absence of him like there is a gaping hole in my chest. Pressing my palms to my eyes, I swallow down the frustrated scream building in my chest. *I hate you,* I tell myself vehemently. *I fucking hate you.*

A noise at the door draws my attention, and I drop my hands, fearing that it's Henri coming back. Nate stands in my doorway, hands shoved deep into the pockets of his basketball shorts and face unusually serious.

"I don't want to hear it," I tell him. He and Henri play hockey together—I can't imagine being roommates will trump that relationship. He's not going to be on my side in this.

"You okay?" he asks, and I'm shocked into silence.

"We broke up," I explain, even though it's painfully obvious he heard. The look he gives me says I am correct in this assumption. "You don't have to tell me, I already know I'm an asshole."

Nate opens his mouth –probably to agree—but closes it again and contents himself with a shake of his head instead.

"Just say it," I tell him wearily. It's not as though he can make me feel worse.

"You're a damn idiot, you know that?" I nod, and he

makes a frustrated noise. "I can't understand you, Atlas. I really can't."

"Might as well not even try." I can hardly understand myself, let alone expect anyone else to. "Things would have ended, anyway. I just sped it along and ended them on my terms, that's all."

Nate's green eyes snap to mine.

"So, what? You broke his heart before he could break yours?" I stay silent because there really isn't anything to say to that. "Wow. Well, on behalf of Vas, I'd just like to say: fuck you. But as your roommate and sometimes-friend even though you're a dick, feel free to text me if you need to talk."

"Aw," I try to tease, but it lacks all conviction and merely sounds sad. Mutely, he shakes his head and leaves my room. Not even the wall between us is enough to mask the disappointment radiating from his room.

Nate and I pack our things silently after that. He'll be the last to leave, driving back to the ranch tomorrow after I catch a flight to D.C.. I can tell he's frustrated with me, but trying to toe the line as someone who is friends with both of us. Instead of trying to talk, he chooses silence and I'm grateful for it. I realize that I still don't know who's supposed to be picking me up from the airport, but I can't bring myself to care. Maybe they'll just leave me there, and I can rot on the floor in the baggage claim until it's time to come back to school.

I TEXT my dad once I've landed and am waiting in baggage claim, but he doesn't reply. There aren't any texts from Henri, either, which somehow hurts worse even though I know not to expect any. When my bag makes it's slow way to me on the conveyor belt, I tug it off and head outside to wait on a bench in the passenger pickup. I should probably call my stepmom, since I can't get in touch with my dad, but I just don't care. I feel awful—foggy-headed and achy, like I'm coming down with a cold and not heartbreak.

Heartbreak—Atlas, you piece of shit. Annoyed with myself and my feelings, I desperately try to think of anything but Henri and the devastated look on his face when I'd yelled at him. I don't deserve to feel sorry for myself. I'm the one who did that to him, and I did it on *purpose*. It doesn't matter that I was only trying to protect myself or how hard the words were to say. What matters is that I said them, and there is no going back now.

A slick little silver Audi pulls up to the curb and the driver taps the horn in a quick staccato. Glancing behind me, I try to figure out who they're picking up. I'm the only one out here. It's only when the passenger window rolls down that I see my brother's face grinning at me.

"Hey!" he yells, and indicates the rear of the vehicle with a wave of his hand. "Trunk is open."

Stowing my luggage, I slide onto the smooth leather seat of the passenger side. After clicking my seat belt into place, I look over at Ethan with eyebrows raised.

"Whose car is this?"

"Mine," he says excitedly, hands rubbing the steering wheel fondly. "Do you want to drive it? I'd let you."

I stare at him, nonplussed. "Yours? You're seventeen, how the fuck—" Realization dawns and I scoff, shaking my head. "Dad bought it for you, didn't he?"

"Yeah," Ethan replies, still in that same giddy tone of voice. He's too excited to hear the anger in mine. "What do you think? Mom was going to come pick you up, but I asked if I could instead. I couldn't wait to show you."

I take a deep breath, tempering my annoyance so as not to ruin his excitement. It's not his fault our dad picks favorites, or that he's the chosen one. It's definitely not his fault that I'm in a bad mood because I broke up with my boyfriend.

"It's pretty cool," I tell him, and he beams as though this is the highest of praise.

"Right? I'm so excited you're here. Do you want to go to the new Marvel movie with me and Ryan? Maybe we could go tomorrow, since weekdays are usually less busy at the theater."

I sit in silence, listening to his idle chatter as we fly down the interstate. Ethan has always been the excitable one of my stepbrothers, prone to going "off to the races" as my stepmom likes to say. He can talk about anything to anyone. Ryan, on the other hand, is both shy and sensitive, disposed to getting teary-eyed over ASPCA commercials. I, of course, fill the role of the angry and unfriendly brother. Together, we are the perfect trifecta.

"Do you think you know what you want to major in, yet?"

Realizing that I'm actually needed in the conversation now, I pull myself out of my stupor to answer his question.

"Uhm, no. Not really."

"Do you have any cool classes, though?"

"Ceramics was a lot of fun," I admit.

"Holy crap, that would be so cool," Ethan agrees, voice rising an octave as he gets himself worked up over the thought. I can't help but smile a little bit—Ethan is contagious. "So, what do you make? Can I see something? Can you make *me* something?"

We talk aimlessly as he drives us home, the conversation bouncing all over the place the way it usually does when Ethan is involved. He's so distracting, I'm able to forget my private misery for the length of the car ride. It's not until I'm home, and in the bedroom that used to be mine but is now a guest room, that the pain resurfaces.

Both of us will be better off in the long run, I tell myself miserably, as I try to fall asleep. Maybe if I repeat it enough times, it'll actually be true.

21

Henri

"HENRI?"

I turn quickly at the sound of my name being called, and heft the armful of binders into the crook of my elbow. Sam Jameson walks toward me, casually dressed in slacks and a blue button-up shirt. As usual, he's smiling at me in a friendly way that I'm sure is meant to put me at ease. Unfortunately, because anyone in a position of power makes me a little nervous, it does nothing to smother the butterflies that live in my stomach.

"Yes, sir?" He raises an eyebrow at me, and my cheeks burn as I correct myself immediately. "Sam. My apologies."

"I've never had to work so hard to convince someone *not* to be polite," he teases. There's no bite to the words, and his eyes are warm, so I relax a little bit.

"I am sorry. This is a hard habit to break. I fear it might take all summer."

Tucking his hands into his pockets, he smiles. "You busy?"

"No," I reply hastily, even though I am a little bit busy. This is the start of my fourth week into the internship, and I'm working with the media team. Today I'm supposed to be learning about the different players and accounts, and the sheer amount of reading I need to do is daunting. The department head also spoke to me about working together on a special project, which is both exciting and intimidating. All of a sudden, "busy" is an understatement.

"What's that you've got there?" Sam asks, nodding to the folders in my arms.

"I am to come up with interview questions," I tell him. "Miss Denise would like to do foreign-language interviews on social media for the non-native players. She is thinking that it would be fun to have me interview in German, French, and Russian, and we can put subtitles for the American fans. She says...well, she says some things that I should probably not repeat to my boss."

Sam laughs, reaching out a hand to pull some of the binders off of my pile.

"Here, let me help you carry. And don't worry, I already know Denise curses like a sailor. It sounds like a good idea— utilize all those languages you've got in your repertoire. Particularly now, when we've got two KHL rookies joining. I would like to speak with you, though, if you can spare a minute or two."

"Of course," I tell him, nerves multiplying as I follow him toward his office. Sam is the nicest of anyone I've worked with here, but he's still technically my boss and being told he needs to speak with me doesn't make me feel great. I'm desperate to do a good job here, and the thought that I might have done something wrong is terrifying.

"No need to look so nervous," he comments, letting me

walk into the office before he closes the door behind us. "I just wanted to check in. Nothing bad."

"Okay." I take a seat in front of his desk—a chair I've sat in many times so far this summer. Placing my media folders on the floor, I rest my hands in my lap and wait for him to speak.

"First of all, how are things going here? Any complaints? How are you liking the job so far?"

"Oh, no, I do not wish to complain. I am liking it here very much. If I do not become a sportscaster, I think perhaps I will try equipment manager. I believe I would enjoy Mr. Brad's job."

"I bet he loves it when you call him Mr. Brad," Sam muses. I smile, and relax a little more. He's so nice to me, it's impossible to be uncomfortable around him. "Is the commute okay? I know you're coming from the university area and that can be a bit of a drive."

"It is not so bad if traffic cooperates." I shrug. "Thank you for asking."

"Learning a lot?"

"Yes! There are many things I did not know that happen behind the scenes. I am only wishing it was the regular season, so I could be a part of it."

"Well, I've got an inbox full of nothing but compliments about you, so if you're looking for a job after you graduate, I'd say this would be a good place to start."

My chest burns like it's on fire at that, and I sit up a little straighter. "Thank you."

Sam clears his throat, fiddling with a pen sitting on his desk.

"Now, I'm not trying to overstep here, but I'm wondering if everything is going okay for you otherwise? Outside of here, I mean."

"You mean at home? At Carter's house?" I'm surprised by this. I would never gossip or complain while I am at work, and certainly not about Carter and Zeke. I would not have anything to complain about, even if I wanted to do so.

"I don't know." He shrugs. "I guess I'm just asking if you're all right. You come to work on time every day and you work hard—harder, in fact, than many of the *actual* employees. You don't complain, and you take direction with a smile on your face. But"—he pauses, fingers teasing the end of the pen again and sending it spinning—"the guy I met almost a year ago seemed a lot happier than the guy sitting in front of me. I just want to make sure there isn't anything I can do for you, that's all."

There is something a little shocking about kindness offered in such a straightforward fashion. I sit there in silence, listening to him speak as my throat slowly closes and my head fills with pressure. I can't even remember the last time I cried, and yet I worry I might start right now. All I can think about is Atlas and how last year I *was* happier than I am now. It seems incredible to me that Sam—who knows me only from these past three weeks of work—was able to pick up on that.

"Oh," I reply, because it's the only English word I'm able to wrap my tongue around at the moment.

"I'm sorry if I'm making you uncomfortable. That wasn't my intention. It's just that I know it can be hard to be so far away from family, and although I'm sure Carter Morgan is an excellent friend, I somehow doubt he's the best guy to bounce emotions off of."

We share a smile at that. I haven't really talked to anyone about what happened with Atlas, yet. I've never been one of those people who talks about themselves—I'm far more comfortable listening and offering advice to others than asking for it. But I'm also not presented with an opportunity to do so very often. I always try and project an air of competence, which occasionally backfires as it then gives people the impression that I don't need help, even when I do.

"I am not uncomfortable," I tell him, even though I am a little bit. Not because of him, though. Rather, because being the center of this type of attention makes me shy. "I, uhm, I do not wish to complain, and I am sorry if I have been in a rotten mood."

Mouth twisting, he runs a hand over his face and sighs. "Henri, that is *not* what I was trying to say. I only want to convey my willingness to listen in the event you needed someone to talk to."

"I am thinking you will laugh at me, when you hear that I am sad because of relationship problems," I tell him, trying for a joke and failing spectacularly. Sam doesn't laugh; doesn't even crack a smile.

"I'm sorry to hear that," he says seriously. All of a sudden, I can hardly wait to keep speaking. The words I'd tucked carefully away all summer pile up in my throat, desperate for air.

"Yes. I thought things were fine, but I was wrong because he has broken up with me." If Sam is surprised to hear my significant other was a man, he doesn't let on. I suppose the most surprising thing about this conversation is that I had a significant other at all. "Atlas—that is his name—is very hard to get to know. He is...what is it, when you are thinking only the bad things will happen? Cyclical?"

"Cynical," Sam corrects quietly, and I nod in agreement.

"Yes, he is cynical. He thinks I will break up with him, so he breaks up with me." There really isn't anything more to say than that. I could tell him that I've barely been able to sleep these past few weeks, and that my heart *hurts*. Nobody warned me that heartbreak was a physical ailment, beyond just the emotional. I miss Atlas so much, my body aches with it.

"That's difficult, especially for someone your age."

I nod, because I've thought this exact thing. Atlas is too young to be so angry about the world.

"Yes, I agree. I have had an easy life, though, and I think perhaps I am not understanding Atlas because of that."

Sam cocks his head to the side, surveying me. "Have you tried reaching out?"

"No. I am too nervous," I admit.

"But you want to?" he prompts.

"Yes, I want to. I want to do better at convincing him to keep me around. I was surprised before, and I did not say any of the things I wanted to say. If he spoke German, I would have done much better."

Sam chuckles. "Correct me if I'm wrong, but I don't see you being much of an arguer in any language."

"Well, no. But you are thinking I should call him, yes?" I fidget a little in my seat, eyes trained on Sam. This isn't how I saw this conversation going, but I mean to see it through, now. I really do want advice.

"I think you could check in; let him know you're thinking about him. Sometimes things don't work out, though, no matter how hard we try."

"I would be happy if he only wanted to be my friend. I only need him around to be happy," I tell him, and earn myself a soft smile.

The truth is, I like having sex with Atlas. He's the only person I've ever found that level of connection with—the only person I've ever looked at and *wanted*. But my favorite things are not the blowjobs or the kissing. My very favorite things are when he holds my hand, or finger-combs my hair; when he brings me ridiculous apple-themed items, and smiles when I call him German nicknames. If Atlas never wanted to kiss me again, I would be sad, but if he never wanted to talk to me again, I would be devastated.

Sam and I talk a little longer, and it's as though I can feel the muscles in my back unlocking. It's as though I've been holding myself still—bracing for impact—and unable to relax. Suddenly, I am exhausted. I want to crawl into my bed at Carter and Zeke's house, and think about dark hair and almond-shaped eyes. I want to think about what I am going to say when I call Atlas, and fall asleep as I let myself dream of maybes.

"Why don't you finish up early today?" Sam suggests, tapping his phone and noting that it's still several hours before quitting time. "You've earned it."

"Could I bring these with me, do you think?" I point at the media files. Sam nods.

"Absolutely. But don't spend all evening working on that. Relax a little bit too, okay?"

After giving him my word that I wouldn't squander my free afternoon working, I leave the building to blinding sunlight and thick, humid heat. I can't wait to get home and change out of my work clothes—slip into something casual and less constricting. Clothes Atlas would prefer to the polo shirt and khakis I'm wearing right now. Sighing, and desperately fighting against the gloom that threatens once more, I slowly walk to my car and stow my homework on the passenger seat.

The drive home, as Sam correctly observed, is long, but

today I don't mind. I use the time to think about Atlas, and
what I'm going to say when I call him, because that decision
has been made—I am going to reach out, and I'm going to do
it tonight. Even if Atlas no longer wants to date, I mean to
convince him that friendship is still an option. What absolutely is not an option is this: no contact, and a yawning
emptiness in my chest.

Carter's car is sitting in the driveway when I get home.
Carefully, I pull up next to it and get out. Neither him nor
Zeke was home this morning when I left for work, since
they'd spent the night in Charlotte for a "mini getaway" as
Zeke called it. I've been feeling badly about it ever since they
packed up the car and left, worried that I'd chased them out
of their own home.

Quietly, I walk in the front door, taking my shoes off and
leaving them in the hall closet next to Zeke's. Carter's appear
to have been kicked in haphazardly, so I take a moment to
straighten those as well. As I always do when I come home—
ever aware of the fact that they might be naked in the living
room—I shout out a greeting to let them know they're no
longer alone.

"Hello, I am home."

"Vas!" Zeke shouts happily from the kitchen, making me
smile. He peeks his head around the corner and beams at me,
walking forward to wrap an arm around my waist and give
me a side-armed hug. This is a new development in the last
few weeks, but I can't say I mind it. Nobody else is
hugging me.

"Hello, my friend. How was your trip?"

"It was a blast. I'll have to show you pictures of the bed-
and-breakfast. It was so nice! We missed you, though. How
was work?"

"It was…" I pause, thinking back to the conversation I had with Sam Jameson. "It was very interesting. I was missing you and Carter—it is strange to be here alone."

Zeke grins and leads the way back to the kitchen where Carter is standing at the stove, stirring something in a pot with a wooden spoon. He's glaring down at it, apparently trying to frighten it into cooking. Zeke reaches over, lips twitching, and takes the spoon back.

"What are we making?" I ask.

"Spaghetti," Carter grunts. "We brought this for you, Vas."

He shoves a paper gift bag across the counter roughly. Sitting down at the island, I pull out a box of chocolates.

"Those are from a local, family-owned business," Zeke explains. "Carter almost made himself sick by eating a dozen at once."

Chuckling, I pop open the box and select a piece. When I hold it out to Carter, he holds up a hand and shakes his head.

"Those are for you," he tells me. "I've learned my lesson."

"Thank you. That was kind of you to think of me." Carter waves this away, too, embarrassed. He comes to sit beside me at the island, watching Zeke drain the water from the pasta. "May I help you, Zeke?"

"I've got it," he replies.

I wait until we are all seated, and their mouths are busy with spaghetti, before I bring up Atlas. Clearing my throat, I set my fork down on the counter and link my fingers in front of me on the island.

"I am going to call Atlas," I announce.

"Fuck that guy," Carter mumbles around a half-chewed mouthful.

"Well, I am just wanting to talk to him. I miss him. I think perhaps we could be friends, if nothing else."

"I get it," Zeke tells me, smiling kindly. "I'd be the same way if our positions were reversed."

"Except I would never have said that shit to you," Carter points out, and Zeke sighs.

"True."

"Even so," I cut in, "I am going to call him after dinner. I am not going to let him get rid of me so easily."

"Be careful," Carter says, voice low as he fiddles with his fork and it clinks against the side of the bowl. "You're a nice guy...I just don't want him to take advantage of you."

I pat his arm to show him I'm grateful. Carter is a good friend—he is unfailingly loyal and feels a deep responsibility for those he cares about. It was this, more than anything, that had me keeping my mouth shut about Atlas and our breakup during my first week living here. But Zeke, ever tuned to the emotions of others, had carefully asked me one night if everything was okay. I certainly wasn't going to lie, so I'd told them some of what happened. Not word for word, but just enough for them to understand. Carter, predictably, had been mutinous on my behalf, though this has seemed to cool slightly in the weeks since.

"I will be careful," I promise, and then promptly change the subject. "Now, tell me about your getaway."

Later, I sit on the edge of my bed, door closed and room dark except for a single lamp on my nightstand. My phone, cradled in my hand, is pulled up to Atlas' contact. Taking a deep breath in, I click the call button and bring the phone to my ear.

22

Atlas

"HEY, YOUR PHONE IS RINGING."

I glance over to see Ryan, my youngest brother, poking his head out of my window. I'm sitting on the roof, having popped out the screen on my window and crawled through to have a smoke without being seen by my stepmom. I've also nabbed a bottle of whiskey from my dad's stash, which I now nudge behind me and out of sight of my brother.

"It's fine," I tell him. It's probably Nate, calling to tell me about cow tipping, or whatever the hell it is they do for fun on a ranch.

Instead of heading back inside to his video games like I expect him to, Ryan puts his palms on the windowsill and begins to crawl through. Pulling the cigarette from between my lips, I reach a hand out to him.

"Careful," I admonish. He glances up at me, before slowly crawling over to where I'm seated. He scoots his butt close enough to me to press his body against mine.

"You're not supposed to be smoking," he says, watching as I put it out on the shingles. I wave a hand through the air, trying to keep any lingering smoke away from him. Making sure the whiskey bottle is still firmly out of sight, I turn back to him.

"And you're not supposed to be on the roof."

"You won't let me fall," he says, shrugging. "Do you want to have a sleepover tonight? We could put the sleeping bags on the floor in my room, and watch a movie on the ceiling with the projector."

"Sure," I agree, and say a silent prayer for my lower back.

"You can pick the movie," he offers. I can't help but smile a little bit at that. Ryan is sweet and gentle, often giving the impression of being younger than he actually is. Sometimes, I worry about him. He's *too* kind. Like Henri.

"Ethan having a sleepover with us?" I ask, trying to distract myself from the pain thinking of Henri brings.

"No. You guys went to the golf course yesterday, so tonight it's my turn to hang out with you."

I snort at that. I've never been so popular as I am this summer—my brothers practically fighting each other over what I'm going to be doing, and who I'm going to be doing it with. I can't say I mind, and I'm already a little bummed, thinking about a day in the future when hanging out with me won't be quite so thrilling for them.

"Why are you so sad?" Ryan asks suddenly, skinny arm pressed against mine and bony shoulder poking me in the bicep.

"I'm not," I reply immediately, even though it's a bald-faced lie. Ryan frowns.

"Mom says you are."

I sigh and rub my eyes. Of course she does. My dad might be fucking clueless and not give a shit, but my stepmom is always two steps ahead of the rest of us. She's also aware of the walls I keep built up between us, which is probably why Ryan is out here talking to me about this and not her.

"I'm fine, Ry."

He huffs a little bit, scuffing his socked foot against the shingles. "Lying is bad," he says testily.

"Okay, fine, I'm just..." I pause, trying to figure out a way to explain a breakup to a kid who still thinks other boys and girls carry cooties. "I had a good friend at school and I told him I don't want to hang out anymore, that's all."

Ryan's nose scrunches up as he thinks about this.

"Why did you do that? You probably hurt his feelings. You need to say sorry," he tells me, in a tone of voice suitable for a lecture.

"Yeah, probably," I agree, wishing I could take a pull from the whiskey. "But it's too late, now. Some things you can't apologize for."

"That's not what Mom says. Mom says if you mess up, you make it right. I have to say sorry to Ethan *all* the time." He groans dramatically. "You don't get to be mean to people just because you're grown up."

"All right, I'll try," I promise, because he'll never let it go otherwise. Besides, the damn kid is right. I told Henri he meant nothing—said it right to his face. I should be begging for forgiveness on bended knee.

"What's your friend's name?" Ryan asks.

"Henri."

"Cool."

I laugh a little bit, feeling marginally better than I did

even just an hour ago. My relationship with my parents might be a clusterfuck on the best of days, but I love my brothers.

"He's from Germany," I add.

"No *way*!" Ryan exclaims, finding this just as exciting as I'd known he would. "That's so cool. You need to say sorry so that he'll invite you to visit, and then you can take me along."

"Sure," I agree, even though I know it'll never happen.

We sit there for a little longer, watching the sun go down over the rooftops. Ryan stays quiet, leaning against me and seemingly happy to just sit in silence with me. If Ethan were out here with us, he'd be losing his mind with boredom. After my butt has gone numb from sitting still for so long, I give Ryan a nudge.

"Let's go in," I suggest. "You can pick out a movie for us to watch tonight."

We crawl back in through the window, and I do my best to keep the bottle of whiskey hidden behind my back. He doesn't seem to notice when I slip it under the comforter on my bed, but walks purposely toward the door.

"It's probably dinnertime," he tells me.

"You go down. I'm not hungry." That isn't exactly the truth, but it's close enough. The actual truth is, I'm not hungry enough to sit at a dinner table with my dad and listen to him talk over and around me like I'm not there. I'm not hungry enough to listen to the barely veiled barbs about what a disappointment I am. In short, I don't need to listen to Dad expand on things I already know. I'll go down later to raid the refrigerator when everyone is asleep. For now, cigarettes and whiskey will get me by.

"Okay. I'll tell Mom you're not hungry," he declares agreeably. I nod, watching as he closes my door on the way out of my room. My stepmom won't buy the *I'm not hungry* line, but neither will she call me on it. She and I will never be close, but we're at the point now where we understand one another. She knows I don't get along with Dad, and that pushing the relationship won't help anything.

With Ryan gone, I pull the whiskey out and finally take a long drink. These last few weeks have been damn near unbearable, helped along only by the alcohol I've been stealing from my dad's liquor cabinet. I'm not sure what it says about him that he hasn't mentioned noticing the missing bottles, even though I've been at it for weeks.

Fingers wrapped around the neck of the bottle, I go looking for my phone after remembering that it had been ringing earlier. I find it and the bottle falls to the floor with a thump, tipping over and spilling whiskey across the carpet. I barely notice. My eyes are trained on the screen of my cellphone, illuminated and showing a single missed call from Henri Vasel.

"Fuck," I mutter, shaking myself out of my stupor enough to bend over and right the bottle. I'm going to have a hell of a time explaining why my carpet smells like a distillery, but that is a problem for future Atlas. Fingers trembling slightly, I call him back.

The phone rings for long enough that I wonder if I missed my shot to talk to him. And serves me right if I did. Sighing, I'm just pulling the phone away from my ear—not intending to leave a voicemail—when the call connects and Henri's beautiful, accented voice greets me.

"Atlas?"

That soft, lilting voice is like a fist to the throat. Closing my eyes, I take a deep breath and reach for calm. God, I've missed him. The only person I've ever missed so badly is my biological mother. It's a terrifying realization—knowing that I care for Henri enough to give him that kind of power to hurt me. I fight against the urge to hang up the phone—my first instinct always being to run.

"Hey," I whisper back, because that's really the best I can do. Henri's silent for a moment, breathing softly. I can practically feel his trepidation—our last encounter looming large between us.

"Is this all right for me to be calling you?" he asks.

"Yeah."

He clears his throat, talking fast as though trying to get all the words out before I hang up or interrupt him. "How are you doing, Atlas? Are you enjoying your summer? How are your brothers?"

My summer has sucked because I miss you, and it's my own fault I feel like shit and it's everything I deserve, I want to say, but don't.

"It's been okay. Not...not great. It's been good hanging out with Ryan and Ethan, though. Ryan and I are doing a camp-out on his bedroom floor tonight."

Henri chuckles softly, the sound as soothing as ocean waves. "That sounds like a good time. I am sure they are missing you when you are at school."

"Yeah. What about you? How's the internship going?"

"It is good to be working. I enjoy it very much. But I...I am missing speaking to you every day. Perhaps we could be friends, yes? I know you do not wish to be with me, but maybe we can still talk. Friends," he repeats.

Sitting down on my floor with my back to the wall, I take a drink of whiskey and close my eyes. Fucking friends. It's a good solution. A way for us to keep in touch and maybe hang out every now and then once we're both back at South Carolina U. A small part of me is grateful he's giving me this out—presenting me with the seemingly perfect solution to the mess I made.

But the greater part of me doesn't want to be his friend. I miss our accidental relationship. Friendship is great and all, but I want to be able to reach over and touch his hair whenever I get the urge. Count the calluses on his palms. Give lazy blowjobs when he's feeling in the mood, and just fall asleep breathing the same air when he isn't. Nearly a full month after I dropped a bomb on us, and I'm growing more certain every day that I made a colossal mistake.

I can either protect myself from the imagined hurt of the future, or live with the very real hurt of the present. I chose wrong.

"Henri, I'm sorry about what I said."

There is a sharp intake of breath from the other end of the phone. Opening my eyes, I contemplate the whiskey bottle again. *Henri wouldn't like it that you're drinking*, I think. Sighing, I push it away and close my eyes again, leaning my head against the wall. Downstairs, I can hear my family sitting down for dinner. Ethan is laughing, probably at his own story or joke, and there is the soft rumble of my dad's voice, probably telling him to quiet down. He's always saying Ethan's exuberance gives him a headache.

"It is okay, Atlas," Henri replies softly.

"No, it's not. I...I was a dick, and I said shit I shouldn't have—shit I didn't even mean. I'm not good at letting people in," I admit, glad that we're having this conversation over the phone and I don't have to look into his blue eyes as I say the words.

"I know, Bärchen. It is okay," he repeats soothingly.

My throat feels tight all of a sudden, and I'm wishing I hadn't shoved the whiskey out of reach. I'm not used to people being this kind and understanding. I'm used to mistakes and apologies being dangled over my head as ammunition for future arguments, not this calm and generous acceptance without a trace of anger in his voice.

"It's not okay," I argue. "You can yell at me, if you want. You *should* yell at me."

"Oh, I am not this kind of person who yells," he says, and I huff a small laugh. "I wanted to hear your voice and talk about your summer. I did not call looking for a fight."

"No, you wouldn't, I suppose," I muse. "I really got lucky the day Dr. Robertson assigned us to be partners."

"That is funny, Atlas, because I am thinking that *I* was the lucky one."

We sit in silence for a minute, breathing softly together. If we were in the same room, I'd ask him what he wanted and wait to see if today was a day when he felt like being touched. I'd ask him if I could spend the night.

"Atlas?"

"Mm?"

"Why are you not wanting to, how did you say it...let people in?"

I don't answer right away. I've never actually told the story out loud, so I'm unsure of how the words fit together. How the hell do I pick the scab off of a wound that's been festering for over a decade?

"My mom—my biological mom, that is—left when I was five years old. She...well, she just brought me over to the neighbor's house one day, asked if they could watch me while she went to the grocery store, and then never came back. She'd bought a single plane ticket, on my dad's fucking credit card, *weeks* prior. Had her bags packed and everything—he never even noticed."

I pause, trailing my fingers over the wet, whiskey-stained carpet. Henri is silent, thank God. I'm not sure I could choke the entire story out if he interrupted with platitudes and sympathy.

"She was, is, from Hawaii, so that's where she went. Just packed up and left. And then it was like...Dad didn't even *care*. He was more annoyed about the trouble of getting a divorce with someone thousands of miles away than he was with the fact that his wife and the mother of his child just left him. He was already dating my stepmom before the divorce even went through, and they were married less than a year later. Ethan was born right after that, and it was...it felt like my dad had just decided his original family was flawed, so he went out and found a new one. A better one."

Needing to wet my throat, I bend forward and reach for the discarded whiskey. I'm not looking to get drunk, but the first time I tell this story isn't going to be when I'm completely sober, either.

"And I look *exactly* like my mom. I don't have super solid memories of her, because I was so young, but I've seen pictures and we are pretty much twins. I inherited all of her Japanese traits."

"She was beautiful, then," Henri comments softly. I let the words sit warm in my chest for a second, bolstering myself to continue.

"Dad hates it. I can tell every time he looks at me that he's wishing I wasn't a walking reminder of the woman who left him. Hell, he probably wishes she'd taken me along. My dad and stepmom are both, like, super blond and they have blue eyes; Ryan and Ethan look exactly like them. They look like a family, and I look like a transplant. Nobody ever assumes we share DNA. I look like the adopted Asian kid."

"That is hard."

"I mean...yeah, sometimes. Mostly because my dad *makes* it hard. He's always saying I take after my mom in everything, which isn't a compliment when it comes from him. It's all: *Atlas, your grades might be better if you took after me more than your mother.* Every single thing I do, that he doesn't like, circles back to my goddamn DNA. I hate it, Henri, I fucking *hate* it. And I know it bothers my stepmom, too, like their marriage has three people in it instead of two."

"It would be difficult, I think, to trust someone not to hurt you, when the one person who is supposed to love you didn't," Henri says, so softly I can barely hear the words. It's hard to breathe again; my throat tight around a golf ball–sized lump. He continues, still in that same low, soothing tone. "I am thinking it would be hard to love others when you are hurt so young."

"I'm really sorry," I tell him, because yes, my family might have broken my heart, but I'm the one who broke his. "I'm just really fucking sorry."

"Bärchen, it is all right. Thank you, but I am not needing to hear apologies, okay? Do you want to talk of something else?"

"God, yes," I say on a groan, and he laughs.

"Tell me something good," he prompts. I walk over to my bed and lie down, getting comfortable. The only good things here are my brothers, so they are who I talk about. Long, rambling stories that probably don't make a lot of sense to him, but nonetheless feel better to say than the one I told about my mom.

"Goodness," Henri exclaims, when I tell him my dad

bought my seventeen-year-old brother a brand-new car. "This is probably a bad idea, yes?"

"Probably." I laugh.

"When I came here for school, Jakob helped me. He bought my car and Mama was not happy about this. She does not trust these American drivers."

"Fair," I concede. "Do you have to work tomorrow?"

I pull the phone away from my ear to check the time. Although he loosened up on the rigid scheduling of his days toward the end of the semester, I doubt that relaxation carried over into the summer. He's probably past his scheduled bedtime right now.

"I do, yes."

"I should probably let you go, then."

He's quiet on the other end of the line, breathing softly. I really don't want to let him go. I want to keep talking well into the night, and hear all the things I've missed out on during these past few weeks of silence. What I really want is a confirmation that this is not a one-off. That I could text him tomorrow and expect a reply; maybe another phone call after work if I'm lucky.

"Perhaps I might call you tomorrow?" Henri asks carefully, and I let out the breath I didn't even know I was holding.

"Sure," I agree.

"Goodnight, Bärchen. Thank you for calling me back."

I can't fight the smile as we hang up the phone, Henri's lovely, accented voice ringing in my ear long after the line goes dead. He doesn't hate me. More than that, though, he still wants to *know* me. I feel almost dizzy with relief. This outcome was too much to hope for, and certainly not what I'd been expecting. And even though we didn't have an explicit conversation about where we go from here, at least I know there will be something. Friends, boyfriends, whatever it is, I want it.

Three weeks without Henri Vasel was more than enough for me.

23

Henri

THE FOLLOWING MORNING, I wake up long before my alarm and immediately reach for my phone. I don't have an active imagination by any estimation, but I can hardly believe that conversation with Atlas actually happened. And, based on my call history, happen, it did. Feeling a little better about our situation now that I know he won't ignore me completely, I send him a text.

HENRI

Good morning, Atlas. I hope you slept well.

ATLAS

i slept on the floor which is to say i did not
sleep at all

The reply came so fast, he must have been looking at his phone when I messaged him. Smiling, I prop myself up against the headboard and text back.

HENRI

And what movie did we watch?

ATLAS

the dark knight

ryan loves superhero comics

HENRI

It was good'?

ATLAS

well christian bale is hot so

Chuckling, I hover my thumbs over the keyboard and try to think of something else to ask. What I really want to ask is if he will be my boyfriend on purpose, not as an accident. I want to ask if he will let me take care of him and treat him kindly—the way he deserves to be treated. Instead, I go with:

HENRI

What are you doing today?

ATLAS

unsure probably something with ethan though

dad has been making noise about going to a car show but i would rather drip battery acid in my eye than do that

might just come down with a cold and lie in bed all day

you?

HENRI

I am working today, and then I will do a workout with my friend Carter. After that, I will make dinner with my friend Zeke. I am teaching German dishes.

ATLAS

like the one you made me?

I smile down at my phone. Last Christmas is one of my favorite memories.

HENRI

Yes! Zeke is a very good learner. Much better than me, who cannot remember the difference between tbsp and tsp.

ATLAS

lmfao well to be fair those are pretty similar

I stare down at my phone in silence, unsure of what that acronym might mean. Across the hall, I can hear the soft noises of someone moving about. Probably Zeke, who usually wakes up earlier than Carter. Sliding out of bed, I pull pajama pants over my boxers and tug on a shirt, before leaving my room and heading downstairs to the kitchen. I've got eggs frying, and bread toasting when Zeke makes an appearance.

"Good morning, Vas," he greets me cheerfully. I pick up the mug I pulled for him and pour him some coffee. My goal this summer is to make sure Carter and Zeke never have to do things themselves that I could have done for them.

"Good morning, Zeke," I reply, which makes him laugh for some reason. Zeke is always smiling and laughing. He is, in many ways, the precise opposite of Atlas. Handing him the mug, I nudge him away from the oven.

"Take a seat. I shall handle breakfast," I tell him. "Carter is sleeping in, yes?"

Zeke snorts. "Yeah. He told me he wants to take advantage of the off-season and catch up on sleep—he's going into hibernation. But honestly, I'm so used to getting up at five, I don't think I could reset my body clock even if I tried."

"I am the same," I agree. "Zeke, do you know what this 'lmfao' means?"

"It means: laughing my fucking ass off," he tells me, taking a sip of coffee and eyeing me over the rim of the cup. "Did you end up reaching out to Atlas last night?"

"I did, yes." The toast pops up, so I'm spared eye contact with him as I talk. Head down, I butter it carefully. "I called him and we are talking for a while. We are going to be friends."

"Is that what you want?"

Carefully, I plate the eggs before pushing it across the island to him. He murmurs a thank-you, takes another sip of coffee, and gives me a politely questioning look. I wish I had a good answer for him.

"I...will be glad to see him still," I answer diplomatically. "But no, it is not what I am wanting. I would prefer a...try again?"

"A do-over?"

"Yes, that." I smile at him gratefully. "Atlas and I did every-thing all wrong, and I am wishing we could have a do-over. We are good together, he and I, and I think we could be better with a little more trying."

"You've got the summer—maybe you could talk and get to know one another without anything else distracting you," he suggests diplomatically.

I nod down at my plate, taking a small bite of toast and

chewing through my thoughts. Carter once told me that Zeke is demi, but *Zeke* has never told me that. I'd like to talk to him about Atlas, because I think he, more than anyone else, will understand what I mean. But stronger than this desire is the worry that I'll overstep and make him uncomfortable. Thinking that maybe the best way to broach the subject is to talk about myself, I set my fork down.

"I have always enjoyed dating, ever since I came here for school. I like to talk to people, and learn new things. But Atlas is the first person I looked at and...enjoyed looking at," I finish, somewhat ridiculously. It's not easy to find an appropriate way to explain that you wanted to have sex with someone for the first time in your adult life. "I am not wanting to scare him, but I am also not wanting to let him go. I worry there will never be another Atlas, yes?"

Rubbing a finger over my brow, I look down at my food and wish I had the appetite to eat. That was a terrible way to explain what I mean, but I can't think of anything better. Zeke is going to think I am a crazy person.

"I think you and I are very similar, Vas," Zeke says carefully, drawing my gaze back to his. "And I think your concerns are valid. There are a lot of people in the world who can go through heartbreak, turn around, and find another person they are just as attracted to. But there are also people that struggle with that—people like myself—and it's perfectly reasonable to want to hold on to that feeling once you've found it. I don't know what I would do if Carter left me. I honestly don't. I'll never love anyone the way I love him. I think I would end up dying alone."

"Well, this is simply not going to happen," I tell him, slightly alarmed at the words. Zeke smiles and takes a bite of egg.

"I don't think so either, but the point remains that I'm probably more likely to be struck by lightning than find another person in the world that I'm attracted to, or that I love as much as Carter. And the same might be said of you."

I heave a sigh of relief. "Yes, you are right. As always, you are right. Thank you for understanding."

"Atlas might understand as well, if you give him a chance."

"Perhaps, yes. Maybe it is as you said, and we shall take the summer to get to know one another the proper way."

Zeke and I finish breakfast, chatting companionably as we eat. Carter has still not made an appearance when I have to go to work, so I leave Zeke with a request to bid him good morning from me, and walk out the door. After parking my car, there is a message waiting from Atlas.

ATLAS

have a good day at work

HENRI

May I call you later?

ATLAS

you may

Smiling, I tuck my phone into the pocket of my khaki pants and walk inside, thinking about Atlas as I do.

THE NEXT COUPLE of weeks pass in a haze of long days working my internship, evenings spent in the company of my friends, and nights on the phone with Atlas. In many ways, I am having the best summer of my life. Never before have I had so much to fill my time, or so many people asking for it.

Feeling absurdly grateful, I walk the halls of the rink with a smile on my face. Everyone I pass greets me by name and an answering smile. I really, truly love it here. Finished for the day, I stop by the practice rink to watch a little bit of their training. Carter is on the ice but not in goal. Troy Nichols is working on one-timing slap shots, fed by one of the coaching staff, and it would be dangerous to have their goalie in the net. Seeing me standing by the boards, Carter skates over.

"Heading home?" he asks.

"Yes. How is practice?"

"Good," he grunts, head turned to watch Nichols. "Once they finish with this, I think they wanted to run through a few face-off drills working from the defensive zone. I'll probably be awhile, still."

"Max is coming over tonight, yes? Zeke mentioned?"

"Oh, yeah, he is. Luke is off doing what-the-fuck-ever." Carter waves a hand and I bite back a grin. He loves to pick at Luke, and pretend not to like him. Carter is not such a good liar that he thinks he is.

"We shall have to invite him another day. Otherwise we will miss out on the pleasure of his company," I say mildly. Carter eyes me, like he knows I'm giving him a hard time.

"Mm-hm," he hums noncommittally, eyes flicking back to where Troy Nichols is still firing missiles into the back of his net. "You heard from housing yet?"

Surprised by the change of conversation, it takes me a second to think through the question and answer him. He leans against the boards with an elbow, eyes still on the ice but attention on me.

"No, but probably this week. I will call Jakob to help me with the forms."

Carter raises a hand in acknowledgment as the defensive coach calls out to him, letting him know he's actually done for the day and they'll regroup tomorrow. Clearing his throat, he turns toward me fully. Knowing Carter as well as I do, I can tell by his expression that he's about to embark on what he considers to be an uncomfortable conversation.

"I want you to stay with us, instead of moving back into the dorms." I sigh, but Carter continues with a scowl before I can interrupt. "It's your last year, Vas, you shouldn't have to stay in the fucking dorms. Our house is more comfortable, and it's close enough to campus for you to still walk to class if you want. You can cook your own food instead of eating the café shit."

"But, Carter, what about Zeke's grandmother? I thought she was to be moving in with you?"

He snorts violently. "Yeah, the two of you could give lessons on stubborn. She won't budge for now, saying she doesn't want to impose on us."

"I do not wish to impose, either," I point out gently. "You have been kind to let me stay over the summer, but—"

"Zeke hates being alone when I'm gone. I hate *leaving* him alone when I'm gone. If you moved in permanently, you'd be doing us a favor and making yourself more comfortable in the process. I'd feel better, knowing you were there."

I pause. Carter isn't a liar—he wouldn't tell me something about Zeke unless it was truthful. Playing for the NHL means Carter is gone a lot during the season, and it's entirely plausible that Zeke finds the loneliness uncomfortable.

"You have already talked to Zeke about this?" I ask carefully.

"Yeah. He loves having you there and so do I. You're already moved in, Vas, just *stay*." I can tell by his expression that he's fast losing his ability to maintain this conversation.

"I will pay you the housing fee that is usually paid to the school," I tell him, holding up a hand to waylay the angry outburst I know will follow that statement. "It is fair, Carter, you cannot pretend it is not. You have given me room and board for a whole summer for free. That is enough. If I am to stay, I will pay."

"You can pay the same thing Zeke did when he first moved in," Carter offers, and I jump on it immediately.

"Okay," I agree, though my confidence wavers when he smirks at me. I thought I'd just won that argument, but now I'm unsure. Carter looks far too happy for someone who just agreed to something he loves fighting me on.

"Great. It's settled, then. Apparently I'm done for the day, so let's get out of here. I'm fucking starving."

Max's car is already in the driveway when I get home, and a quick glance inside the vehicle confirms he is already in the house. After going through my usual motions of putting my shoes and coat away, I find Zeke where I usually do: the kitchen. Max is sitting on one of the island stools, looking serious as he carefully places pepperoni slices on a pizza.

"Hello, my friends," I greet them.

"Vas!" Zeke replies exuberantly, walking over to give me a side hug.

"Hey, Vas," Max greets me, sharing a quick smile before he goes back to putting pepperoni equidistance apart on the pizza. "I came a little early, so we made pizza."

"That looks delicious," I tell them truthfully, walking over to the sink and washing my hands. "How may I assist?"

When Carter gets home, the kitchen is ringing with

laughter and music; there are two homemade pizzas in the oven and one being cleaned up off the floor. I look up from where I am kneeling on the hardwood, searching for stray cheese.

"I thought you were right behind me," I comment, earning a grunt in reply.

"Got caught up talking to some of the guys. What happened there?"

"Slipped off the pizza spatula thing," Max explains, lifting up the item in question to show Carter. "Don't worry, we've got another started."

He gestures to the dough spread out on the island. Carter leans over to steal a few toppings and pop them into his mouth, before walking over to rest against the island next to Zeke. I go back to cleaning up the floor and the cabinetry, while Max finishes putting the toppings on the next pizza. He talks aimlessly as he does, him and Carter falling into their usual NHL chatter. Once I'm satisfied that the pizza mess is sufficiently cleaned up, I leave to dispose of the towels into the laundry and take a detour to my room to change. After pulling on a pair of shorts and a T-shirt, I have a sudden inspiration.

Taking a quick photograph of myself in the bathroom mirror, I text it to Atlas.

ATLAS

oh my god am i witnessing the death of the khaki right now

HENRI

I wore the khaki pants to work.

ATLAS

for shame

no polo shirt though i am so proud

HENRI

I was provided two uniform shirts to wear
during my internship, and I get to keep them.
Two new polo shirts for my collection.

ATLAS

dear god they had no idea the monster they
were feeding

Smiling, I tuck my phone into my pocket and head back downstairs. Everyone has moved to the living room as we wait for the food to be ready. When Max sees me walk into the room, he straightens and clears his throat.

"So, I've got news," he says. Walking over to the couch, I take a seat next to where Carter and Zeke are sitting so close together, they appear to be conjoined. "When I was in Detroit a few weeks ago for rookie training camp, Luke came with me."

I nod, because I'd already known this. Max left the day after graduation to join his NHL team for a few weeks of training. Next week, he'll be flying back to stay for good, as the pre-season training begins in earnest. Carter, too, will be a busier man once more, the summer flying by and scattering my friends. My heart hurts, as it always does, when I think about how little I will see their faces soon. I smile at Max, not wanting him to know the reminder made me sad.

"Yes, Luke sent me a few photographs," I tell him.

"So, yeah, he's actually going to come with me when I move. We found an apartment. Together," Max clarifies when nobody seems shocked by this pronouncement. Carter is the first to rally.

"I'll pray for you," he says, and then grunts from what I suspect was an elbow in the ribs from Zeke.

"That's great," Zeke tells Max. "Did Luke find a job?"

"Well, so that's where he's at right now, actually." Max sits forward, voice rising excitedly. "He's interviewing for a job with the Tigers! He's been applying *everywhere,* and had a couple virtual interviews, but this is the first one that led to a second interview. He flew out yesterday to meet with them!"

I have no idea who the Tigers are, but I can recognize the enthusiasm in Max's voice as a good thing. I beam at him.

"This is fantastic news. I do not see how they cannot offer him a job. Luke is very talented."

Max smiles back. "I've been worried about it, to be honest. Luke can't just sit at home and relax, he has to *do* things. I was...well, I was worried he wouldn't want to come with me if he didn't get a job, I guess."

Carter snorts, drawing everyone's attention. "I don't think there was any stopping him from going with you," he says, which I happen to agree with. "He would have folded himself up into your suitcase."

"I am very happy to hear this. I would not have wanted you to go alone," I tell Max, and when his eyes meet mine, I can see the unspoken words between us. He hasn't told Carter and Zeke what he shared with me last year, about what happened to him, nor has he brought it up again with me. He smiles a small, soft smile like he knows where my head is at.

"Zeke and I have news, too," Carter says suddenly, and his mouth twists into a decidedly wolfish grin. "Vas is moving in with us. Permanently."

"For the school year," I correct, as Zeke's head whips toward me on a gasp, and a wide smile blooms on his face.

"Really? You agreed?"

"Yes, but I will be paying—"

"—half of the utilities," Carter fills in happily. I frown at him.

"Well, yes, but I had agreed to pay the same rent that you asked from Zeke," I remind him.

"Right. Which was half of the utilities and nothing more," Carter replies smugly. I gape at him. Zeke sends me a mildly commiserating look.

"I told you he won't take your money," he mumbles. Max, for his part, looks like he's fighting a silent battle against a smile and losing.

"You tricked me," I say to Carter, impressed with him, while also feeling annoyed at myself.

"Sure did," he replies without a trace of apology.

Zeke's pizza, just like everything else he makes, is delicious, and earns him no less than three appreciative *I love yous* from Carter. It doesn't matter how fervently I wish for time to slow, however. Eventually the food is consumed, the kitchen is cleaned, and the day ends. I give Max a ridiculously long hug, trying to convey how much I care for him and how hard it will be when he is gone.

"Ich liebe dich," I tell him quietly. He makes a low sound and squeezes me a little tighter. Max doesn't speak German, but he doesn't need to, to understand the sentiment.

"I'll still be around," he whispers into my shoulder, like my sudden melancholy is apparent to him. "I'll text you."

"Yes, we will still talk," I agree, even though I know it won't be the same. Just like when Carter left school. The loss of him at practice every day was like suddenly finding myself without my left hand. I would look for him in the net and feel a jolt of disappointment when I saw Micky there in his place. It will be the same with Max, I know. Perhaps worse, since I have played right wing to Max's center for the past three seasons. How on earth am I supposed to play without him?

"We will fly out to watch when you play Carter's team," Zeke pipes up, and I share a grateful smile with him.

With Max gone home to call Luke and hear about his interview, Carter and Zeke retreat to their bedroom where I can hear the soft murmur of voices and the occasional burst of quiet laughter. After showering, I stretch out on my bed and call Atlas.

"Henri," he answers, and I immediately feel less sad than I did before.

"Hello, Bärchen, how are you this evening?"

"You will never guess what happened," he says, and then launches into a ridiculous story about a backyard baseball game gone wrong. A slow smile creeps across my lips as I listen to him talk about his brothers and a broken window.

"So, I am guessing your dad is likely unhappy about this?" I ask, and am rewarded with a throaty laugh from Atlas.

"Pissed! To be fair, it was kind of nuts to be playing baseball in the backyard. Especially with Ethan, who's wild to the point of danger. But it was fun, and my stepmom wasn't even mad about it. It was so funny, Henri, we were standing there just...staring at the window and trying to decide if we should make a run for it, and she came out the back door with the ball in her hand."

"Uh-oh," I muse, smiling.

"Right? But she just tosses it to Ryan, points away from the house, and says: *aim that way, please.* Fucking *hilarious.* Of course, Dad blew his top when he got home. He's convalescing in his sitting room now, probably drinking a bourbon and ruminating on how much better his life would be without kids."

"I am thinking your dad is a little unreasonable." Atlas snorts violently. "To be honest, though, I am unsure how my own parents might react to a broken window. I was a very well-behaved child."

"You? I simply cannot believe that."

"I know," I agree seriously. "I am full of surprises."

Atlas laughs again, and I miss him so badly it hurts. I miss the way his dark hair shines like it's oiled, and the way his mouth only seems to soften for me. I miss kissing him, and touching him, and the way it felt to let him do it to me. I sigh, because those things are gone.

"What's wrong?" Atlas asks.

"It is nothing. I am being silly. Tell me more about your day."

He huffs. "Henri, come on. Tell me. You don't sound like yourself."

"Oh, it is only that I had to say goodbye to my friend today. Max is very talented, as you know. He is to play hockey for the NHL, and will be going to Detroit soon. I am happy for him, but I am also sad for myself because I will miss him very badly. It is selfish."

He's silent, and I imagine I can feel the quiet judgement. I should only feel proud of Max; glad of his good fortune and talent. I should not think of myself at all, because it has nothing to do with me. Opening my mouth to say this to Atlas, he cuts me off with a firm, "Don't be an idiot."

I laugh. Atlas is so much like Carter, it is sometimes worrisome. I imagine they'd get along well, if they ever met. They could sit in a quiet room and glare at one another.

"You are literally the least selfish person I know," he

continues hotly. "You're allowed to miss your friend. Jesus, and people think *I'm* hard on myself. And just because he's going off to be a hockey star, or whatever, that doesn't mean he won't miss you just as bad. You guys practically live in each other's pockets during the season. You can't tell me he won't be sad when he looks over at his new teammates and realizes you're not one of them."

"Well, now I feel worse." I sigh, and Atlas laughs again. How lucky for me to have heard it so many times tonight. "I worry for him, too. I would feel better if Carter or I were with him."

"Isn't he with that Luke guy?"

"Yes. He will be going along."

"So, everything is fine," Atlas says firmly. "You can't always worry about everyone else. You'll drive yourself mad."

"You are right. My mother tells me I am a caretaker. She tells me it is born from my desire to make other people happy. She tells me I must try not to be these things all the time."

"Your mom the doctor, right?"

"Correct."

"She sounds kind of cool," he says quietly, and I wonder if he's thinking of his own mother. My poor Atlas. If only that were a hurt I could soothe.

"Yes, she is cool. People are always surprised, yes? Jakob and I did not follow in their footsteps. We are both choosing to do something different. Most people think we will be doctors, too."

"You would be a terrible doctor," Atlas says honestly.

"Yes," I agree, smiling helplessly at the ceiling.

"You're way too empathetic. You'll be great at sports media, though. You're the perfect guy to be impartial. Not to mention, you practically live and breathe hockey. And you're killing it at your internship."

I open my mouth to demure, but the fact is, he's right. I am doing very well at my job, and have been told many times over. I decide to take the compliment instead of arguing it away.

"Thank you. I have other news, as well."

"Oh?" The word comes out on a yawn, and there is the faint rustle of cloth in the background, as though he's cozied up in bed. My poor heart is never going to survive this night of longing.

"I am not returning to the dorms for my final semesters. I will be here, at Carter and Zeke's house. Carter tricked me into it, so I shall remain living here under quiet protest."

Atlas snorts. "Better than the dorms, though. You'll be able to make all the fancy German bread you want."

"True."

"And sleep in a bed that's bigger than a prison inmate's," Atlas continues.

"True," I whisper, thinking of all the enjoyable nights he and I spent in my small, dorm-sized bed; the mornings we woke up pressed together simply because there was nowhere else to go. Atlas yawns again, and I take pity on him, loath though I am to hang up the phone. "You are tired, Bärchen. Let us get some rest and we shall speak tomorrow, yes?"

"Okay," he replies sleepily. "Text me in the morning?"

"Always," I promise, remaining on the line with the phone pressed to my ear so that I can listen as he falls asleep.

24

Atlas

WHAT STARTED off as a summer promising to be the worst of my life, has somehow managed to be the best. Perhaps it's that they're getting older, but this is the first time I've ever felt quite so enamored with my siblings. Nearly every single day this summer was spent in one or both of their company, and had it not been for that, I'm not sure I would have survived. At the very least, I would have ended the summer as an alcoholic.

Add in the fact that Henri and I are now speaking daily, and really, what the hell do I have to complain about?

Dad drives me back to the airport, awkwardly trying to make stilted conversation. I apply only half of my attention to the chatter, and eventually he stops trying. I'm glad. It's hard to talk when all I can think about is the fact that soon I'll be back at school and in the same postal code as Henri.

I want to see him, while feeling afraid of what might

happen if I do. In all our chats, he hasn't mentioned wanting to meet up, and neither have I. We've carefully danced around the topic of school, using classes and hockey to distract us from the fact that we can no longer use distance as an excuse not to connect.

I know I made a mistake. I know I hurt him, and that's not something I can easily forgive myself for. Henri has, but I can't. And if I do—what then? I still don't trust relationships, myself, or other people.

But I trust Henri, and that's what matters.

Feeling sick to my stomach, I unclip my seat belt as Dad pulls up to passenger drop-off. He gets out of the car and pulls my suitcase from the trunk, before shoving his hands into his pockets and standing awkwardly next to me.

"Well," he says, "let me know if you need anything."

"Okay. Thanks." I give him an uncomfortable, one-armed hug which he returns belatedly, only as I start to pull away.

"Have a good semester," he calls to my retreating back. I wave a hand in acknowledgment of the words, but can't trust my voice. Any reminder of school starting, and being back on the SCU campus, tightens my throat to the point of discomfort. At this rate, even if I do see Henri, I'm not sure I'll be able to force any words out.

The flight to South Carolina is unremarkable, as is the Uber I pick up from the airport. By the time I'm walking through the front door of my shared house, I'm feeling distinctly travel worn. I need a hot shower, hot food, and a warm bed in an air-conditioned room. Hefting my suitcase, I head up the stairs toward my room. I'm the last of my roommates to arrive, as indicated by our house group chat. Nate drove in yesterday morning, and the two newest roommates

—replacing those who graduated last semester—moved their stuff in the day before.

My room looks exactly the same as it did when I left it. Small and nondescript as it is, I can't help but feel a tug of something like happiness when I look around. I like it here. Dropping my suitcase on the floor, I open it up and pull out the bare minimum of supplies needed to wash an airport off of one's skin, before heading into the bathroom for a shower.

I do less showering, and more standing under the hot water in a trance. Henri's already here and tucked happily away in the spare room of his friends' house. He'd gone home to Germany for a quick visit with family before classes start, and even with that time change between us, we'd somehow managed to talk every day. I'd told him I'd be back in South Carolina today, and he'd responded that he'd be back a couple days prior—neither of us took it any farther than that. No offers to grab coffee or meet up for dinner. If we are friends, it is quite possible that Henri prefers we remain the virtual kind. I can't blame him.

Walking back across the hall to my room, toiletries clutched in my hand and towel flung over one shoulder, I step in to find Nate stretched out on my bare mattress.

"Did you miss me?" he asks, smiling wide beneath his summer tan. His eyes look impossibly green against that brown skin, and his brown hair is shot through with sun-bleached strands. He looks like he's just come back from Australia, not a ranch in Montana.

"Not particularly," I tell him.

"I named a horse after you. New filly—mean as all hell. Bit me on the shoulder," he rattles off. As usual, he's completely unperturbed by my rudeness. "So, her name is

Atlas. Better than Daisy, which is what it was when we bought her. I have never met a horse less like a daisy."

"You named your horse Atlas because it bit you," I summarize, feeling oddly pleased with this. He grins. "Fair. Have a good summer, then?"

"I did! The best—the literal fucking best. You?"

"Fine."

Nate thinks about that answer for a second, parsing through the tone and trying to figure out whether that "fine" leans more toward good or bad. Swinging his legs slowly over the side of the bed and sitting up, he pats the bare mattress.

"Sheets?"

Tossing my damp towel over the dresser, I bend over my suitcase once more and pull out the new set of sheets. Nate takes them silently and together we make up the bed. That done, he carefully lies back down and pillows his head under his arm, watching me. I sigh.

"Okay, fine. I talked to Henri," I admit.

"Mm-hm," he hums. "Called him to yell at him some more?"

"To apologize." Nate's eyebrows shoot upward. Frowning at him, I start unpacking my suitcase. "So, that's that. We're friends."

"I saw him yesterday when the team got together for a meeting with Coach Mackenzie. He's captain this year—Vas, that is. Not Coach."

"Oh. That's cool." I don't know what, if anything, being captain of a hockey team entails, but I know Henri was probably thrilled and embarrassed by the achievement in equal measure. I bet he tried to talk his coach into giving the job to someone else.

"Vas looked like he wanted to fucking melt into the floor when Coach announced it. Everyone agreed it should be him, though. We love that guy."

"Yeah," I agree, because I'm well aware of how highly Henri is regarded by Nate and his teammates.

"Vas is looking good, too." My head snaps up. Nate is still draped across my bed, fingers idly playing with his cellphone as he talks in a casual, offhand way.

"Okay." There really isn't anything else to say to that.

"You are an impeccable conversationalist," he notes. I toss a pair of rolled-up socks at his face, but he bats them away with the reflexes of an athlete. "You going to meet up with Vas?"

"Probably not."

Nate sighs and stretches, wincing a bit. He sees me catch it and lifts one shoulder in a small shrug. "Broken ribs."

I blink at him, trying to perform the mental calculus that will make that add up. It doesn't.

"I didn't think you'd started practice yet," I say slowly, still trying to remember how his training schedule went last year.

"No, we haven't. Not until tomorrow. Ranch accident." He grins at me, inviting me in on the joke. I don't laugh—remembering the moment two years ago when Nate came back from Christmas break with twenty-seven stitches in his arm after he was kicked by a horse and its hoof cut him. Ranch accidents seem to happen too frequently for my taste.

"Fuck. How long are you out?" Nate looks at me like I'm insane. I can't see how that was the wrong question. Playing hockey with broken ribs seems like a distinctly bad Idea.

"I'm not telling Coach. Bruised ribs are nothing—I'm not missing any games during my last season."

"Broken," I correct.

"Whatever. Same thing." He grins again. Again, I don't return it. As far as I'm concerned, there is a big leap between bruised and broken. "Listen, it's nothing. Don't tell Vas."

"Jesus, I won't. I already told you I'm not going to see him."

"Right." Sitting up, he rolls his eyes. "But see, I know how much you love hearing my opinion, so—"

"No."

"*So*," Nate continues, raising his voice a little bit in case I try to interrupt again, "my opinion is you need to pull your head out of your ass, and go talk to him."

"We do talk," I grumble.

"Atlas, I'm telling you right now, if you want something to change, then you're the one who's going to have to make it happen. You told Vas to fuck off, and he's too nice and respectful to fight you on that. If *friends* is really what you want, fine. I'll shut up about it. But if it's not, you have to talk to him. *You*."

I can't even be annoyed at the unsolicited advice. He's right. Henri could give Victorian etiquette lessons to gentlemen in the nineteenth century, he's so proper. Any overtures past our virtual relationship will have to come from me. I told him to leave, which means it's on me to ask him to come back.

"Yeah," I agree morosely. Do I want to get back to what I had with Henri? Yes. Am I sure that's the best decision for him and myself? No. Relationships scare me. Feelings scare me. Fucking *Henri*, with his floppy brown hair and pretty blue eyes, scares me. I am so beneath him, it's a miracle he looks at me at all.

"I'd better go. I want to grab my shit from the bookstore before I head over to Marcos' apartment."

He tries to stretch again, but only gets his arms halfway above his head before he flinches and drops them back to his side. His shirt pulls up with the minor movement, and I catch a glimpse of a black bruise snaking around his pelvis. Did he hurt his hip, too? Maybe I *should* tell on him to Henri.

"Nate, let me see that fucking bruise." I take a step toward him and put a hand out, meaning to catch the hem of his shirt. He shoves my arm away.

"I've got to go."

"Wait a second, who the hell is Marcos?" I yell after him as he walks down the stairs.

———

HENRI

I am taking German this semester.

ATLAS

sounds tough think you'll pass?

HENRI

By the skin on my teeth.

ATLAS

LMFAO

by the skin OF your teeth

HENRI

Ah, yes. When I read that back, I see now that teeth do not have skin.

ATLAS

why are you taking german?

have you been lying to me this whole time and you don't actually speak german

> do I even know you at all??

HENRI

I am actually Czechoslovakian spy, here to infiltrate the NHL. I am working my way up to become commissioner. Then, I will control hockey as I wish and will create a super team of all the best players. We will be the best team in the world. We will take over.

ATLAS

......that was oddly specific

HENRI

Delete these messages.

ATLAS

is your name even Henri

HENRI

My name is Dvořák Alžběta Drobný but this is confidential. I will now have to kill you.

ATLAS

stop it right now I can't fucking stand you

HENRI

Atlas, this is only a joke. You must learn to not take things so serious.

ATLAS

oh my god

HENRI

I tried to make up the most crazy of names.

ATLAS

you succeeded

I'M a little ashamed of the smile on my face as I sit on my bed and text back and forth with Henri. People who grin at their phones are idiotic. But it's impossible not to, especially when Henri's in this goofy sort of mood. He always seems so hesitant to tell jokes—like he's worried people won't pick up on the humor—so when he does, it feels like a rare, special treat.

HENRI

German they teach in school here is different than German we speak in Germany. It will be interesting.

ATLAS

huh so like it's proper german but you speak slang?

HENRI

Perhaps? We are only in the third week, I will have to keep you informed.

ATLAS

god yes what the hell will I do without german class updates

HENRI

And you? How are classes going? You have told me nothing of what you are studying this semester.

ATLAS

well, I decided to go heavy on the art courses

taking a bunch of pottery/ceramics/painting things

HENRI

What! But this is incredible! I am happy you will be doing what you want. You did not enjoy Creative Communications.

This is such a grossly incorrect statement, it's laughable. The class was a drag, sure, but the company more than made up for it. I'd subscribe to a lifetime of Creative Communications courses if it meant Henri was sitting next to me.

ATLAS

thanks I'm excited it should be fun

they have open wheel nights over in the studio

My heart is pounding as I type. The moment the instructor had mentioned that we were free to come in during the open session—and free to bring a guest—my thoughts had immediately gone to Henri. It had taken a Herculean amount of self-control to refrain from texting him right then and there, asking if he'd like to join me. That was two weeks ago, when classes started.

Today, I've decided to say fuck self-control and ask him if he wants to join. The thought of Henri leaned over a pottery wheel, hands mucked up with clay and lips pinched in concentration is enough to get me half-hard and aching with want.

HENRI

What does this mean? Open wheel nights?

ATLAS

sorry

like a pottery wheel

it's just nights when the studio is open for us to come fuck around and make stuff and we are allowed to bring guests

you should come with me sometime

Locking my phone, I drop it down onto the bed beside me and breathe out hard. I've seen the man's dick, for fuck's sake,

I should *not* be nervous about asking to spend time together in a classroom. The chime of my phone startles me. Two measured, deep breaths and I check it.

HENRI

When and where?

Shall I wear the khaki?

25

Henri

ZEKE IS SITTING on the floor in the living room, books spread out around him, and laptop balanced on his knee. When I reach the bottom of the stairs, he glances up at me, smiles, and does a double take.

"Are you going out?" he asks, sounding startled. Rightly so, too. I've only gone two places since the semester has started: school and hockey practice.

"Yes. I am going to make pottery with Atlas."

Zeke's already round eyes widen further. "Really? Like a date?"

"Oh, well, I do not think so," I hedge, smoothing my hands nervously down the front of my blue polo shirt. "I think it is only a fun thing to do with friends."

"Huh," he replies, mouth twisted as he chews on the inside of his cheek. "Pottery, you said?"

I sigh, because I know exactly why he's asking. "I do not

think I have the correct clothing. But Atlas tells me we will be wearing aprons, so I think perhaps this will be fine?"

"You can always do a load of laundry when you get back."

"True." Nervously, I comb my fingers through my hair before brushing them down across my jaw. I shaved in preparation for the evening, but perhaps I should have left the hair. Atlas used to like it when I was a little scruffy. "Well, I shall get going. Have a good evening, Zeke."

"You too! I'll stay awake and wait for you, so I can hear how everything went." He smiles cheerfully, and I relax enough to return it.

The arts classrooms aren't in a building I've ever been to. As such, I park in the wrong lot and end up having to walk twice as far as I would have done, had I known where I was going. It's a good thing I got here thirty minutes early, otherwise I might have been late.

Instead, when I push open the door of the studio, I'm alone except for a young lady who barely glances up at me before she focuses back on her work. Stepping off to the side, I clasp my hands in front of myself and settle in to wait for Atlas. It feels unusually warm in the room, and my heart is beating a little too fast for someone who hasn't moved in several minutes. I work to regulate my breathing, and have just about managed it, when the door opens and Atlas walks in.

He's wearing dark jeans and a dark shirt, and his black hair shines in the extreme light of the room. Almond eyes ringed in black find mine like a blow to the stomach. I force myself to smile, because that's what you do when you greet your friends.

"Hello, Atlas," I say, far quieter than I'd intended. I hadn't forgotten that he was beautiful, precisely, but there's a difference between remembering something and having it right in front of me.

"Hey. Thanks for coming."

He looks so uneasy, it's obvious I'm not the only one unsure of how to act. Being friends seemed like a more manageable task when we didn't have to look one another in the eye.

Atlas' eyes jump from mine and land on my pants. He doesn't smile, but I can see the shadow of the expression on his face anyway.

"I'll get you an apron," he offers, and some of the tension breaks.

"I would be most appreciative."

Trailing after him, I try not to stare too obviously at the back of him, but it's difficult. I want to do more than look. I want to touch. When he turns around to hand me an apron, my face flushes guiltily. Friends don't look at their friend's backsides.

"Thank you."

Atlas looks around the room, notes the presence of the girl, and leads me over to a pair of wheels as far away as the room will allow. Patting the seat to indicate where he wants me, he wanders off through a pair of double doors. Putting my apron on, I sit down and watch for him to return. He doesn't take long, walking back into the room with two lumps of clay in his hands.

"Here you go," he says, plopping one down in front of me and settling the second on his own wheel.

When he takes a seat next to me, his leg brushes mine. Fingers clenched painfully together in my lap, I wait for him to walk me through the steps. It is extremely hard to concentrate, particularly when he reaches across me and his arm brushes mine. There is a distinct possibility that I will not survive this night.

"Perhaps you might show me how to do it, before I try for myself?" I suggest. I've already forgotten half of the instructions, and it really is very hot in here. My back is sweating.

"Sure." He sets the wheel to spinning and wets his hand. "You want to make sure you're sitting close to the wheel, and keep your elbows in tight. Hands like this"—he holds his arms out to show me—"and push the clay forward. Let's assume we're making something simple, like a bowl. When you've coned up, you can use your thumbs to level the top— like this."

Watching carefully, I nod even though his eyes are on his hands and he doesn't see it. Having him demonstrate was a bad idea. Now, I'm sitting here listening to his voice, and watching his hands, and every inch of my body is aching.

"You see?" he asks, and I nod, even though I do not see. "Give it a try."

Taking a deep breath, I situate myself in exact mimicry of how he's positioned. He reaches over and helps me get the wheel spinning, watching as I wet my hands and put them on the clay. The moment I do, I realize this is a lot more difficult than he made it seem. I squeeze too hard and the clay shoots upward into a cone. I try to compensate and end up over-doing it, my thumbs creating a deep indent into the top. I huff.

"Goodness," I mutter, frowning down at my hands. "This is not right at all."

"Here, it's all right." Atlas reaches over to help me, voice heavy with humor. I breathe hard through my nose as his hands touch mine, gently directing.

I cannot do this. I simply cannot.

"Atlas." He jolts, even though my voice is low. His hands slide away from mine and he leans back, bending over his own wheel once more.

"Yeah?"

"It is nice to see you. I have missed you."

This feels like a safe introduction into all the words I've been saving for him over the summer. He doesn't reply right away, but continues molding the clay with sure hands, dark head bent low.

"You know I'm sorry, right?" he mumbles, talking directly to the pottery wheel. I've stopped paying any attention to my own; instead, letting the clay spin through my palms aimlessly.

"Yes, Atlas, I know this." I know it because he's said it. Many times. Far more times than I needed to hear it. "Thank you. I am sorry, too, that you did not feel as though you could trust me."

He sighs and sits up a little bit. "I don't trust *anyone*, but that's my problem. I made it yours and treated you like shit, and I'm sorry for that."

"Thank you," I repeat. "No more of that, now. I don't need to hear apologies for things that are forgiven."

Movements confident, Atlas uses his fingers to create a hole in the center of his project and I watch, mesmerized, as it begins to hollow. He focuses on the clay for a few moments, and I allow him his silence.

"I miss you, too," he says finally, and if the air hadn't already been feeling thin in here, it surely is now.

Giving up entirely, I take my hands off the molded lump of clay and reach out to rest one on his forearm. His eyes flick upward toward mine, wary. Luke once said Atlas is a feral alley cat, and I see it now—the cautious stillness of his body and the suspicion in his eyes. Too late, I realize I've gotten clay all over his arm.

"Sorry," I tell him. Slowly, as though giving me the opportunity to push him away, he reaches a hand out to slide his thumb across my jaw. I can feel the wet, cool texture of the clay, a direct opposition to the way my skin feels as though it's on fire.

"Now we're even," he says, and then adds, a little more quietly, "You shaved."

"Yes, I was very undecided. I was thinking shaving meant I put some effort in, but I am also thinking that you told me you like my scruffy chin."

Atlas' lips twitch as though he wants to smile. His fingers are still on my jaw, so gentle he's barely touching me at all. He gives another swipe of his thumb before dropping his hand and spinning his wheel back into motion. I fear there is no helping my own, so I merely settle in to watch him.

"That sounds like quite the dilemma, but you needn't have bothered worrying. I like you both ways."

I smile at the side of his face, unable to decide what I want to watch more: his expressions or his hands.

"Nate told me I should pull my head out of my ass and talk to you." He exhales harshly. "So, that's what I'm doing. Because I miss the shit out of you, and things are kind of miserable when you're not around. I'm going to mess up, though, Henri. I will. And I'm fucking terrified that you're going to leave me, but me hurting you wasn't the way to handle that. I know I don't deserve a second chance, but I'd like to ask for one anyway."

I wish he'd look at me, but I know why he isn't. I can't imagine these words are easy for him to say, if the raw, pained edge to his voice is any indication.

"But even if that's not possible, maybe we could stay friends," he adds, sounding resigned and hopelessly sad.

"Bärchen, I am really wishing you spoke German so I could say romantic things without sounding like a fool." I succeed in teasing a smile out of him at that, and some of the tension melts out of his shoulders. "But I will have to do my best. You are always talking about me leaving, always worried about this. But you told me to go at the end of last semester, did you not? And if you will remember, I did not go far. I messaged you and called you and bothered you all summer, yes?"

A soft chuckle, and he sits up to look at me fully. I lean a little closer to him, scuffing my stool across the concrete floor. The clay on my face has dried, and is starting to harden on my hands as well. Neither one of us seems overly invested in pottery at the moment.

"I know it is hard to believe when people tell you things, so I will not do that. I will show you, yes? I won't tell you that I won't leave you. I will simply stay, and perhaps that will speak for itself. I am sorry for the people who have not treated you well, because they no longer get to know you and that is a terrible thing."

"Fuck," he says on an exhale, swiping his hand across his cheek and smearing clay. I hurry to continue, because I'm not quite finished yet.

"I am not this person who gets bored and goes looking for someone new. I am never wondering if there are better people out there for me. I have only ever wanted you, Atlas."

"*Fuck*," he says again, and reaches for me. Dirty hands clasped tight to my face, he pulls me to him.

Balanced as we are on uneven metal stools, the kiss is awkward. I can't get my hands on him the way I want to, and I can't pull his body into mine. But he tastes just how I remember, and when I brush my tongue across his lips, he makes a desperate sound and kisses me harder.

"Sorry. I'm sorry," he says on a gasp, pulling away sharply. "I should have asked first. I know you don't always want... Sorry."

Those lovely eyes are wide, lashes unbelievably dark on his pale face. There's clay in the hair around his ears, and brushed across his cheekbones. I'm sure I don't look much better. I touch the pad of a finger to the side of his chin, wishing I could tell him that I love him.

"One day, I will tell you something," I promise. "You will not believe me if I say it today, so I will wait for now. But, one day."

He looks quizzical at that, but doesn't press me. I sit forward to kiss him again, because apparently that is allowed.

"What're you making, there?" he murmurs against my mouth. We look down at the misshapen pile of clay on my pottery wheel.

"Abstract art," I say confidently, making Atlas snort. "It will speak to everyone differently."

"Mm," he hums, a teasing tilt to his mouth as he looks at me. "And what does it say to you?"

"It says *let us leave the pottery to Atlas, who is a professional.*"

I get a laugh, a full smile, *and* a kiss from that joke, which leaves me feeling very pleased with myself. Atlas bends over his wheel, fingers flying confidently through steps he hadn't gotten around to showing me yet. I watch silently, every now and then locking eyes with him when he glances over at me. There is a very faint flush on his cheeks, as though he's uncomfortable with my scrutiny.

"Okay," he mutters to himself, wiping his hands down the

apron and reaching for a wire. Fascinated, I watch as he removes the clay from the wheel. The steps are completed so quickly, it's apparent he's done them dozens of times before.

"What did you make?" I ask him. He shrugs.

"I guess just a bowl. I didn't set out to make anything specific. The open studio thing was just a ploy to hang out with you and talk. I didn't actually expect us to take the pottery part seriously."

Chuckling, I look down at my filthy hands and back up to Atlas' face, which is covered in the remnants as well. I really don't want the evening to end here. I want to get him alone and make up for a summer's worth of kissing. I want to fall asleep the way we've done a handful of times, breath mingling and skin touching.

"Do you want to come back to my place?" he asks carefully, picking at his fingernails nervously. "We could clean up and maybe hang out for a bit... Or not, it's up to you."

"Yes," I answer swiftly. He could have suggested we find the nearest body of water to clean off that way, and I would have agreed. As long as we remain together, I am up for anything. "Yes, that sounds excellent. I shall drive, yes?"

26

Atlas

HANDS SHAKING SLIGHTLY, I clean up our station. Henri, despite the apron, has managed to get clay on both his pants and his polo shirt, as well as up his forearms. Not to mention, what I smeared all over his face and into his hair. I want to take him home, stand him in my shower, and clean off every inch. Then, I want to lay him out on my bed and cover the same ground with my mouth.

Pump the brakes, Atlas, you've only just started to figure things out, I think, trying to talk myself down.

Silently, we leave the building walking side by side. I don't grab for his hand, still a little unsure about exactly where we are, and needing explicit words to explain what he needs.

"Henri," I whisper, as he leads me across the lawn. It's dark, and the campus mostly empty.

"Yes?"

"Can you tell me exactly what you want? Like, are we..." I trail off, leaving that sentence for him to finish. I have a feeling I know what he's going to say, and the possibility leaves me a little queasy. *You want this,* I remind myself sternly.

"Well, I think that is maybe up to you. I have not made it a secret, what I want."

"Together," I fill in.

"Boyfriends," he adds slowly, as though he's testing the word to see if it can hold our weight.

"Okay," I agree, fighting back the flash of nerves. "Okay."

Henri, probably hearing the abject terror that one word holds, slides his hand into mine and squeezes my fingers. Once we're seated in his car, I point him toward the exit we'll need to take to go back to my place.

"Do you remember where it is?" I ask him, knowing he only came over a handful of times. Most of our time together was spent tucked away in his dorm.

"If you wouldn't mind directing," he requests, so I do.

Nate's truck is the only one in the driveway when Henri pulls in. I can see the light from the television filtering through the front window as we walk up the step, and let ourselves in. Nate's sprawled out on the couch, remote resting on his stomach and face turned toward the TV. He glances over at the sound of the door and breaks out into a wide smile. I don't fool myself into believing it's because he's excited to see me.

"Vas!" he exclaims, proving my theory correct.

"Hello, my friend," Henri greets him, inclining his head slightly. "How are you this evening?"

"Good, good. You guys kiss and make up?"

"Yes," Henri says without hesitation. It shouldn't be possible, but somehow Nate's smile grows.

"We're going upstairs," I interrupt. Eyeing Henri's dirty

clothes, I sigh. "Nate, you got any sweats that he could borrow that aren't covered in clay?"

Nate looks like he might faint with happiness. Walking over, he slings an arm over Henri's shoulders and pulls him into his side. "I would *love* to lend you some clothes, Vas. Spending the night?"

"Stop. And no touching," I snap, shoving his arm off of Henri. He merely laughs and gestures us to follow him as he walks up the stairs. We hover in the doorway as Nate fishes through his closet. He selects a few things, tossing them over his shoulder at Henri, who catches them easily.

"Thank you. I shall wash them and bring them to practice, yes?"

"Whatever works." Nate shrugs. "I'll be downstairs. You guys have fun."

He bumps Henri's shoulder as he passes and waggles his eyebrows suggestively at me. I scowl at him, waiting until he's back down the stairs before turning to Henri.

"You go first," I offer, feeling ridiculously awkward. This is my house. It was my idea to come back here, and this is *my* Henri—no reason at all to feel nervous. And yet, the eggshells are scattered about, and I'm doing my best to walk tentatively over them.

"I shall be quick," Henri promises, and slips into the bathroom.

I wait for him in my room, sitting stiff on the edge of my bed. He's as good as his word, the shower cutting off mere minutes after it turned on. I stand to meet him, just as he turns the corner into my bedroom.

"Nate is making a joke," he tells me, and points to his chest. The shirt Nate loaned him has the motif of a riderless horse and the words *Save a horse, ride me* emblazoned across it. I pinch my lips together to keep from laughing at the put-upon expression on Henri's face.

"No collar, either," I point out. "It's unnatural, at this point, seeing you in anything but a polo shirt. Who even are you?"

"I am a cowboy," he replies solemnly, once more pointing at Nate's shirt.

"Jesus." I breathe out hard, grappling with the visual of Henri on a horse, tight jeans gripping those impressive thighs. "Now that's a thought. I'll be right back. Make yourself comfortable."

Grimacing, I snatch up my clothes and skirt past him toward the bathroom. That sounded like I'm expecting to come back from the shower, and find him naked and waiting for me, stretched out on the sheets. God, fuck this awkwardness. Why can't things just be exactly the way they were before I screwed everything up?

Cranking the heat on the water, I scrub all remnants of clay from my skin. I also take a minute to wash my hair and say a prayer of thanks for how lightly I grow body hair. No manscaping needed, so I'm in and out of the shower in under five minutes. Standing in front of the mirror, I do a quick visual inspection of myself, decide it probably can't get much better, and walk back across the hall.

Henri's seated in almost the exact spot I vacated when he'd come in—perched on the edge of my bed, back straight, and palms resting on his thighs. He looks over when I walk in.

"This feels strange, does it not?" he asks immediately. I sigh, relieved.

"Yeah, it does."

"I have some thoughts," he says. I snort, taking

another pass at my hair with the towel before tossing it onto the dresser. When I sit next to Henri, he immediately puts a hand on my leg. "I think, because it is too late to be driving home, I should be staying here tonight. And perhaps we might kiss again, and I would really like to hold you, and we could talk a little more if you wish."

Checking my phone, I note that it's not yet 10 p.m. "You're right. *Way* too late for you to drive home. You'll have to stay. No more talking though, because I think I'm going to have an allergic reaction if we continue."

We crawl into bed, sliding below the sheets and wordlessly rolling onto our sides to face each other. Without even making a conscious decision to do so, I reach a hand out to slide my fingers into his hair. He groans at the contact, leaning forward and kissing me.

"Atlas," he whispers, rolling me so I'm on my back and he's on top of me.

"I missed you," I whisper back, eliciting another groan.

"Ich habe dich mehr vermisst," he says, barely getting the words out before his mouth presses against mine with greater urgency.

Fuck it. I slide one hand under his shirt and up his back, refamiliarizing myself with the softness of his skin and the planes of his muscles. He rocks against me, the movement so gentle it's barely movement at all.

"Atlas," he repeats.

"Go on," I tell him. Closing my eyes, I lose myself in the feel of his hair and the weight of him, pressing me down as he rocks his hips. I catch a whiff of his hair when he kisses a careful line across my cheekbone.

He still smells like lemons.

I BARELY SLEEP through the night, constantly waking up and reaching across the bed to make sure Henri was still there. He was.

And there he is now, still sleeping peacefully despite the morning light filtering through my small window. One of his legs is resting between mine, hair rough against the inside of my thigh. His bare shoulder is just visible above the blanket, which is pulled up under his chin and held tight in a fist. I hadn't expected open wheel night to go the way it did, but I sure as hell don't have any complaints.

Regretting that we can't laze around in bed all day, I put a hand to Henri's hair. He comes awake almost immediately, one eye slitting open and a quick smile on his lips. *Happy to see me*, I note, and relax a little bit. It's going to take some getting used to on my part, being given so much selfless affection and feeling as though I deserve it.

"Good morning, Bärchen."

"Morning. Sleep okay?"

"I did, yes. I slept very well. I have not slept this well in many months."

Chuckling softly, I tuck a hand under my cheek to raise my face off the pillow.

"Laying it on a little thick," I tease, even though he's right. Everything—including sleep—is somehow better with him around.

"I have class this morning." He sighs, rolling over to grab his phone from the pocket of Nate's sweats, which were tossed to the floor last night.

"German class?" This earns me a sharp nudge with his toe. I toss my leg over his hip to spare my calf, still idly threading my fingers through his hair. "I have class, too. Not until nine, though, so I think we've got a little time. You'll probably want to go home and change, though?"

I've never seen Henri go to lecture in anything other than his polo shirts and khaki pants. If he wears Nate's borrowed clothes, everyone in his classes would probably die from shock.

"Yes, I suppose I should. I texted my friend Zeke that I was not going to be home last night, but he is probably waiting for me this morning. He is likely wanting to hear what happened. We are very similar, him and I. He understands when I tell him that you are the only one for me."

"I have no idea what to do when you say things like that," I admit, shifting in discomfort. It's not even the words that bother me, it's the way he says them with utter conviction.

"I will tell you. Here is what you do: you put your hand like this"—he demonstrates by placing his palm against my cheek, fingers curled gently around my ear—"and you kiss me, obviously."

"Obviously," I repeat softly, as he leans forward to do just that.

"And then you say: Henri." He stops, and it takes me a long moment before I realize he's waiting for me to repeat his words.

"Oh, right. Henri—"

"You are the most handsome of men. The smartest. The most skilled at hockey." Another pause.

"You are the most handsome, smart, and skilled at hockey," I repeat obediently.

"And then you kiss me again! Simple," he exclaims, before muffling my laughter with his lips.

"I'll keep that in mind for next time." Sitting up, I stretch and bend over him, reaching for my shirt. Something bangs against the wall I share with Nate, followed by a muffled curse. Henri laughs.

"Nate is fun. I am not sure I could be living with him, though. You are a brave soul."

I walk Henri down to the door in my shirt and boxers, resting a shoulder against the wall to watch him slip his shoes back on. Rising back to standing, he steps close enough for me to put a hand on his hip and squeeze.

"Together?" I ask.

"Together," he repeats. "Always."

EPILOGUE

5 Years Later
Henri

RUNNING A HAND DOWN MY CHEST, I smooth my tie. In front of me, Bryan is fiddling with his camera gear and muttering under his breath. Behind me, Detroit's NHL team is in the locker room after a very hard-fought-for win against Toronto. The door opens, and a still-dressed Max Kuemper steps out with a smile already on his face. I return it, but refrain from giving him the hug I'd like to bestow. I can hardly play favorites in front of a live audience.

The post-game interview is, as always, quick and remarkably unimaginative no matter how hard I try to make it interesting. Max provides well-spoken and thoughtfully quiet answers for the camera. It's not until we cut the live feed that his smile meets his eyes and he steps forward to engulf me in a very sweaty, very welcome hug.

"Hello, my friend," I greet him, tightening my arms as

best I can around his chest guard. We so rarely see each other in person these days, and the pain of missing him has yet to get any easier.

"God, I fucking love it when we play Toronto," he says, letting me go and beaming happily. "How are you?"

"Well, I can't say I care for the outcome of that game, but I can't complain otherwise. And you?"

Max laughs. "I'm great. Really great. Hey, did you see—"

"That Coach Mackenzie and Anthony Lawson were married?" I fill in, still unable to use Coach's first name no matter how many years it's been since I've played for him. Old habits, I suppose. "I am, in fact, astounded that it has taken so long."

"Right?" He snorts, shaking his head. "I'm so happy for them, though. I wish we didn't have to fly back tonight. I would have liked to catch up with you."

"Yes," I agree. "But I do have news—good news, I think— on that front. I'll be covering All-Star weekend this year, which means that you, Carter, and I will all be in attendance. I'm assuming Zeke will be joining him, and Luke with you?"

"He wasn't sure whether he was going to make the trip, but now he will! Holy shit, this is going to be incredible. Have you told Carter?"

"I have not. I was thinking it might be a fun surprise."

Another forceful snort. Max's face shines with delight. "Fun for us. Carter hates surprises."

"Indeed."

"So, I take that to mean Atlas will be coming as well?"

"Indeed," I repeat. Max's smile turns playful.

"Any other wedding announcements on the horizon?" he asks.

Max, who has always been the better communicator between my two oldest friends, is well aware of how I feel about marriage. Specifically, how I feel about marriage to Atlas. He knows that I purchased a ring over two years ago, and that I have yet to make use of it.

"I am playing the long game," I respond, making him laugh again. Checking the watch I received as a birthday gift from my brother, I grimace up at my friend. "If you had not gone into overtime *and* a shootout, we would have had more time. I thought you were an All-Star, Max—could you not have scored sooner?"

Grinning, he puts a hand on my shoulder and pulls me into another hug.

"I'll see you in February," he confirms. "Drive home safe tonight."

Max re-enters the locker room after a final, cheerful wave, and I make my own exit from the arena. Atlas will long be home by now, probably stretched out on the couch, watching something other than a hockey game. It's bitterly cold outside, with fat snowflakes falling lazily from the dark sky. Sitting in my car and giving it a few moments to heat up, I send a quick text to Atlas to let him know I'll be there soon.

ATLAS

Drive safe. Want something to eat?

HENRI

I can make something when I get home.

ATLAS

I'll do it. Did your team win at the hockey?

HENRI

No, Max won at the hockey tonight.

Leaving now. See you soon. I love you.

Locking my phone and slipping it back into the pocket of my suit jacket, I put the car in drive and carefully leave the parking lot. My phone doesn't buzz with a return text, and I hadn't expected it to. I try to tell Atlas as much as possible how much he means to me. That I love him, and I treasure every year we've spent together. He doesn't tell me he loves me back, but I don't need him to.

I hear the words in the way he supports my career, even though it means late nights and extensive periods apart. I feel the words in the quiet, accepting way he treats me. He never pushes, or asks for more than I can give. He is, in all ways, the perfect partner. I do not need to hear *I love you* to know it is true.

When I get home, the front light is on and the TV playing low. As I suspected, he's on the couch, legs tucked under a blanket and a mug cradled in his hands. One of his own, handmade mugs, unless I am mistaken.

"Hello, Bärchen," I greet him fondly, leaning over the back of the couch to kiss the top of his dark head. I shrug off my American accent the same way I shrug off my suit jacket. I've worked hard the last few years, making sure my broadcasts are all easily understood by dampening my accent. Atlas prefers for me to sound German, though, so I happily don't have to pretend at home.

"Hey. Soup in the kitchen for you. It's in the microwave—should still be warm."

Grabbing my soup, I settle next to Atlas, who lifts the blanket obligingly. Tucking it around my legs, he leans heavily against me. Feeling sentimental after my conversation with Max, I wrap my arm around him and rest my cheek against his head. The TV is muted, casting light over the dark room. Atlas makes no move to turn the volume back up, merely snuggles into me, breathing softly as I sip from my mug of soup.

"I ran out of ChapStick today," he says suddenly, as though he's continuing a conversation we'd already been having.

"Okay. I can pick some up tomorrow?"

"My lips get really dry in the winter, you know?" I nod, because I do know that. I'm unsure why I'm being told this story, but am willing to see where he is going with it. The way he's talking, I already feel as though I've missed a few pertinent sentences. "So, I checked the bathroom thinking maybe we had some spares. And then I couldn't find any, and so I thought *maybe Henri has one in his drawer.*"

Atlas stops talking, and I stop breathing. Atlas and I share everything, but by some mutual, unspoken agreement, our bedside tables are strictly our own. It is the only place in our house I felt comfortable that Atlas wouldn't stumble upon the engagement ring I'd bought.

"I see," I murmur, waiting him out in the hope that maybe he is telling me this for a different reason. Maybe Atlas, who is allergic to romance, did not recognize a ring box when he saw it. He sits up, tucking a leg underneath himself and looking at me with a frown on his face.

"I love you," he says in a stern, almost forceful voice. "I know I don't say it. I *should*, but it's not easy for me."

"I know that. I do not need you to say it."

"Except, apparently you do, because you have a ring and a receipt dated *two years ago*," he says, voice thin and anxious. "Why haven't you asked?"

"Because I did not know what you would say," I tell him

truthfully. He breathes in sharply, eyes widening. My hand, which had gotten dislodged when he moved, is resting on his shoulder. I squeeze it, gently. "Atlas. I would have bought that ring and asked you to marry me the day we graduated had I thought you might say yes. I have always been sure of you—of us."

"You thought I'd say no."

"I thought that I would give you time," I correct gently. "Just because I knew you were it for me, does not mean that you were at the same place. I did not want to give you an impossible choice."

He stares at me for a moment, before repeating his earlier words: "I love you."

"I love you, too." I smile at him. I didn't need to hear it, but it feels nice all the same. "Now, about—"

"If someone were to ask me something—anything—I'd probably say yes," he interrupts. "I'm feeling pretty agreeable."

"Oh? I suppose there is a first time for everything." Atlas' lips twitch. I touch a finger to his cheek, smoothing the pad over his skin. "Atlas."

"Yeah?"

"You are the world to me. You are a blessing, and a gift. I am the happiest man alive with you beside me. Atlas—my love, my Bärchen—would you marry me?"

"Yes," he whispers. "Of course I will. You're it for me, too. You've always been it for me, even when I was too dumb to see it."

"Atlas, you have been holding out on me. That sounded like a wedding vow. I thought I was the romantic one?"

He laughs, hooking an arm around my neck and pulling me in for a kiss. It would have been nice to skate with Max tonight. To play one more game, the way I long to do when I'm sitting in the broadcasting booth and missing the past. To score a goal and hear the crowd cheer. But even that dream pales in comparison to this. I do not need anything else, so long as I can have my Atlas.

THANK YOU

The biggest and most heartfelt thank you to Kim Ruge. I cannot express enough how much I appreciate the German language, and regional knowledge you provided. Hearing that you related to Henri was the best feedback I could have received. Thank you doesn't begin to cover it, but I'll say it again anyway— thank you! It goes without saying, but any mistakes or discrepancies that might have wormed their way in are mine, and mine alone.

Thank you to Maya for the very timely, and sage advice to *just put it away.* This book was not easy, and I was all set to trash it and start over. I'm glad you talked me out of that, and even more glad that you still speak to me after listening to me worry about it for months.

Thank you to every single person who has adored Henri right from the start. I think it's pretty clear how much I love him, and that always makes it a little harder to share.

ABOUT THE AUTHOR

JJ is a Colorado native currently living the beach bum life. She spends most of her time listening to the characters in her head and putting them on paper. If you don't find her writing, she will be reading too many books, and watching too much hockey. She loves traveling, horseback riding, fitness and any outdoor activities (particularly if the ocean is involved).

instagram.com/authorjjmulder

patreon.com/JJMulder

bsky.app/profile/jjmulder.bsky.social

ALSO BY J.J. MULDER

The Offsides Series

Changing the Game

Square to the Puck

Between the Pipes

From Coast to Coast

SCU Hockey

Shots on Net

Save the Game